# Desperate Measures

LOVE, PASSION AND PROMISE BOOKS
are published by
The Madaris Publishing Company
P O Box 28267
Jacksonville, FL 32226



ISBN 978-1-7344558-3-0

10 9 8 7 6 5 4 3 2 1
Printed in the United States of America

Cover design by Rebecca Marie, The Final Wrap
www.thefinalwrap.com
Formatting by Elaine York, Allusion Publishing
www.allusionpublishing.com

**Love, Passion and Promise**
**An Imprint of the Madaris Publishing Company**

# Desperate Measures

MEN OF ACTION BOOK 2

BRENDA JACKSON

Dear Readers,

In 2013, I introduced my readers to the Grangers; namely father, Sheppard Granger, and his sons – Jace, Caden and Dalton. The success of that series prompted me to write spin-off books for the Protector Series, which featured bodyguards – Striker, Quasar and Stonewall. These bodyguards or protectors were introduced in the Granger books. In 2020, I came back with another spin-off series from the Grangers and The Protectors – **The Men of Action**.

Book 1 of the Men of Action Series**, Entangled Pursuits**, was a huge hit with my readers. Now I am bringing you Book 2, **Desperate Measures**. This is Dak Navarro and Amelia Courson's story. It is packed with plenty of action and romance. Both Dak and Amelia were introduced in the Protector Series.

**NOTE** - Coming in 2022 is the 3rd book in the series – **Infinite Possibilities** – which features the hero my readers have come to know and love from my Grangers and Protector Series – Roland Summers. What's next after the Men of Action Series? Stay tune for a brand new 3-book series, **THE DEFENDERS**. Three hot attorneys that are taking Oregon by storm and the women by choice. These three heroes- Locke Dangerfield, Shogun Duke and Macayle Wasilla - are Sheppard Granger's "adopted" sons.

I hope you enjoy Dak and Amelia's story in **Desperate Measures**.
Brenda Jackson
www.brendajackson.net

If you would like to receive my newsletter, visit my website at –
www.brendajackson.net
Also, check out my FREE app – **BRENDA JACKSON** -
on your smart phone!

**IN LOVING MEMORY OF THE MAN WHO WILL ALWAYS AND FOREVER BE THE LOVE OF MY LIFE**
**GERALD JACKSON, SR.**
**FEBRUARY 11, 1951 - DECEMBER 15, 2013**

# *Dedication*

To the man who will always be the love of my life, Gerald Jackson, Sr. My first. My last. My everything.

To William M. Raines Class of 1971 – This is our 50$^{th}$ Class Reunion Year! Vikings, we are still ichiban!

To the members of my 8$^{th}$ grade class at Northwestern Junior High School in Jacksonville, Florida, who were enjoying my stories even back them. Because of your encouragement, I kept writing. Thank-you!

To all my readers everywhere, please continue to stay safe.

Love bears all things, believes all things, hopes all things, endures all things. - 1 Corinthians 13:7

## BOOKS IN THE GRANGERS, THE PROTECTOR AND MEN OF ACTION SERIES BY BRENDA JACKSON

### THE GRANGERS

*—A Brother's Honor*

*—A Man's Promise*

*—A Lover's Vow*

*—Captivated by Love*

### THE PROTECTORS

*—Forged in Desire*

*—Seized by Seduction*

*—Locked in Temptation*

### MEN OF ACTION

*—Entangled Pursuits*

*—Desperate Measures*

*—Infinite Possibilities – coming in 2022*

# Chapter 1

*THEY'D BEEN SENT TO kill him.*

*He was surrounded by five men and each one was wearing a belt of knives around their waist. Only two had guns in their hands—both aimed at him—but that didn't necessarily mean the other three couldn't quickly reach their weapons if necessary. Thinking quickly, he refused to accept that he would die here, in this God-forsaken countryside, by their hands.*

*He was ready to make a deal, anything that would prolong his life for a little longer. Suddenly, words spoken by one of the men stopped him. The thug was speaking Ukrainian. He knew there were a few Ukrainians living in South America, but he hadn't expected to find any this far north. Too bad nobody had told this guy that he spoke more than twenty languages—including Ukrainian—so he understood every word being said. The man was reminding the others that their commander had ordered he be taken alive. If he was harmed in any way, there would be grave consequences. The commander wanted the pleasure of killing him himself.*

*That made him wonder who their commander was... and what had he done to get on the man's bad side? Granted he'd worked undercover for the USN, the United Security Network, a clandestine agency of the United States government, for the past five years. It figured that during this, his last assignment with the Network, something bad would happen. Sooner or later, the bad guys would figure out a way to get to him; that he wasn't invincible.*

*His attention was quickly drawn back to his precarious situation when one of the men began advancing on him, holding a syringe in his hand that was big enough to bring down a damn bull elephant. If the guy thought he was going to stick him with that thing, he had another think coming. They might as well kill him now. Because there was no way in hell he would allow himself to be taken alive—drugged or otherwise.*

*When the man holding the syringe came within range, he attacked, becoming a fighting machine, kicking the syringe out of the man's hand, then breaking the man's neck with one blow. Then the others ganged up, and....*

Dakota Navarro jerked up in bed and glanced around, then rubbed his hands down his face that was now soaked with sweat. He'd had that damn dream again. For years, he had managed to push it to the back of his mind, a place where he never had to think about it. Kovalenko and his band of cutthroats were all dead. He'd come out of that ambush alive, but not without a few scars. But he'd survived and that was the most important thing. That assignment—he'd been in South America to prevent the assassination of the president of Argentina and the subsequent coup attempt—was a thing of the past. Every member of his team, the In-flight Unit of the USN, had made it out alive. Most people hadn't ever heard of the United Security Network. Whereas the CIA's job was to collect and distribute foreign policy intelligence and analysis, the USN was where the real action was. It basically took that intelligence and analysis and secretly worked behind enemy lines—usually in on-the-ground-combat to protect the United States and their allies from terrorism. Dak had been recruited by the USN after serving as an Army Ranger for five years. The USN had sought him out after he'd developed a number of high-tech security devices for the US government during his stint as a Ranger.

That had been ten years ago. Now, as CEO of Navarro Technologies Incorporated, an electrical and mechanical engineering firm that specialized in advanced technology, he was a very wealthy businessman. And he was still creating high-tech security devices–some for-government use, some for the private sector. He worked hard and played harder and enjoyed jet-setting all over the globe. He had business interests in almost every country...and women waiting for him in each one, too. Life couldn't get any better than that.

So why was knowing that he was only ten miles away from one woman—one *irresistible* woman—stressing him out? Because he had an itch that only she could scratch? Or because she was someone he had to stay away from? After all, her brother, Stonewall Courson, was one of his best friends. And Stonewall would hang him by the balls if he knew the images that flashed through Dak's head whenever he thought about his sister. In his dreams, he'd made love to her, over and over, in every position known to man...as well as a few his creative mind had conjured up.

Easing out of bed, he went into the bathroom and splashed cold water on his face, then returned to the sitting area. He liked this beach bungalow. It was roomy and just a few feet away from the ocean. Sliding into his jeans, he decided to go outside and sit for a spell. It was a beautiful June night. The smell of the ocean was strong and the sound of the waves lapping against the shore filled his eardrums. The night was so dark, he could barely see the beach. Miami Beach. He was here for another friend's wedding. And since he was pretty sure she was a friend of the bride-to-be, it would likely only be hours before he saw her.

*Dr. Amelia Courson.*

Had it actually been two years since he'd last run into her at Stonewall and Joy's wedding? She had to be the sexiest doctor he'd ever seen. Hell, she could take his pulse anytime. Check his heartbeat. Touch anything else she wanted to feel. He'd happily strip naked in front of her, so she could examine all of him. Dak chuckled. Like that would ever happen...though it would be nice. He'd fly from his home in Vermont to Virginia in a quick second just to have her give him a physical.

Easing down in one of the wicker chairs on the porch, he stared out at an ocean he couldn't see, recalling how he and Stonewall had met. He'd hired Amelia's brother a few years back to act as his bodyguard when someone from Dak's past had made his way into the present. Dak had known the USN would get to the bottom of it in short order. In no time at all, they'd discovered that there had been no connection between this guy and his past as a USN agent. Instead, he'd been a former business associate who was holding a grudge about a business deal that hadn't gone his way. Still, it hadn't been fun. But during those nine months, his relationship with Stonewall had moved beyond that of client and bodyguard to become one of good friends. Stonewall was one of the few men he could trust. So Dak considered it the worst kind of sin to be lusting after the man's sister. His reputation with the ladies was legendary and Stonewall knew it. Hell, he'd even been featured, in a number of high-profile magazines, as the wealthiest jet-setting playboy. His name had been linked to numerous actresses and models, but only short-term, just the way he liked it. He didn't do long-term relationships with women. And that was the main reason he could not get involved with Amelia.

He recalled how Stonewall used to speak of his sister, whom he fondly called Mellie. Dak figured she had to be a looker—Stonewall told him she'd once been Miss Charlottesville and Miss Virginia. She had even competed in the Miss USA Beauty Pageant, coming in third place. She had used all the scholarships she'd earned in the pageants to pay her way through medical school.

So Dak should not have been surprised to find her smart and beautiful when he had finally met Dr. Amelia Courson for the first time. What had surprised him, however, the day he'd walked into the rehearsal for Stonewall's wedding, the day he'd first set eyes on her, was that he'd wanted her, badly. When he'd found out who she was—and that she had to be off-limits—it had nearly killed him to stay away from her. But he'd managed...barely.

It had been tough, since they'd both been part of the wedding party and had been paired together. Whenever she smiled at him, flashing those knock-out, sexy-as-hell dimples, Dak had felt things he'd never felt before. His attraction to Amelia had been immediate, arresting and totally unorthodox.

Stonewall's description of his sister hadn't done Amelia justice—she was strikingly beautiful. Everything about her was damn near perfect. Gorgeous body, ideal height, classic features, stunning smile, and on top of that, she was a great conversationalist. And just to test his libido, her bridesmaid's dress appeared as if it had been tailored to her body. The way the material had molded to her curves should have been outlawed, and those strappy high heels she wore revealed a great pair of legs. No doubt about it, Amelia was every man's fantasy girl. In less than five minutes, she had become his.

But it was when they'd danced together that he knew he'd gone too far. The feel of her in his arms, holding her close, had made him feel things he'd never experienced before. His desire for her, his need to sweep her into his arms and carry her away somewhere private, was almost overwhelming. He'd been so unsettled after that dance that he'd fled the wedding reception the moment Stonewall and Joy had left for their honeymoon. He just hadn't been able to take any more temptation without acting on it.

That had been two years ago. And he hadn't seen or talked to Amelia since. He hadn't even asked Stonewall about her. Yet, Amelia Courson had occupied a large part of his mind from that day on. Sometimes, just out of the blue, he would remember their dance, holding her in his arms, inhaling her scent, focusing on how well their bodies had connected...and he'd get worked up all over again. And that wasn't like him.

He'd gone to bed almost every night with the image of her wearing that bridesmaid's dress in his head. Of course, in his dreams, she wasn't wearing it long. Not surprisingly, he would wake up aroused. He had tried dating other women to put her out of his mind, but that had turned out to be a total waste of time. None of them could keep his interest...which meant that it had been a long time since he'd gotten laid. If he was ever going to be able to move forward, he had to find out if his intense desire for her was real, or just some sort of fluke. After all, it had been two years. He had to get on with his life, one way or another.

Standing, he inhaled deeply, loving the scent of the ocean that flowed through his nostrils. Just the thought of seeing Amelia Courson again had other body parts coming to life as well. He had a feeling when he went to bed again, those memories of a night he nearly lost his life would be long gone, pushed away by thoughts of the beautiful face he couldn't wait to see again.

• • •

When Amelia Courson walked into her grandmother's home, she found her brother and sister-in-law already in the kitchen helping Granny Kay. Mellie loved it whenever her grandmother invited everyone over for breakfast or dinner. It was an opportunity for them all to slow down and enjoy each other's company, for a change. All of them had demanding jobs, so low-key time together was at a premium. Mellie was a doctor at the hospital, Joy, a lieutenant with the Charlottesville Police Department, and Stonewall, a bodyguard with Summers Security Firm. And tomorrow, they would all be flying out to attend the wedding of Andrew Logan and Antonia Oliver in Miami. Since Stonewall and Joy were in the wedding party, they'd head out first thing in the morning, while Mellie and Granny Kay would follow them later that afternoon.

Mellie loved her brother and adored her sister-in-law. And the two had announced last month that they were expecting their first child in January. It was wonderful for Mellie to see her brother so happy. That's the way she wanted things for herself one day and wouldn't settle for anything less. But she had plenty of time to get serious about someone. She was only thirty-three, after all. Hopefully she would come across her Mr. Right in the next couple of years.

"What's this I hear about you taking an entire month off from the hospital," Stonewall asked, once all the platters of food had been placed on the table, everyone seated, and grace had been said.

Mellie glanced over at her brother. "You heard right. I'm long overdue for a break. I've spent so much time at the hospital lately, I'm burned out. It's time I had some time for myself, instead of always taking care of everyone else."

"That's a good idea," Granny Kay said. "I was beginning to worry about you, Mellie. These days employers want their employees to keep doing more and more, while offering less."

Mellie smiled over at her grandmother. "Management didn't like it. In fact, I think they were going to refuse me the time off. But they finally saw I meant business when I submitted a transfer to another hospital."

Joy chuckled. "I bet that lit a fire under their feet."

Mellie chuckled as well. "Sure did. They immediately hired two additional doctors, and I withdrew the transfer. But because we now have enough staff, they couldn't argue when I insisted on taking time off. Still, I plan to leave town for most of those days. That way, there's no way they can call me to come in."

"Where are you headed?" Stonewall asked as he poured syrup onto his pancakes.

"No place in particular. After the wedding, I might hang around Miami Beach for a few days before returning back here to repack and take off elsewhere. I was thinking of visiting Whitney in California." Whitney was her best friend from college, who now worked as an attorney on the west coast. "I'm even thinking about taking one of those cruises out of Baltimore."

Granny Kay lifted a brow. "You can do that at the spur of the moment? Without a reservation?"

Mellie nodded. "Yes. Do you want to come with me, Granny Kay?" Mellie asked her grandmother, while looking through the platter for the crispiest pieces of bacon that she could find.

"Heavens no. I'm flying back on Sunday morning. Carlton said he would pick me up from the airport. He wants me to attend his family reunion with him."

Mellie couldn't help but smile. Some people found it hard to believe that her seventy-five-year-old grandmother still dated on a regular basis. Katherine Courson looked good for her age, and lately, Granny Kay had even more dates than Mellie. Of course, she blamed it on her job at the hospital. She hadn't gone out in months. And whenever she did go out, it was usually with Craig. He was a fellow doctor at the hospital who wasn't ready to let others know he was gay. That was his right, and she didn't mind hanging out with him, or accompanying him to various hospital functions.

In a way, it was a good thing her grandmother wouldn't be joining her if she decided to take a cruise. Who knew? Maybe she'd meet someone. And if she did, she intended to walk on the wild side for a change. She'd been so busy with work, she hadn't had the chance to let loose in years. Heck, she couldn't even recall the last time she'd slept with a man, or even been attracted enough to one to consider it.

Suddenly, her thoughts shifted to a certain handsome man, whose gorgeous body and sexy smile made her think of him often...too often. She hadn't seen him in two years, since Stonewall and Joy's wedding. But he'd been on her mind constantly ever since. He'd also taken up a lot of room in her dreams.

Glancing over at her brother, she asked, "Will Dak Navarro be at the wedding, Stonewall?"

Her brother looked at her curiously. "Why are you asking?"

"Because I'm curious. So please stop 'big brothering' me and tell me. I can take care of myself."

Stonewall didn't say anything, and Mellie knew why. He knew, better than most, about Dak Navarro's reputation with women.

Still, she wasn't lying when she'd told him she could take care of herself. When he'd been eighteen, Stonewall had gone to prison for being in the wrong place at the wrong time. That meant Mellie and Granny Kay had been left to fend for themselves in a neighborhood that was no longer safe. So, they'd both started going to the gun range, to learn to shoot, and had taken a series of self-defense classes.

By the time Stonewall was released, the neighborhood had gone through a revitalization and resurgence. A lot of the abandoned homes had been renovated, and new businesses had opened. The riff-raff was eventually driven out. Now the Magnolia Oaks community was the most sought-after diverse area in Charlottesville, consisting of young professionals, artists and revelers who enjoyed the numerous nightlife hot spots in the area. Granny Kay's home actually quadrupled in value. She loved being one of the eldest neighbors amid 'a sea of young folk', as she put it. Her new younger neighbors adored her and spoiled her rotten, and Granny Kay did the same for them.

Mellie had made the move at the right time and purchased a house on a street shaded with huge magnolia trees, just around the corner from her grandmother. She loved her home and was glad she'd made the investment when she had. And living so close to Granny Kay made it easy to check up on her, even while they both had their own space. And, as far as men were concerned, she could take care of herself there, too. She had no trouble recognizing a jerk a mile away. She knew when a man was drawn to her looks and nothing else.

She recalled a time as a teenager she'd felt sorry for herself when it seemed all the men in her life had deserted her. Namely, her father, her grandfather and then Stonewall when he'd gone to prison. Seeing she was headed toward

'abandonment issues' when it came to men, Granny Kay had taken the bull by the horn and shown her granddaughter that when life throws you lemons, you make lemonade. Granny Kay had lost the same three men – son, husband and grandson - but she'd persevered, stayed grounded and became stronger. Mellie knew that her grandmother was her role model, and Granny Kay had taught her that no matter what, life goes on and only the strong survived.
"I know you can take care of yourself, Mellie," Stonewall interrupted her thoughts to say. "But..."

"But what, Stonewall?" She figured it was a good thing they were having this discussion now and not at the wedding, just in case the intense attraction she'd felt for Dakota Navarro hadn't been a figment of her imagination. And even if it hadn't been, that didn't mean she had to do something about it. Heck, he could very well be bringing a date to the wedding.

Her brother didn't say anything for a moment, but just studied her. Finally, he added, "I couldn't help noticing at my wedding, that you and Dak were very much attracted to each other."

Mellie just grinned. "Hey, you were the groom. You should have only had your eyes on the bride—not noticing what was going on between me and Dak."

Stonewall leaned over and kissed Joy on the cheek. "Trust me, I couldn't take my eyes off my beautiful bride, but I didn't miss the looks you and Dak were giving each other. Anybody who saw you two together would have noticed."

"I didn't notice," Granny Kay chirped.

"Umm, neither did I," Joy added.

"Well, she was, and he was. I saw them both," Stonewall said.

"And like I said—" Mellie replied, grinning, glad to know the attraction had been mutual and not just a whimsical moment created by her brain, "—you should have only had eyes for Joy. I can take care of myself."

Suddenly, a thought occurred to her. "I hope you didn't say anything to Dak about it, Stonewall." Was that the reason she hadn't seen Dak again since that night? He'd practically disappeared after the reception, and she hadn't seen him since. In a way, she had expected a call. He could have easily gotten her phone number from Stonewall...or maybe not.

"No, I haven't said anything. Even though I don't act like it, I do know you can take care of yourself."

Mellie smiled. "If there's anyone you need to be concerned about, Stonewall, it's Dak."

Stonewall lifted a brow. "Meaning?"

She placed her glass of iced tea down. "Granny Kay didn't raise a fool. If—and that's a big if, since I haven't seen or talked to Dak in two years—he and I decide to take our attraction to the next level, he'll discover real quick that I'm not like any other woman he's known before. So, you might want to consider warning him about me."

Joy giggled, Granny Kay let out a laugh and Stonewall actually looked worried. Mellie was pleased to see that her brother's concern seemed to be for his friend, not her.

# Chapter 2

DAK KNEW THE MINUTE Amelia entered the church, but he refused to glance over his shoulder to look at her. He had, however, saved a spot next to him on the pew, hoping that she would take it. Drew didn't have any family and had made Granny Kay an honorary grandmother. As a result, the older woman would be escorted in by an usher and led to the front row.

He picked up Amelia's scent the moment she began walking down the aisle and knew the moment she paused by his pew. When he glanced up at her, he immediately felt a deep kick in the gut. She was more beautiful than he had remembered. Her glossy black hair appeared longer and now fell past her shoulders. He balled his hands into fists, stopping himself from reaching out and sifting his fingers through the luxurious strands.

"Is the seat next to you taken?" she asked in what sounded like a breathy voice.

"It is now," he said, standing and moving aside so she could sit beside him.

Once seated, she smiled and said, "Thanks."

"It's my pleasure, Amelia." He knew all her family and friends called her Mellie, but he liked the name Amelia and thought it suited her better.

"How have you been, Dak?" she asked, in a whispered tone.

"I've been fine. What about you?"

"Overworked. Putting in far too many long hours at the hospital," she said.

"Sounds like you need to take some time to relax."

"Trust me, I intend to."

Before he could respond, the wedding began. He tried not to notice how close they were sitting, or that whenever she shifted, their thighs or legs would touch. When that happened, he felt a rush of sensation race through his body. More than once, he glanced down at her hands that were clutching a small purse. They were beautiful hands, with fingernails that were polished a candy-apple red, matching her lipstick. A short while later, hearing a couple of sniffles, he glanced over and saw her crying. Weddings obviously made her cry. He recalled she'd cried at Stonewall and Joy's wedding, too.

Reaching into the pocket of his jacket, he pulled out a handkerchief and handed it to her. "Thanks," she said, dabbing her eyes.

"No problem."

After the minister presented the couple as Andrew and Antonia Logan, Drew swept Toni off her feet and into his arms. Everyone stood as he carried her out the church and was followed by the wedding party.

"What a beautiful wedding," Amelia said, still sniffling a little.

"Yes, it was," he agreed, as they waited for the church to empty. There had to be more than three hundred guests here today.

"I loved how both Toni's grandfather and her father gave her away. I've never seen that before."

"It was different, but in a good way," he admitted.

"I think she made a beautiful bride, Dak."

"No question about it."

When it was time for them to leave, Dak offered her his arm. He knew he was making it appear as if the two of them were together. That was okay with him. And since she took it, she obviously didn't mind anyone making that assumption.

Once they were outside the church, they mingled among the other guests while the sun beat down on them. The temperature had to be in the high eighties, and as he loosened his tie, he had to admit to himself that he missed Vermont weather. He glanced down at Amelia, to see if the heat was bothering her at all. She looked gorgeous. Absolutely. Totally. Completely. "You look nice," he said.

She smiled. "So do you. Are you going to the reception?"

"Yes. Are you?

She nodded, and he warmed up even more at the sight of the dimples that appeared in both of her cheeks.

"Do you need a ride?" he asked, hoping she did.

"No. I have a rental."

"If you'd like, I could always bring you back later to get your car." He wasn't ready for her to be out of his sight. Already he'd noticed several men's eyes on her.

"Let me check with Granny Kay. She's an official part of the wedding party, and they'll probably hang back a while for pictures."

"Sure."

As he watched her walk off, he couldn't help appreciating her gorgeous legs, made even more tempting by the stilettos she wore. And he saw that he wasn't the only man looking. But it was more than just her legs—it was her walk, so elegant and graceful. The way she carried herself was absolutely irresistible. He could easily see how she'd won those beauty pageants. She was a natural beauty and had a radiant glow about her.

He tried to keep the frown out of his face when he saw several men turn to brazenly look at her as she walked back to him after talking to her grandmother. For all they knew, she could be his girl or his wife. He was certain they had seen the two of them walk out the church together, with her holding on to his arm. He was going to have to say something...

Suddenly, he wondered what the hell was wrong with him. He was not someone who got territorial when it came to women.

"Granny Kay will be riding to the reception with Stonewall and Joy in their limo," Amelia said upon returning. "I was right. They have a ton of pictures to take."

"My rental car is parked over there," he said, offering her his arm again.

She took it and they walked seemingly in sync over to a Mercedes sports convertible. "Nice car," she said, when he opened the door for her.

"Thanks. But like I said, it's a rental."

"Still, I understand you own quite an assortment of cars."

He figured Stonewall had told her that. "Yes, I do. Collecting cars is a hobby of mine."

"Sounds fascinating. Any favorite model?"

"Not really. I just go after whatever catches my eye." *The way she was doing*. "If it gets too windy for you, just let me know. I can always put the top up," he said, backing out of the parking space.

"Are you kidding? Considering this heat, any breeze will be welcome," she said.

He nodded, noticing that several of the men who'd checked out Amelia earlier were watching her leave with him. He smiled...and just barely resisted the urge to pump his arm in triumph.

• • •

Mellie leaned back against the headrest and closed her eyes. She loved the feeling of having the wind on her face and blowing through her hair. But it wouldn't last for long. The reception was being held nearby, in the ballroom of a hotel on Miami Beach. She let her thoughts drift back to the beautiful wedding. She'd especially loved the vows Drew and Toni had written and said to each other.

She opened her eyes and glanced over at Dak. The snap, crackle and pop of attraction were still there. Nothing had changed since the last time they'd seen each other two years ago. He could still push her buttons, make her heart race and do things—real serious things—to the area between her legs.

"I understand Drew and Toni are flying to Antigua for their honeymoon."

"I know. He asked me about it."

"You've been there before?" she asked him, knowing she wouldn't be surprised if he had. Stonewall had told her and Granny Kay all about Dak's technology company that specialized in creating high-tech security devices for government and private use. He had business interests world-wide, and was a successful and very wealthy businessman.

"Several times."

"I bet it's nice."

"It is. Stonewall stayed with me there a few times, while he was my bodyguard."

Mellie nodded. "The two of you traveled a lot of places together. He mentioned that you don't care to stay in hotels," she said.

They had come to a traffic light, and he glanced over at her. "That's right, I don't. They're just so impersonal. I travel a lot, and I find it much more comfortable to stay in a place that's mine. So, I tend to purchase a home in countries I visit often." He laughed. "As a result, I own quite a few."

That's what she'd heard. And they were all beautiful and elegant and usually had staff at his disposal. "What is your favorite place to visit?" she asked him.

He smiled and the depth of that smile touched her all over, even in places it shouldn't. "My home in Vermont. I'm rarely there, but whenever I return, I'm struck with the feeling that it's where I belong."

Stonewall had told Mellie all about Dak's Winding Rivers Estate in Vermont. He'd said that it encompassed five hundred acres of the most beautiful land he'd ever seen. Sunny hillsides, lush valleys, huge lakes and scenic streams—the estate had it all...including a monstrosity of a house that sat right in the middle of it. That was the house Dak considered home.

"So—" Dak said, changing the subject, "—tell me about Amelia Courson."

She glanced over at him. His eyes were on the road but he was obviously waiting for her to respond. "What do you want to know, that you probably don't already? I've heard Stonewall in action. He likes to talk about me."

He chuckled. "Your brother is proud of you."

She smiled. "We are proud of each other. I'm sure you know we lost our parents when they were vacationing in this very city and a hurricane hit. I think of that every time I come to Miami."

"I can imagine."

"We were young, and Granny Kay and Grandpop became our legal guardians. Then a year later, Grandpop was gone. He never got over losing his only child—my father—who died of a heart attack. Granny Kay said it was actually the grief that killed him."

"I can believe that," he said. "I recalled when my father died...my adoptive father, Michael Navarro. He'd always been larger than life, and it had been so hard to watch him shrivel up to nothing when cancer took over his body."

She nodded. "I'm sorry. How old were you?"

"A lot older than you were when you lost your parents. I was twenty-three and had made Army Ranger the year before his cancer was diagnosed."

She knew the Rangers were the most elite-fighting force in the army. Still, she had trouble imagining the smooth, suave, debonair man sitting next to her taking orders from anyone. But there was no doubt in her mind he'd looked just as sexy in his uniform as he did in his expensive, tailor-made suits, like the one he was wearing now, that looked as if it had been created just for him. And it probably had. "I'm a doctor. And though I love what I do..." Mellie said. "Doctors can burn out really easily. They're great at taking care of others but often fail miserably when it comes to taking care of themselves."

"And you've been failing in that area, right?"

"Yes. But I plan to remedy that."

"How?" They'd come to another traffic light, and he glanced over at her. Why could she feel the intensity of that gaze on every part of her?

"I'm taking off all the days I've accumulated this year. I don't want to risk losing that time off, and if I wait much longer, I might. In all, there are sixty days. I'm taking thirty of them now and will use some in October, when the church will be honoring my grandmother for her years of service, and then save the rest for around the holidays. I'm having a niece or nephew who I'm hoping will come a little earlier than his or her January due date. I want to be around to help Joy and Stonewall any way that I can."

"Sounds like you've got a lot of plans, Amelia."

"Not too many. I've just decided to take care of myself for a change."

"That's a wise decision."

At that moment, they pulled into the parking lot of the hotel where the reception was being held. "Are you staying at the hotel?"

The fact that he asked, probably meant he wasn't. "Yes, I'm taking it you're not."

"No. I've rented a house on the beach."

Mellie wished she'd thought of that. "Sounds perfect."

"It is." He brought the car to a stop. "I figure the reception will be over around five. Will you go out with me afterward?"

She noticed he didn't say where they would be going. But that was okay. She could certainly take care of herself. "Yes, Dak, I'd like that."

# Chapter 3

DAK COULDN'T BELIEVE IT. He'd shared more about himself—and his past—with Amelia than he had shared with anyone else, woman or man. The only person he'd ever spoken to about his father was his pilot Sylvester, or Syl, as he was usually called. And that was mainly because, at one time, Syl and his father had been friends, working together on the police force. Hell, he'd even told Amelia about his father's death of cancer...and that was a subject he avoided at all costs. Michael Navarro would always have a special place in Dak's heart because he'd been the man who'd saved him, both mentally and physically.

Before Dak was a year old, his sixteen-year-old biological mother had given him to his seventeen-year-old biological father to raise, when he'd refused to help parent their child and pay child support. Larry Smalls hadn't known the first thing about raising a child, or how to treat a woman, either. Dak's biological father had always been in and out of relationships, and he had drilled the idea into his young son's mind that women should never be an important part of a man's life. They were fun for a while, but actually getting into a relationship killed a man—his sense of freedom and his soul. Then, to drive his point home, he would talk about Dak's mother—the woman who had obviously forgotten all about him, who'd never come back to check on him or find out how he was doing. Larry had used her as a prime example that women were selfish and couldn't be depended on; that they were useless, except in bed.

Just after Dak turned seven, his father had been shot and killed while trying to cheat a man while playing a serious game of poker. When social services had come to collect Dak, he'd managed to escape through a bedroom window and had lived under a neighbor's house in Coachella, California for weeks before he'd done something really dumb. In truth, his mistake had turned out to be a blessing, and definitely a life-saver. He had gone into a bakery without a penny to his name, but had walked out with a pocket full of cookies. He had barely made it out the door when a man, an off-duty cop, had grabbed him. That man had been Officer Michael Navarro.

Michael was Spanish-American, and his family had migrated from a place near Barcelona. To this day, Dak owed Michael Navarro everything. The police officer who'd lost his wife Tabitha, three years before they met, had needed Dak in his life as much as Dak had needed him. Luckily for Dak, Michael had been dating Janice, an attorney at social services, and she'd made the process of Michael becoming Dak's adoptive parent fairly easy. Dak hadn't liked his name of Charles Smalls, so Michael had fixed that, too. On his eighth birthday, Dak had gone from being Charles Smalls to Dakota Navarro. The name Dakota had been Dak's idea. The first time he and his adoptive father had gone camping together, they'd visited Cascade Creek in South Dakota. Although there had been many more camping trips in the years that followed, that first one was one Dak never wanted to forget, and so, he'd chosen the name Dakota to always remember.

Michael had allowed him to participate in activities he'd only dreamed of. He went to church regularly, played sports and even had a tutor to help him catch up in school. Once he got back on track, he'd more than caught up—he had surpassed other kids and had graduated from high school at sixteen and gone straight to college. After that, he'd enlisted in the army as an officer and following in Michael's footsteps, he had quickly made Ranger. He used to love listening to his father recount his times as an Army Ranger and had known that he wanted to be one as well.

"Here you are, Dak."

Bringing his thoughts back to the present, Dak glanced up at Amelia. They were in the ballroom sitting at a table and she had left to grab a plate of appetizers for them. The dinner wouldn't start until the bride, groom and wedding party arrived. They were still at the church, taking pictures. Other attendees were slowly trekking in, but for the moment, he and Amelia had a table all to themselves.

Dak glanced down at the plate she slid in front of him and smiled. "Thanks. Everything looks good."

She chuckled. "At least we won't starve while we wait. I figure it will be another twenty minutes or so before everyone gets here."

He nodded and studied her features as she nibbled on a cracker topped with chili cheese dip. As his gaze followed a string of cheese wafting past her lips to her chin, he was tempted to lean in to lick it off.

Forcing back the urge, he glanced around the room and saw the Granger brothers enter the ballroom with their wives, along with Carson, Sheppard's wife. Practically everyone knew the story of how Sheppard Granger, who'd been in jail serving time for a crime he hadn't committed, had befriended a group of younger inmates, becoming, in some cases, the father none of them ever had. While in prison, Sheppard's three sons, Jace, Caden and Dalton, had been raised by their grandfather. Not only had Sheppard been Drew's best man today, but he'd also been Stonewall's best man two years ago.

Dak stood when he saw the group headed their way. "Please join us," he invited.

"Thanks," Dalton said. "We might need to add more chairs. Margo and Randi will be joining us as well."

"There's plenty of room," Dak said, grabbing two other chairs. Margo and Randi were married to Stonewall's two best friends, Striker and Quasar. Since Striker, Quasar and Sheppard, like Stonewall and Joy, and Granny Kay, were part of the wedding party, they would be sitting at a reserved table at the front of the room.

Margo and Randi soon joined them and over the next few minutes, while he and the Granger brothers talked sports, the women passed around cell phones showing recent pictures of their kids. He and the brothers also talked business. A year ago, Granger Aeronautics had exclusively designed and built a one-of-a-kind luxury jet for Dak's company. It was a beauty and he'd been more than pleased with the final product.

It was not only a smooth sailing aircraft, but also state-of-the-art. His jet had all the conveniences of home with several specific amenities he'd requested. It also had speed. A number of people hadn't understood why he would need a plane that traveled so fast, but Dak had known Dalton Granger would understand. Very few people knew that he and Dalton had first met years ago, when they'd both been in their twenties and working undercover for the USN.

Whereas Dak's role in the agency was on-the-ground combat and operational maneuvers, Dalton was one of those agents used to mix, mingle and eventually identify those wealthy billionaires whose money was used to back the terrorists. The good thing was that neither their roles nor their identities in the agency were ever revealed. Even that time Dak had been ambushed by Kovalenko and his band of cutthroats, it had been dark, and he'd been wearing a mask. They'd known him only by his code name—Raven. Thankfully, Kovalenko and his men were all dead. Dak had fought them off, killed a few before his team had shown up just in time to finish them off. Kovalenko, the cutthroat's commander, had gotten away and evaded capture for years. However, according to the USN, the man had finally been captured and was now dead.

Moments later, everyone stood and began clapping. The wedding party had arrived.

• • •

"This has been one special day," Mellie said as Dak led her over to a table in the back of the night club. It was one of many clubs in Miami Beach that provided live entertainment. Their table had a beautiful view of the ocean. And although it was close to eight, there was still plenty of daylight left. "Drew and Toni looked so happy," she said.

"Yes, they did."

As soon as they were seated, a waitress came to take their drink order. That would be all they would have. The dinner at the reception had been more than filling and had been followed by several decadent desserts. After the reception, Dak had taken her back to the church to get her car and said he would pick her up from the hotel at seven thirty. That had given her time to shower and change into comfortable clothes—a sundress and sandals.

He was wearing a pair of slacks and a buttoned-down shirt. He'd left the first two buttons undone to reveal a very sexy chest. Dakota Navarro was in perfect physical shape. And he seemed to like the way she looked, too. She felt his gaze on her the moment she'd met him in the hotel's lobby, and it hadn't left her since. In fact, he'd told her twice already how nice she looked.

She glanced around the nightclub. "It's crowded. I understand the band is pretty popular."

He nodded. "I heard them when I was in LA last year. I understand they dropped an album a few months ago."

There was no need to tell him that although she loved music, she hadn't taken the time to just sit and enjoy it for a long time. By the time she arrived home from the hospital, all she had energy to do was shower and get into bed. If she was lucky, she might get eight hours of uninterrupted sleep. But too often, she'd be awakened by a call from the hospital, asking her to come in to cover for someone.

"I look forward to hearing them tonight," she said. She tried not to stare at Dak's features but couldn't help herself. She loved his dark chocolate complexion and the way the lantern in the middle of the table seemed to glow across his handsome features. His eyes were dark, nearly the color of midnight and his nose was perfect. But what she liked more than anything was his neatly trimmed beard, and the way it drew attention to a pair of luscious lips.

"Amelia?"

She blinked, realizing he'd been talking to her, while she had been held mesmerized by his lips. "Yes?"

"I asked what all you have planned for the next thirty days?"

Before she could answer, the waitress returned with their drinks, and she was glad for the interruption. She needed something to drink, at least a sip. She'd grown far too warm just sitting here with him and seeing his mouth had only made her hotter. "Nothing special...other than I intend to go as far away from Charlottesville as I can get."

He lifted a brow. "Why?"

"Let's just say that if people at the hospital knew I was still in town, they would call me if an emergency came up. So, I'm putting myself out of range. I honestly need time to take care of myself."

He nodded. "I can see that. On a happier subject, are you looking forward to becoming an aunt?"

A huge smile covered her face. "Immensely. I don't care if it's a boy or a girl. But it will be Auntie's baby, and I intend to spoil him or her rotten. That's a given."

"You like kids?"

"I love them. Hopefully, I'll have some of my own one day. Not anytime soon, though. I'll need a husband first, but I'm not in a rush for one of those, either." She didn't have an issue with women who had a baby on their own, but she wanted her child to have both a father and mother, the way she'd had during the early years of her life. Garrett and Vivienne Stonewall Courson had been the best, and although Mellie had been young when she'd lost them, she still remembered how her father would read her bedtime stories before her mother would tuck her in at night. She also recalled all the quality family time they'd spent together. The older she got, the more she appreciated the memories.

"What about you, Dak? You like kids?"

He shrugged. "What's there not to like? And if you're asking if I ever intend to have any of my own, the answer is yes. But like you, I'm in no hurry to settle down."

When the lights suddenly dimmed, she knew the band was gearing up. As they performed, Mellie let herself truly enjoy the music, even tapping her feet in tune to the beat. What she'd told Dak earlier was true. Today had been a special day. And not just because of the wedding. She'd loved being able to spend time with friends she hadn't seen since Stonewall and Joy's wedding - Like the Grangers. Although they lived in the same town, their paths rarely crossed. She had been invited to Sheppard Granger's birthday party last year, but had to miss it, because she'd been called in to work at the last minute.

"Will you dance with me, Amelia?"

The way Dak said her name always sent a shiver of intense longing through her. She knew he'd mastered a number of languages, so whenever he spoke, even good old American English, he did so with sensuality. And whenever he spoke her name, he did so with deep masculine awareness, and in a voice that stroked every single hormone in her body. She thought back to the last time they'd danced together at Stonewall and Joy's wedding. Being held in his arms was a memory that had a permanent place in her mind.

"Of course, I'll dance with you, Dak," she said, her heart racing nearly out of control.

He stood and took her hand. The moment they touched, a sizzle rushed through her, ending at her lower extremities, and from the way he was looking at her through a pair of dark, mesmerizing eyes, she knew he'd felt it too. She wished she could ignore it but couldn't. As he led her to the dance floor, she could feel her sex throbbing. And as he pulled her into his arms, her entire body went on red alert. And she realized that the overwhelming attraction she'd felt the last time they'd danced together had not been a figment of her imagination.

"You look beautiful," he whispered against her ear. He was so close, his warm breath sent shivers down her body.

"Thanks. You look quite handsome yourself." No lie. This man was the stuff of every woman's dreams. Their fantasies, too.

He tilted his head and chuckled, and it sounded more like a groan from deep within his throat. The sexual chemistry flowing between them was so thick, she could barely stand it. Blood didn't just flow through her veins, it rocked. How long had it been since she'd been this attracted to a man? This turned on by one? The answer was quick in coming. Never.

She'd dated, although not much lately. No one had really even caught her interest in the last few years—not since she'd first met Dak. The moment Stonewall had introduced them to each other at his and Joy's wedding rehearsal, and she'd looked into Dak's eyes—even knowing his history with women, at least what she'd heard or read about—she'd felt an overwhelming attraction she hadn't managed to get past. Since they'd been partnered off for that wedding, they'd done a lot of touching, which had only amped up the temptation. And then, when Joy had requested that her bridesmaids dance with the groomsmen they'd been partnered with, things had become hotter. The moment Dak had taken her into his arms, she'd been a goner. And now, two years later, she was back in his arms again, and the sexual chemistry was even stronger than before.

Mellie suddenly drew in a sharp breath when she felt Dak's fingers skim across the back of her dress, drawing seductive circles and making her pulse kick in every way that it could. If she didn't know better, she would think that he knew there was a particular spot on her back that was one of her most sensitive erotic zones. When touched, it could rev up her desire in mega-seconds.

His fingers were inching closer, and she was about to moan his name, but then the music stopped. Drawing in a deep breath, she took a step back, thinking he was about to lead her back to their table. Instead, another slow number began playing and suddenly, they were slow dancing together again. He held her closer and thankfully, his hands moved from her back to wrap around her waist.

She could feel his body, hard and aroused, pressed solidly against her, and it made her head spin. Then the second dance led to a third—all slow dances. It was only when the band went into a fourth number, one with a faster beat, that he took her hand and whispered, "It's time to get out of here."

After taking care of their bill, he led her out of the nightclub. When the night air hit her skin, along with the scent of the ocean, she finally regained some semblance of control. "Where to now?" she asked.

"I think I need to get you back to the hotel," he said.

He led her over to his car and put the top down. She loved the feel of the wind in her face and closed her eyes. She thought about the last time she'd made love with a man, but the details were sketchy. It had been a long time ago, definitely before she'd met Dak two years ago. And she couldn't even blame it on the long hours at the hospital. She'd had no interest, because no other man compared to Dak. She could admit that now. It was Dak who'd filled her nightly fantasies, with his hands, his tongue, his.... Well, they'd been some dreams.

"We're here, Amelia," he said. She opened her eyes and saw that he had parked in one of the parking spaces in front of the hotel.

She looked over at him. "Would you like to come up for a nightcap." They both knew she was offering him more than that.

He drew in a deep breath, and then he reached out and softly caressed the side of her face with the pad of his thumb. "Yes, I want to, but I better not, Amelia."

She didn't ask why, when it was obvious that they wanted each other. She had an idea, but figured it was something he needed to work out for himself. Yes, she was Stonewall's sister, but she was also the woman Dak wanted and the woman who wanted him. A woman who was old enough to make her own decisions.

In the meantime, though, she would give him something to think about. Something to remember.

She leaned toward him, and she could tell by the look in his eyes that he hadn't expected such a bold move from her. Good. He would discover she was full of surprises. His lips parted and then it was on. The moments their lips touched, the desire that had held them in its grip all day, possibly for the past two years, surged forward, taking over her senses. And from the way he was kissing her, he was feeling the same way. The way his tongue was mating with hers had her moaning, purring, and outright groaning. His mouth was hot and demanding, his lips, sensual and thick, and his tongue...his tongue tasted incredible, so uniquely male, so like she'd figured Dak would taste. Totally delicious.

He was taking her mouth with a hunger that she felt all the way to her toes, especially at the juncture of her thighs. Each carnal lick and stroke of his tongue came close to sending her over the edge. If he kept it up for much longer, she would have an orgasm here, right now. She'd heard of women who'd come during a kiss, but she'd never been one of them. Honestly, she'd never believed such a thing was possible. Now she did.

Refusing to climax from a kiss in a parking lot, she abruptly pulled her mouth away and leaned back in her seat. His breathing seemed to be just as choppy as hers. She glanced over at him. After that kiss, would he change his mind about her invitation to come up to her hotel room? And did she still want him there? Because now, she knew that this wasn't the time. That kiss had blown her away, but for a reason other than desire.

Mellie knew Dak had a reputation with the ladies. And still, for reasons of his own, he'd refused her invitation. So regardless of their obvious attraction, Mellie needed to step back. She didn't want him to have any regrets and a guilty conscience the morning after. And knowing Dak, he would have.

So instead, she quickly opened the door, and said, "Thanks for a lovely evening, Dak. Maybe I'll see you at the next wedding, whenever that will be. Goodbye."

She swiftly got out of the car and raced across the parking lot to the hotel, ignoring his calls for her to stop. She needed this distance and so did he. If she heard from him again, she would deal with it then.

And if she didn't...? Then, as she'd said, maybe their paths would cross again at another wedding.

# Chapter 4

"*THANKS FOR A LOVELY evening, Dak. Maybe I'll see you at the next wedding, whenever that will be. Goodbye.*"

For the third straight day since returning home to Vermont, Dak paced around his study as Amelia's final words to him continued to ring in his ears. Why was he letting her get to him? Would it matter if he didn't see her for another two years? He stopped and rubbed his hands down his face. Maybe the question he ought to be asking himself was whether or not he could wait that long to see her again. Especially after the kiss they'd shared, the kiss he couldn't get out of his mind.

Just remembering it caused pleasure to the nth degree to shoot up his leg, hitting him straight in his groin. That kiss had been unexpected because she had initiated it... and he hadn't seen it coming. But it had been a pleasant surprise. And really, it didn't matter who'd made the first move. The deed had been done and he hadn't been the same since.

*But she was Stonewall's sister.*

If he'd been able to ignore that very important part, he could have solely concentrated on her delicious taste and the way her tongue had stroked his. Their kiss hadn't lasted nearly as long as he'd have liked, but it'd sure had the intended effect. Ever since that night, thoughts of her sent him to bed with heat coursing through him. Twice, he'd woken up in need of a shower. No kiss had ever affected him that way before. If nothing else, it should be a firm cue for him to stay back, stay away and leave Amelia Courson the hell alone. But he couldn't. Hell, he didn't want to. That kiss had gotten into his system, and the intensity of it was making him crazy. He wanted more—a whole lot more. He figured it would take more than one night to expel Amelia Courson from his system once and for all.

He continued pacing. Then why was he hesitating in sending her flowers, the way he did any other woman he desired? After all, this was why he had a system—so he didn't have to think about it too much. When there was a particular woman he wanted, he would simply send her an invitation to share his world for a week, in some exotic location. The invitation specifically spelled out the rules of the liaison so there would not be any misunderstanding.

If a woman accepted the invite, she knew what she was in for...as well as what she wasn't. He pushed the thought out of his mind that since meeting Amelia two years ago, he hadn't issued any invitations. As hard as it was for him to believe, he'd gone two years without having a woman share his world—or his bed.

Thinking of Amelia's plan to take some solid time off from the hospital, he realized that if he was going to make a move, he needed to do it now, before she made other plans. Pulling his cell phone out of his pocket, he proceeded to make the necessary call. A few minutes after providing all the necessary information with his personal assistant, Jefferson Perkins, the man then asked, "Will you be sending an invitation as usual, sir?"

Dak would normally send a pre-printed note card inviting the woman to join him. Usually, the invitation read...*You are invited to share my world for a week in a non-committed affair. If you accept, please RSVP*. The woman would then be given a specific date and automated-reply phone number to call. He knew some women considered his methods impersonal, but once he and his companion took off in his jet, he made it as personal as it could get. As far as he knew, he hadn't left any of his partners disappointed. For that week, he treated his lady like a queen. And by the time the trip ended, she was happy and satisfied, and so was he.

Yet, he couldn't see sending that kind of impersonal invitation to Amelia. He would write her a note himself. "No. Please send a courier to pick up a letter later today."

After ending his call with Jefferson, he went to his desk, sat down and wrote out a personal invitation, signed it and then sealed the envelope. Then he summoned a member of his household staff to make sure it was given to the courier when he arrived. Once that was done, he sat down and let out a long breath. It was done. He had strayed away a little with the wording of this invitation, but the vital message points had been the same. He was asking Amelia to agree to a seven-day non-committed affair.

It wasn't that he didn't want the happy ending so many of his friends had. But he'd just seen too much, lived through too much, to risk it. His biological father had taught him that women should never become too important. A man could have fun with a woman but expecting anything more just led to disappointment. And he'd seen, by watching his dad, Michael Navarro, the kind of heartache that could happen when a man let a woman into his life. Michael had grieved the loss of his wife for years after she'd passed. Even though Dak and Tabitha had made his days more bearable, it was obvious to anyone who knew him that he wasn't the man he'd been before.

Dak was determined to never experience that kind of pain. So he made it a point to never let a woman get too close. And he hadn't. But Amelia was tempting him.

Dak knew what he had to do now and figured he might as well get it over with. His call was answered on the second ring.

"Hey Dak."

He released a deep sigh the moment he heard Stonewall's voice. Better to get it over with quickly. "I'm sending Amelia an invitation to share my world."

As one of his closest friends, Stonewall knew what that meant. However, just in case he'd forgotten, Dak added, "You know how I operate. I see what I want, and I go after it."

There was a long pause. Then Stonewall said, "Mellie is an adult who can make her own decisions about things."

Dak was surprised Stonewall was taking it so well. "Glad you feel that way."

"Mellie gives me no choice when it comes to her personal affairs. However, I will give you this warning, Dak."

Dak leaned back in his chair and rubbed his bearded chin. He figured Stonewall would threaten to break Dak's damn neck if he hurt his sister. “What’s the warning, Stonewall?”

“Mellie is not like the women you’re used to dealing with. You might want to think twice before inviting her anywhere. She won’t put up with your bullshit. Don’t say I didn’t warn you.”

“Duly noted, Stonewall.”

“Fine. We’ll talk when you get back.”

Then there was a click in Dak’s ear, and he could have sworn he’d heard Stonewall chuckle.

• • •

“Delivery for Amelia Courson.”

Mellie glanced at the woman standing on her porch. She was holding a huge beautiful arrangement of mixed cut flowers, with a card that evidently was to accompany them. “Thanks. Hold on a second and I’ll grab your tip.”

“No need. It’s been taken care of. Enjoy your flowers.” The woman hurried back to the private car. A private car and not a florist van?

She frowned as she stared at the flowers for a long minute before closing the door. She glanced around her living room, looking for the perfect spot, and then placed them on the sofa table where they would be seen every time she walked into the room. Taking a deep breath of the colorful blooms, she smiled. She’d smell them throughout the house, even if she couldn’t see them. They had such a lovely scent.

As she admired the flowers, she recalled something she’d overheard a few years back. Stonewall had been telling his best friends, Striker and Quasar, about Dak's technique when it came to pursuing a woman. He would have an arrangement of flowers delivered to her with an official printed invitation, asking her to share his world in a non-committed fling. Usually, the affair lasted no more than a week, and the woman would accompany him—on his private jet, of course—to some exotic country where he would wine, dine and bed her. At the end of the week, he would return her home and she would never hear from him again, while he moved on to his next conquest. Mellie figured the only women who would take him up on such a thing were those adventurous types who weren't looking for a lasting relationship any more than Dak was.

She stared at the invitation, amazed that the man had had the audacity to send her such an invitation. What kind of woman did he think she was? But when she tore open the envelope, she realized the invitation was handwritten, not printed. At least he'd done that much.

Then she read the words...

*Amelia,*
*I enjoyed your company this past weekend and I hope you enjoyed mine. I think it's wonderful that you've taken some time off, and as it turns out, I have some free time ahead of me as well. My plan is to fly to one of my favorite countries for much needed R&R. I'd love to help you relax and unwind by inviting you to join me for a week. If you accept my invitation, please let me know by calling me at my personal phone number below. I need your response within 48 hours so I can make*

*the necessary arrangements. I will be leaving Saturday morning.*
*Looking forward to hearing from you,*
*Dak*

Mellie couldn't help but chuckle. Dak was slick, she'd give him that. At least he hadn't sent an impersonal invitation with the flowers, the way he was used to doing with other women. She also noted the invite didn't say anything about a non-committed type of affair. Still, his intent was clear. He was inviting her to engage in a no-strings-attached fling.

The question was, what was she going to do about it? She was definitely tempted to accept his invitation. Though, if she did accept, whether they shared a bed would be her decision and not his. Tapping her chin with the envelope, she considered her own actions, inviting him to her hotel room for a nightcap, knowing full well what the outcome would have been. She had wanted him and had had no reservations about sharing a bed with him then. He had been the one to pull back, though she figured his friendship with Stonewall had a lot to do with his actions. So, what had changed? And did it matter?

Regardless of who issued the ultimate invitation, the result would be the same. But no one could force her to do anything she didn't want to do. Still, the thought of spending time with him in some exotic place was definitely something worth considering. She *did* need to relax and unwind, and if she shared his bed while doing it, what would it hurt? She wanted him. She had, for two long years. So, she had no problem sharing his bed. But she'd be the one calling the shots. After that fiasco with Dr. Ivan McIntosh, she'd never again follow any man blindly.

She and Ivan had met when she'd been doing her internship in St. Louis. She'd soon learned that the relationship had meant more to her than to him because he'd had an agenda. He had her believing they would become medical partners, even convincing her to put money down on a building that would be their private practice.

Mellie had trusted him to do the right thing and when it was time to finalize everything, he'd decided he wanted to go in alone. The only problem with that was that he didn't feel he owed her the twenty-five-thousand dollars she'd given him as a down payment for the building.

She'd considered taking him to court, but knew that if Stonewall ever found out about it, he would have beaten the money out of Ivan, or made his life a living hell. And the last thing she wanted was for him to get into trouble because of her. The only people she'd confided in were Granny Kay and Whitney. Her grandmother was sure her prayers, that Ivan would one day realize his error and pay her the money back, would work. Mellie was not holding out for that to happen.

That had been close to eight years ago. Now she was a woman who wasn't easily swayed. Those days of looking for love were over.

Dak was a man, and she was a woman, and they were attracted to each other. That's how human anatomy worked. It was simply the law of nature.

Besides, Granny Kay would be the first to tell her that life was too short not to try different things and embrace new experiences. And Granny Kay lived that way herself.

She was nothing less than an inspiration. Years ago, while she'd been in her sixties, Katherine Courson had persuaded her granddaughter to join her in taking up martial arts, not to mention accompanying her to the gun range for target practice, taking line dancing and even trying out bird watching. Skydiving was still on their bucket list. Her grandmother was not one to let grass grow under her feet, and she would be the first to encourage Mellie to follow her lead.

But still...

Although Dak's invitation was tempting, she had to think carefully about what her final decision would be.

She tossed the invitation on the table next to the flowers, deciding she usually thought best while shopping. So, she grabbed her purse and went out to do just that.

• • •

"And you're sure the delivery was made at the right address, Jefferson?" Dak asked, placing his cell phone on speaker while he played pool. His entertainment room was one of his favorite places in the house, with one of the largest pool tables made, a wet bar that wrapped around one section of the room, a mini-bowling alley, a movie-size television screen and an indoor rock-climbing wall.

"I'm positive, sir. The courier company we used indicated their representative placed both the flowers and the card in Ms. Courson's hand on Tuesday, at eleven-fifteen a.m., Eastern Daylight Savings Time."

Dak nodded as he stretched over the table, more focused on what Jefferson was saying than getting his ball in the corner pocket. His note had been delivered nearly two days ago, which meant Amelia was deliberately not responding to his invitation—his handwritten invitation! He'd even included his personal number. If she was playing games with him, he didn't like it.

"Will you still be flying out on Friday, sir?"

For a minute, he'd forgotten Jefferson was on the phone. "Yes. Give Sylvester instructions to have my jet ready to go. Destination is Bali, Indonesia."

"Yes, sir."

No longer in the mood to play pool, he hung his cue stick in the holder on the wall and went over to the bar to pour his favorite drink—bourbon. There were a number of other women he could invite, and it wasn't too late to do just that. He went to look up a few numbers on his phone, then stopped. He didn't want any other woman on this trip. He wanted Amelia. But he wouldn't ask her again. No woman was worth that.

He had just taken his glass of bourbon and was moving to sit down in one of the chairs when the security beeper went off.

He had just reached for the remote when the attendant at the gate buzzed him. "What is it, Dusty?"

"You have a visitor."

Dak rolled his eyes. Jennifer Rowe, the model who'd been his last 'guest' three years ago, didn't seem to understand that their time together was long over. It was nothing personal. He just wasn't willing to give himself to any woman for more than seven days. It was enough time for him to have some fun, but still easily walk away. No woman got issued a second invitation.

Jennifer had called yesterday, telling him she would be in the area, then asking if she could stop by. He had told her no. Evidently, she hadn't been listening. His estate was off limits, and he'd told her that more than once. So why was she pushing him?

"A woman, right?" he asked.

"Yes, sir."

"Please tell Ms. Rowe that she's not allowed on the grounds."

"It's not Ms. Rowe, Mr. Navarro."

Dak cocked a brow. "Then who the hell is it?"

"A Dr. Amelia Courson. She says she's here to make a house call. Do you still want me to send her away?"

Dak stood and placed his glass of bourbon down with a thump, trying to ignore the sexual hunger that sprang to life inside him. Amelia was here? Why hadn't she followed the instructions on the invitation he'd sent. He would send a private car to pick her up and take her to the airport where he and his jet would be waiting for her Saturday morning in Charlottesville. No part of his invitation had indicated she should show up here. Hadn't he just explained to Jennifer yesterday that his estate was off limits?

"Mr. Navarro, do you want me to send her away?"

He had half a mind to tell Dusty to do just that. But he wouldn't. He would have a talk with Amelia and explain that, in the future, he would expect her to follow directions. In the meantime, he'd make arrangements for her to stay at a hotel in town. "No, Dusty. By all means let the doctor make her house call. Please have one of your men escort her here."

"Yes, sir."

When he clicked off the intercom, anticipation thickened the very air he was breathing, whether he liked it to or not. How had she found out where he lived? He was certain Stonewall hadn't given her his address. He was about to leave the entertainment room and go upstairs, so that he'd be there when the door opened, but then thought better of it. She had come uninvited, and he refused to greet her at the door as if he'd been expecting her.

If Dr. Amelia Courson had the nerve to enter his private territory, then this room was where his security man would bring her.

# Chapter 5

"REMAIN RIGHT HERE, MISS...I mean, doctor," the security man who identified himself as Silas said.

"Sure thing," Mellie said, pulling her luggage behind her as she entered the foyer of Dak's home...or maybe she should say, his mansion. She could fit four of her houses right here in his foyer. From what she could see of his living room from here, it was four times as large as the foyer. Then she saw the double staircases.

She shook her head. Stonewall had told her and Granny Kay how huge Dak's house was. What would a man, living alone, need with such a huge place? And she'd bet the portraits hanging on the walls were all originals. There was a huge painted portrait of a Hispanic man in a cop's uniform who looked to be in his late thirties. She knew, without being told, that he was Dak's father—the man who'd given a lost little boy a chance to have a good life. And, looking around, Mellie had to admit that Dak had made the most of it.

"Mr. Navarro is in his entertainment room. He asked that I bring you to him," Silas said.

Mellie smiled at him. Although he was a large man who didn't seem to smile much, he seemed rather nice. "Please lead the way."

Deciding to leave her luggage where it was, she followed Silas, glancing around as she went. Okay, not only was the house enormous, it was also gorgeous. She remembered him telling her Saturday night that he didn't spend as much time here as he'd have liked. Well, she had news for him. If she lived in a place like this, she'd probably never leave. Granted, it was night and most of the lights were dimmed or turned off, but given the beauty of what she was seeing, she could only imagine how incredible the place was in the light of day.

They walked through a corridor off the kitchen. Since the lights were on, she could see inside it. Wow. This kitchen could easily be featured on a magazine cover. She recalled Stonewall telling her that Dak loved to cook. He also liked growing his own herbs and vegetables in his garden on his estate. There was a lot about him she didn't know, but she'd find out over the next week or so. Although he hadn't specified a time frame in his invitation, she figured it would likely be the same as invitations he'd issued to other women. Seven days was the max.

Silas paused at a set of double doors, and when he opened them, she blinked. An extravagant looking staircase that matched the two off the living room led down to Dak's entertainment room. That was definitely too fancy for her taste. "You first, doctor."

She moved in front of Silas and could hear the sound of soft music as she got closer to the bottom. Then she saw Dak. This was the first time she'd ever seen him wearing anything other than a tux, a business suit, or dress slacks and a shirt. But here, in the comfort of his own home, he had on jeans and a pullover shirt. And he was leaning over a huge pool table, lining up a shot.

Why couldn't she take her eyes off him, his stance, his perfect physique and the way he looked in casual clothes? Her entire body instantly heated. Maybe showing up unannounced hadn't been such a good idea after all.

"Doctor Courson is here, Mr. Navarro," Silas said from behind her.

That's when Dak's head shifted in her direction and a pair of dark, smoldering eyes met hers.

Smiling, she said, "Hello, Dak."

• • •

Instead of returning her greeting, Dak shifted his gaze from Amelia to Silas. "That will be all," he said to the man.

"Yes, sir."

When his security guy left, Dak shifted his gaze back to Amelia, trying to regain his equilibrium. He'd momentarily lost it when she'd flashed him a dimpled smile. "What are you doing here, Amelia?"

She came down the last two stairs and he tried not to show any reaction to what she was wearing. Like him, she was dressed casually in a pair of jeans and a crisp white blouse. His mouth watered. If he'd thought she was curvy before, those stretch jeans showed him the real deal. And her blouse clearly emphasized what a nice pair of breasts she had.

She crossed her arms over her chest, which made them even more attractive. "Excuse me? Did you not invite me here?"

Placing his cue-stick aside, he leaned against the pool table. "No, I didn't. I invited you to share my world. Had you followed the instructions in my invitation, you would have called the number I provided to you. Then I would have told you that my jet would be picking you up Saturday morning at your airport in Charlottesville. At that time, I would have also given you the itinerary so you'd know where we would be going so you would know what to pack."

She nodded. "Okay. But did you honestly think I would have boarded a jet with you and flown heaven knows where, without us first spending time together on the ground?"

He frowned, thinking of the number of other women who already had. "I don't see why not."

"Well, I do. The longest period of time we've spent together was Saturday at the reception, and afterward at that nightclub for drinks. I need to get a feel for what sort of guy you are before I fly off anywhere with you."

Dak released a frustrated breath. She was just being difficult. That was how it worked—no other woman had ever complained. In fact, she even had an advantage. Her brother was a friend of his. So, she'd know he was a solid guy. And he'd love to show her just how solid...

He pushed those thoughts from his mind, trying to stay on point. "That's not how the invitation works, Amelia."

"Sorry, but that's how my tentative acceptance works."

*Her tentative acceptance*? Drawing in a deep breath, Dak looked away from her, trying to regain control. Picking up his cue stick again, he returned to his game of pool. It was either that or walk across the room and kiss her. Their one and only kiss hadn't left his mind. In fact, even after several days, he'd swear he could still taste her.

"What hotel will you be staying at while you're here?" he asked, lifting his head to look at her.

"Are you trying to be funny?"

Dak didn't have to glance at her to know she'd moved closer to him. Her scent had given her away. "Do I look like I'm joking?"

Amelia then surprised the hell out of him by coming closer, leaning over the table to look directly in his face. The moment his gaze connected with hers, he almost forgot to breathe. The temptation to draw her into his arms was one he could barely handle.

"Umm, you seem unhappy about something. Since I'm sure it has nothing to do with me, it obviously has to do with your game here."

He frowned. "What about my game?"

"It needs improvement."

There was no way he could argue with such a preposterous statement, so he simply laughed. She smiled, flashing those dimples. "I know how to play pool, Amelia. Ask your brother."

"So do I, Dak. And you can ask that same brother."

He leaned against the pool table. "So you think you can play better than me?"

She shrugged. "I didn't say that. What I said was that your game needs improving. And I should know—I was trained by the best. And before you ask, it wasn't Stonewall."

"And who do you consider to be the best?" he asked.

"Mario Arnold."

Dak recognized the name immediately. The man had been the national eight-ball champion for a number of years. "The two of you know each other?"

She nodded. "We dated in high school and are still good friends. A date with Mario always had us hanging out in some pool hall."

Why did the thought of her and some guy she'd dated way back in high school unnerve him? "Where is he now?"

"Mario lives in New Hampshire. He's married with three kids. I went to his wedding." She smiled. "Mario owns a huge pool hall, one that attracts celebrities who are looking for some real competition."

He nodded, wondering if she cried at the man's wedding, too. "So, you think you can beat me at pool?"

"Don't twist my words, Dak. All I said was that your game needs improvement."

Dak didn't say anything for a minute, then he reached to the wall and pulled down another pool cue. "I want to see what you can do."

She took the cue from him, then walked over to the wall and put it back. "The first rule of pool is to never let your opponent select your cue for you. You select your own," she said, looking over the assortment in the case before taking one out.

"Whatever. Ready?" he asked, chalking his cue.

"I am. Are you?"

• • •

He won, but barely. Amelia had been a worthy opponent, and some of her moves had been so smooth and her concentration so riveting, they'd held him spellbound. It was a wonder he'd come out the winner. Each time she stretched, his eyes stretched with her. And when she concentrated on a shot, she had a tendency to lick her lips, which drove him crazy. He'd been so very tempted to pull her into his arms and lick them for her. When he made a good shot, she'd only smile...and wrinkle her nose. That was the only indication she gave that things weren't going her way.

What he liked was that she didn't engage in endless, unnecessary chatter like some women. Not that he'd ever played pool with a woman before. Typically, pool was a man's game, but she played it well. Even better than Stonewall. And she'd been right when she'd mentioned his technique needed some improvement. He noticed how, in some shots, she rose on the balls of her feet. So he decided to try it and found it gave him the leverage to make difficult shots a bit easier. Right now, he'd bet she wished she hadn't said anything—that switch is what had helped him win.

"Congratulations, Dak," she said, placing her cue back in the case.

"Thanks. You played a good game."

"Yet you still beat me."

She hadn't said it in a sulky tone. In fact, she seemed fine with losing. That was a first for him. "Still, you almost had me. Mario taught you well." He pushed aside the question of what else Mario might have taught her. He had no right to feel envious. When she'd been in high school, Stonewall had been serving time and hadn't been around to protect her.

"Yes, he did." She glanced at her watch. "It's late. If you wouldn't mind showing me to a guest room, I'd like to shower and get to bed."

It looked like she was staying then. And it *was* late. A glance at the clock on the wall behind his bar indicated it was after midnight. Had they been playing pool that long? Obviously, they had. Because he hadn't been expecting anyone, he'd already allowed his household staff to go home until next week, after his trip. He still had half a mind to suggest she go to a hotel, after all, but knew it would be a waste of time. Had he made a mistake by not heeding to Stonewall's warnings about his sister?

"Come on then, I'll show you to your room." The thought that he wouldn't be showing her to *his* room seemed odd at best. After all, before the week was out, they would be sharing a bed. However, if she felt she needed to get to know him better, then he would tolerate that minor indulgence. "Where is your luggage?"

"In your foyer."

He climbed upstairs to the main floor and found her luggage right where she said it was. He couldn't help wondering what she had packed when she'd had no idea where they were going. Taking the handle of her bag, he said, "Come on." Then he moved toward another set of stairs. "You'll be using the first guest room on your right."

Nodding, she moved ahead of him and he followed her, drawing in a deep breath of her scent with every step he took. He tried to avoid staring at her, but he'd never seen so tempting an ass. He knew she wasn't deliberately swaying her hips—it seemed to be perfectly natural. But damn, it did something to him. He honestly couldn't picture her wearing scrubs. She was one hell of a sexy doctor.

When she opened the door to the room she'd be staying in, he heard her sharp intake of breath. Joy had had the same reaction to it when she and Stonewall had stayed for the weekend to celebrate Dak's thirty-fifth birthday. Stonewall had refused to let Dak celebrate alone, so he and Joy had made the trip. And by the time the weekend was over, Dak had no doubt that Lieutenant Joy Courson was the best thing to ever happen to his friend.

"I hope it meets your approval, Amelia," he said, walking past her and rolling her luggage into the room.

"It's beautiful. Joy and Stonewall told me you had a beautiful home, but—"

"You had to come see it for yourself?"

She frowned at him. "I told you why I was here."

He studied her posture. Like her response, it was defensive. "I take it you're not seriously seeing anyone."

"If you're trying to piss me off, Dak, you're doing a darn good job of it."

"Why would I want to do that, Amelia?"

But she just glared at him. "I don't know about the women you usually socialize with, Dak, but if I was involved with someone, I wouldn't be here. Nor would I have kissed you last weekend."

She had to remind him of that kiss. Shoving his hands into his pockets, he simply stared at her, not believing that he was actually letting her stay. Especially when all he wanted to do was cross the room, pull her into his arms and kiss her. He would start slowly, savoring her lips, then he would go for it. By the time he finished with her mouth, she'd know, without a doubt, that she'd been claimed.

"Join me downstairs for breakfast in the morning around eight. I'd like to show you around," he said.

"I'd like that."

He nodded and went to walk past her to leave the room, but her scent caught him, and the urge to kiss her became overwhelming. He stepped toward her and she didn't back up. Instead, she asked, "Is there anything else?"

He smiled. "Yes, this."

And then he lowered his head to hers and claimed her lips, just the way he'd thought of doing every night since he'd last seen her. Unable to stop himself, he deepened the kiss, wrapping his arms around her waist and drawing her closer to him. The whimper that escaped her throat only fueled his desire. He removed one hand from around her waist, and pushed it through her hair, releasing the band holding her ponytail. He loved seeing her hair loose and flowing around her shoulders.

He wasn't sure how long they could have stayed that way, but when he skimmed his hands along her back, she broke off the kiss and stepped back, drawing in a deep breath. Her eyes were glassy, and her lips swollen. She wore his kiss well.

"Good night, Dak," she said, taking another step back.

He smiled. Maybe now she'd realize the dangers of showing up to a man's house uninvited. "Good night, Amelia. Sleep well."

And then he left the room, pulling the door shut behind him.

# Chapter 6

THE SOUND OF THE alarm on her phone brought Mellie awake. It was seven o'clock. That would give her an hour to shower and get dressed before meeting Dak downstairs. It had taken a while for her to fall asleep last night. That kiss.... It was no wonder she hadn't been able to sleep. That kiss had left her revved up and ready to rock. Sitting up in bed, she saw she'd received a text that morning from her grandmother. Mellie had sent her grandmother a message last night, letting her know she'd made it safely to Vermont.

Granny Kay had been out on a date, and so had only sent Mellie a smiley face emoji to let her know she'd gotten her message. This morning, her grandmother had added to her text, telling Mellie about the wonderful time she'd had with Mr. Carlton, and finishing with the hope that Mellie would enjoy her time with Dak. The one thing Mellie appreciated about her grandmother was that she treated her granddaughter like an adult, one who was mature enough to handle her own business. Granny Kay only gave advice when Mellie asked for it.

She sent her grandmother a smiley face emoji, then slid out the bed. She'd only unpacked the things she thought she'd need for today. She would find out from Dak just where they were headed, and then, if she needed to go shopping, she would. No biggie. She liked to shop.

A half hour later, dressed in a pair of khakis and a top, she descended the stairs wondering where Dak's bedroom was located. Following the scent of coffee, she walked toward the kitchen and found him there, already at the stove. "Good morning, Dak."

Turning to her, he smiled. "Good morning, Amelia."

Hopefully, that smile meant he was in a much better mood than he'd been when she'd arrived last night. She knew he hadn't been happy with her just showing up, but that was too bad. She had her reasons for coming. And it didn't hurt to keep him on his toes. He was far too used to getting his own way all the time. "Something smells good."

"I hope you're hungry," he said, turning back to the stove.

"I'm starving," she said honestly. "I haven't had anything to eat since lunch yesterday."

He turned back around and gave her a level stare. "Why didn't you say anything about that last night? I would have fed you."

"I was more concerned with whether or not you'd kick me out. It was a rough flight, and I was tired. I wouldn't have had the energy to find a hotel last night even if I'd wanted to." Not that she'd had any intention of doing that.

"Yet you played a game of pool with me."

She shrugged. "I'm never too tired to play pool. It's one of those games that helps me shift my concentration from exhaustion to competition."

"I see."

She doubted that he did. Few people did, especially the other doctors she worked with, who knew they could often find her during her lunch hour at the huge pool hall across the street from the hospital. "Anything I can do to help?"

"No. I don't want you to pass out on me before I can feed you."

Mellie rolled her eyes. She had never passed out and wasn't about to start now.

Deciding it was time to bring up the elephant in the room, she asked, "So, if I choose to do that 'see the world' thing with you, where will we be going?"

She needed to make sure he understood she hadn't decided yet, but so far so good. He had respected her wishes and hadn't tried to seduce her last night. She wasn't counting that kiss, although it nearly blew her mind, and filled her with sexual awareness every time she thought about it. She had initiated a kiss with him Saturday night, so now they were even—at least with the number of kisses they'd shared. There was no way the one she'd given him was anywhere near as impactful as the one he'd given her last night.

"Bali."

*Wow!* She never dreamed she'd ever go there. She knew it was an island located in Indonesia, one known for its volcanic mountains, beaches, coral reefs and rice paddies, and that when her chief of staff and his wife had visited there two years ago for their thirtieth wedding anniversary, they'd come back raving about it. Looking at the photos he'd shared, she'd thought the place was too beautiful for words, but also too extravagant for her budget. Although she didn't have a student loan, thanks to her scholarships, she didn't have as much in her savings account as she would have liked...thanks to Ivan. She wanted to open her own practice one day and that took money.

"Bali sounds nice."

"I believe that it is. The place I plan to stay is one of my most recent acquisitions. I had a few security measures installed and I want to check things out."

If this was a recent purchase for him, did that mean that he'd never taken a woman there? And why did it please her so much that she would be the first...that is, if that was the case and she decided to go? Still, right now, there were more points in her 'Go' column than in her 'No Go' one. He hadn't tried persuading her to sleep with him last night and this morning he was preparing her breakfast. So far, Dakota Navarro had been a perfect gentleman.

Mellie continued to watch him at the stove, trying not to notice how his jeans fit his delectable backside, or the way his t-shirt clung to his broad shoulders. Seeing he didn't need help in the kitchen, she pulled out her phone and checked her messages. Joy had texted her and so had Whitney. Other than her family, Whitney was the only person she'd told about what she was doing. Her best friend had seen Dak at Stonewall's wedding and had agreed with Mellie's estimation of him—he was hot! Whitney's text only contained two words...Want details.

"Did you want to eat in the sunroom off the kitchen?" he asked, gesturing to the room.

She nodded and slid off the stool. He handed her a plate and she followed him. The food looked good—pancakes, sausage and bacon and cheese eggs. Yes!

"How did you know I like cheese eggs?" she asked.

"I know that Stonewall prefers his cooked that way, so I took a chance you would, too."

She did. Granny Kay always prepared cheese eggs for her and Stonewall when they were growing up. The fact that Dak knew that about her, made her feel warm and tingly inside. "I do. Thank you."

"Here we are."

Mellie glanced around at Dak's sunroom. It was in the shape of an octagon, with walls that were made up predominantly with large panes of glass, and a beautifully tiled floor. The view outside of the windows showcased a beautifully landscaped yard under a gorgeous Vermont sky. It was as if she'd just entered heaven.

• • •

"Is anything wrong, Amelia?"

Dak watched as she glanced all around. "This room is beautiful, Dak. It doesn't look real. The view outside is like something in a painting or a postcard. Who has a waterfall in their yard? I've seen fountains before, but never a waterfall. It has to be more than one-hundred feet tall."

He didn't say anything for a minute as he placed his meal on the wicker table. "It's actually one hundred and forty. I designed it myself."

Her brow lifted. "You did?"

"Yes. Come on and eat before your food gets cold. I started the coffee earlier. How would you take yours?" he asked, walking over to the coffee cart.

"Black with sugar is good."

Dak chuckled as he poured. "Just the way Stonewall likes his."

Why did he keep bringing up her brother? Did he subconsciously assume that mentioning Stonewall would keep him in line and remind him just who she was? Namely, his friend's sister?

Instead, he should be trying to take Amelia for who she was—the beautiful woman he wanted. And that desire was growing by the second.

Work kept him too busy to date much. When a social affair called for a plus one, he'd find a companion, but it was only for the night, and meant nothing more than that. The only time he gave up any of his real, uninterrupted time to spend with a woman was one week each year, when he'd whisk her away to some exotic locale. And then it was over.

He was basically a loner and liked things that way. Serious relationships could get messy. Women wanted men to fall in love and he didn't think he was capable of loving anyone.

"There are a lot of things Stonewall likes that I don't," Amelia said, interrupting his thoughts.

"Such as?" he asked, returning to the table with their coffee.

"He loves raw oysters, and I don't. He also likes beer and I detest the stuff."

He slid into the chair across from her. "Anything you like that he doesn't?"

"Yes, pickles. Oh, and cauliflower. No matter how you prepare it, he won't touch it." She paused a moment and then asked, "Ready to say grace?"

There was no need to tell her that he hadn't ever said grace until he'd met Stonewall, who'd explained it as part of their upbringing. Granny Kay had certain rules during dinner and saying grace was one of them. You didn't dare place anything in your mouth without first giving thanks for it. Since his time with Stonewall, Dak had gotten used to doing it, and the few times he'd almost forgotten, he could have sworn he'd caught a glimpse of Granny Kay's frown out the corner of his eye. Like all of Stonewall's friends, he loved the old woman.

"I'm ready," he said, bowing his head.

Her prayer was a little longer than the ones Stonewall would mumble. He cocked an eye open when she not only blessed the food but also the hands that prepared it. The corners of his lips lifted in a smile. She was talking about him—his hands. Stonewall had never included that part.

"Everything looks good, Dak. I never took you for the domesticated type."

That made him wonder just what type she *did* take him for. He figured after spending a week with her, he would find out. Then again, she'd hinted more than once that the jury was still out as to whether or not she would fly to Bali with him tomorrow. He shrugged. If she didn't, some other woman would. Even if it was last minute. But then, he grudgingly admitted that he didn't want some other woman. He wanted Amelia to spend a week with him. That was the only real chance he had to finally get her out of his system.

"I love cooking. It's one of the pitfalls—or pleasures, as I see it now—of being Michael Navarro's son. Dad loved to cook and passed his passion for it on to me."

"Tell me about him."

What? His hands went still as he held his fork halfway to his mouth.

He kept his family history private—always. He didn't share his background with anyone, if he could help it. Then he remembered the conversation he and Amelia had had last weekend. On their way from the wedding to the reception, they had talked, and he'd shared portions of his past with her. It had been right after she'd confessed to losing her parents during a hurricane in Miami. Talking about his father at that time had seemed natural.

He could tell her any discussion of his father, other than what he'd already let slip, was off limits. But then, he could clearly recall one night in Dubai when he'd talked too much. That evening, over a bottle of bourbon that had given Stonewall one hell of a hangover, Dak had let his guard down and shared a lot about himself. Stonewall had done the same. In their lifetimes, both men had seen and done a lot. Some of those experiences had made them stronger, others had made them cautious. That night, Dak had explained to his hungover friend the reasons why he preferred not to make any woman a permanent part of his life. Had Stonewall ever said anything about it to Amelia? No. He wouldn't have...

"What do you want to know about my father?" he asked. It no longer surprised him that whenever he mentioned his father, he would immediately think of Michael Navarro—not Larry Smalls. Larry had only been in his life for the first seven years and Dak's memories of that time weren't good. There was Larry's excessive drinking, and the constant moving from place to place whenever rent was due. Dak remembered going to bed hungry most nights and getting a backhanded slap if he complained. Then, of course, there was Larry Small's constant sermons on the evils of women and relationships. For Dak, living with Larry had been hell. And the man who'd had the greatest positive impact on his life had been Michael Navarro.

"Whatever you want to tell me."

He brought the fork to his mouth and began eating, thinking about it. It was strange that she should make that request while they were out here, in this private place, where he could glance out at the waterfall he'd built in his father's honor. What was even stranger was that he was even entertaining her question. He figured Stonewall had told her some things and she wanted him to fill in the rest. She'd caught him in a good place. Whenever he came out here, he felt his father's presence even though Michael Navarro hadn't lived long enough to see it.

As he finished chewing, he glanced over at Amelia. She was watching him expectantly. *Hell, why not?* "I owe Michael Navarro everything, Amelia. Before he came into my life, my biological father, Larry Small, and I moved from place to place, barely keeping ahead of the bill collectors. I never even went to school, because we never stayed in one place for any length of time. Needless to say, Larry didn't look after me very well."

"You called your father, Larry?" she asked.

Dak nodded. "He told me not to call him anything else, because he was too young to be a father. Larry told everyone I was his little brother. My mother had me when she was sixteen, but she didn't want me. When Larry wouldn't help out with child support, she decided to give me to him. He was just barely seventeen then." He shook his head. "I guess she wanted him to see how it felt to raise a kid alone."

He paused for a minute. "Larry had been raised by his aunt, who told him she wasn't taking care of a baby. I understand that before my first birthday, we moved from New York to California. He followed a group of his friends there. Larry couldn't ever keep a regular job. Instead, he'd rely on his luck at poker to keep food on the table and a roof over our heads. Unfortunately, that didn't always work. And on those days, I'd do everything I could not to be around him, so he wouldn't take those losses out on me. It was as if it was my fault that he was a lousy card player. Then there would be no food for a while, until he could sweet talk his way into staying at some woman's house for a night or two. He never stayed any longer than that—he didn't believe in lasting relationships."

Dak figured there was no need to tell her what Larry thought of women, or that Dak's mother, the one who had deserted him, was the perfect example. Larry had told Dax that the only thing a woman was good for was sex. That had been a lot for a young kid to take in, especially one who didn't even know at the time what sex was.

"Then one night, I was home alone with no food, as usual. Larry had gone out to play poker, and he'd promised me he'd bring home hamburgers, fries and milkshakes to celebrate after he won." Dak shook his head, remembering. "There were some nights that I was so hungry I couldn't even sleep. That night was one of them. I was waiting for him, hoping he'd bring food that never came. Instead, a policeman and a lady from social services showed up sometime after midnight. They told me Larry was dead."

"Oh, how sad," she said in a soft, pitiful voice.

He wanted to resent her pity, but he couldn't. She was only showing compassion. And since she was a doctor, compassion probably came easy for her. "When the lady told me to go into my room to pack my things, I escaped through my bedroom window."

"How old were you then?"

"Seven."

"Where did you go?"

"I ended up living under a house three doors down, stealing clothes off people's lines when I needed something to wear, and hosing off with their water whenever I needed a shower."

"How did you eat?"

"I would steal food whenever I got hungry." He knew he wasn't painting a pretty picture, but it was a truthful one that few people knew about.

"What about your mother? Did she ever come back?"

"No. She never did. I always knew who she was because Larry told me about her. He even kept a picture of her around, but since he used it for dart practice, it didn't last long. But she had to be contacted before Dad could officially adopt me. Instead of wanting me, she signed me over to him without even coming to see me."

He didn't say anything for a minute, and then let out a long breath. "I dropped by to see her after I graduated from college. I was determined to prove that everything Larry had told me about her was lies and that there had been a good reason why she had given me away."

He took another bite of his food and chewed while thinking, then swallowed. "I discovered she is a very educated woman. She eventually got her PhD in Engineering and Technology. I guess she's the reason I'm good at both. Anyway, she said she was proud I'd made something of myself, but that when I was born, she wasn't ready to be a mother. She had plans that didn't include a baby. She hadn't known Larry had been killed until she was contacted about the adoption. At the time, she was still pursuing her career goals and wasn't ready to be a mother then either, so she was quite happy to let Michael adopt me."

"When you finally met her, after college, was she interested in having a relationship with you then?" Amelia asked.

"No. She had been married for a number of years and had more kids. She hadn't told her husband about the mistake she'd made at sixteen, and she'd said that she would appreciate it if I didn't try to become a part of her life. She felt it was too late for that."

Ignoring the angry look on Amelia's face on his behalf, he continued. "I told her I wouldn't and left. To her, I was just a mistake. I knew then that Larry had been right about her." Unfortunately, Dak had soon learned that what Larry had told him about women, in general, had often been true.

Amelia didn't say anything for a minute, but he knew she had more questions. He could see them in her eyes. Finally, she asked, "So how did you meet Michael Navarro?"

He leaned back in his chair. "I'd been living under the house for a couple of months. One day, I went to a bakery, hoping to swipe a couple of donuts and cookies. Michael caught me. He'd been in the shop at the time. I hadn't even known he was a cop until he told me, since he'd been out of uniform. It had been his day off."

Dak could clearly recall that day. He'd figured his life was over and would either be sent to family services or a youth detention center. "Dad told the owner of the bakery that he would take me to police headquarters himself. But he never did. Instead, Michael Navarro took me to his house and fed me. It was the most food I had ever eaten in a single day."

"Wasn't he breaking the law by not turning you in?"

He shook his head. "On the way home, Dad called his lady friend, Janice, to help. She was an attorney with Social Services and knew her way around the law. Janice and Dad used their connections with family services and the police department to find a way out of the situation. In the end, Dad applied to be my foster parent."

"He sounds like a nice man."

"Michael Navarro was the best. What he did for me was life-changing. He'd lost his wife, Tabitha, to cancer three years earlier, and they hadn't had any children. I want to believe he needed me as much as I needed him. He told me he did."

He watched her bite into a piece of crisp bacon and immediately felt heat settle in his gut. He felt the best way to get rid of the problem was to continue talking, since she seemed to be all ears. "Dad was Spanish-American and proud of it. He taught me to speak Spanish and, thanks to him, I got involved in activities at school. We even went to church—a Catholic one. Then, after he'd been my foster parent for a couple of years, he officially adopted me. I went from being Charles Smalls to Dakota Navarro."

She lifted a brow. "Charles? Your name is Charles?"

"It used to be. I told Dad I wanted it changed legally because being called Charles brought back bad memories for me. That's when I legally became Dakota Michael Navarro. It was my decision to take Dad's name as my middle name."

"Stonewall said you started college at sixteen and speak a number of languages."

It seemed Stonewall had shared a lot with his sister. "Yes, I was lucky. I'd aced a lot of placement exams, but didn't want to go away to college. I was still pretty young so I attended the local junior college, which allowed me to live at home and spend time with Dad. I enjoyed learning other languages and took several foreign language classes in college. Once I graduated, I went into the military. I wanted to be an Army Ranger, just like Dad had been. Because I had a college degree under my belt, I was able to enlist as an officer and that's when I picked up a few more languages. I thought of making the military a career...and then Dad got sick and died."

There was no need to tell her anything more. His life had come to a standstill with Michael's death. Not long after that, he'd been recruited by the USN and had been a part of that agency for five years. When his career with them ended, he discovered that all the money his father had left for him had been invested. There hadn't been enough to make him filthy rich, but there was plenty to give him a damn good start. He'd used that money to grow his skills as a businessman, and he'd discovered his ability to speak several languages was beneficial in his career. Other countries were happy to do business with Americans who spoke their language and understood and respected their cultures. Within five years, he'd made the Fortune 500 list and his wealth was still growing by leaps and bounds.

Deciding to bring any discussion about him to an end, he asked her, “Do you like being a doctor?”

# Chapter 7

MELLIE TOOK A SIP of her coffee. "I love being a doctor. My father was a dentist and Mom was his assistant. I know they would have loved it if I'd followed in their footsteps, but I didn't relish the thought of looking into someone's mouth all day. I wanted to do more. I like taking care of people and knowing how to heal them. But medical school is expensive, and I couldn't expect Granny Kay to worry about my dream, especially when she'd used most of the insurance money from my parents' death to pay for a lawyer for Stonewall when he got into trouble. It didn't keep him from going to jail but it kept him from doing ten years instead of five."

Dak nodded. "But he did eight."

Mellie couldn't help rolling her eyes. "Yes, he did eight because he kept getting into trouble. He and Striker were sworn enemies."

"Now they are the best of friends."

Mellie chuckled. "The best. I believe in another life that he, Striker and Quasar were brothers. Granny Kay and I have Sheppard Granger to thank for that."

She took another sip of her coffee, then added, “So I had to figure out a way to get to medical school myself. And with part-time jobs and student loans, I managed it. And yes, I truly love it. I didn’t go into any specific medical specialty, because I wanted to experience it all—the joy of suturing a wound, delivering a baby or finding a potential issue in someone before it can become a problem. I get a lot of joy from what I do...as long as I’m not taken advantage of by the hospital administration while I’m doing it.” She glanced at her watch. “Breakfast was good. At least let me help with the clean-up.”

He stood. “Nope. That’s what dishwashers are for. Then we’ll do the tour.”

Mellie nodded. She’d known Dak was a private person. Stonewall had made that pretty clear to her and Granny Kay when he’d told them what it had been like to work for Dak as his bodyguard. Dak had hired Stonewall a few years back when someone from his past—a former business associate who was holding a grudge about a business deal that hadn’t gone his way—had tried to kill Dak.

Now, in the light of day, Mellie had to admit the truth to herself, that the main reason she’d shown up, uninvited, the way she had was to see if she could break through that thick layer of privacy. She couldn’t imagine spending a week with Dak if she’d failed. Her time with him had to mean more to both of them than just sex. He had to be willing to share more of himself than his body. Why that meant so much to her, she wasn’t sure. She just knew that it did.

It took an hour for Dak to give her a complete tour of his home. It would have taken less time if she hadn’t 'ohhed' and 'ahhed' in every room they entered. Each one was a masterpiece, the decor perfect and the furnishing exquisite. He not only had an entertainment room in the basement, but a theater room and gym as well. To get there, they had to go down a separate set of stairs that were just as extravagant as the others. And below a third set of stairs, there was even a huge ballroom.

He'd explained that once in a while, when business affairs dictated, he would host parties to celebrate any successes his companies might have had. She could just imagine him, with a host of prominent and elite CEOs of various corporations and their wives or significant others in attendance, dancing the night away, enjoying themselves, all while Dak was making rounds with a forced smile on his face, inwardly counting the hours left before they would get the hell out of his home. He played the game when he had to but avoided it when he could.

In her line of work, she often had to do the same thing. Unfortunately, many of the doctors she worked with were pompous asses. And because she tended to go alone whenever there were gatherings or parties, they'd see her as an easy mark. To keep the peace, she would put up with their nonsense for a short time, and as soon as she could cut out, she did. Once she'd made an appearance, she was gone.

"Now for a tour of the outdoors," Dak said, breaking into her thoughts.

He led the way through the kitchen and out a door that opened into an eight-car garage. Several cars were parked inside, all of them impressive. "We will use this to get around," he said, heading toward a golf cart.

"What made you decide to move to Vermont?"

He glanced over at her, and Mellie caught her breath. Damn, she wished that she could control her reaction to him.

"A business deal. I got bored being stuck inside the hotel, so I decided to take a drive and check out the countryside. It was breathtaking. When I saw this property, which had once been a farm, was for sale, I bought it. I had the farmhouse and other structures torn down and built the home I wanted."

She nodded. "The waterfall off the sunroom.... You mentioned you designed it. What gave you the idea?"

He didn't respond, and for a minute, she had doubts that he would. Obviously, the answer was a personal one for him. When she was about to switch to another topic of conversation, he said, "I designed it in memory of my dad. He loved waterfalls and over the years, he'd put together a photo collection of the numerous ones he'd seen. Most of them were in other countries, places he'd visited when he was in the military. He tracked down a lot of them in the States, too. And most of those, we saw together."

Dak paused a minute, then cleared his throat. "We went to Niagara Falls one summer—it was incredible. But my favorite trip was to Yosemite. We camped out there for a week and had a blast."

She wondered if he realized how much happiness was in his voice whenever he talked about his father. In a way, it was sad that just before she was about to lose her family, he'd been gaining his. But she couldn't be anything but happy that Michael Navarro had entered Dak's life when Dak had needed him the most.

"I had that waterfall built so that whenever I go out there, and see how the water flows over it, I think about the way it represents my life...and my time spent with such an awesome man."

"It's a beautiful tribute, Dak."

When he said nothing, she knew it was time to change the subject. "How many acres do you have here?"

"Five hundred."

Half an hour later, Mellie had to admit it was the most beautiful land she'd ever seen. Sunny hillsides, lush valleys, huge lakes, scenic streams and then that breathtaking waterfall were just a few of the things that made this place so unique. He told her about the horses he owned and wasn't surprised she knew how to ride.

"My parents took us to a dude ranch somewhere in Wyoming one summer," she told him. "We had so much fun. Dad loved horses, and Mom loved seeing Dad relax."

"My dad loved horses, too," Dak said. "For a couple of years, he was part of the mounted police force. I still have a lot of pictures of him on horseback."

Since he'd brought up the subject of his father again, she decided to ask, "Your father never wanted to remarry?"

He didn't say anything for a minute. Then he let out a deep breath. "No. For years I thought that he and Ms. Janice would marry. She went a lot of places with us. But then one day, she stopped coming over. When I asked him about it, he said that she deserved more than a man who would forever love the wife he lost, a man who couldn't make room in his heart for anyone else. I think he grieved the loss of his wife until the day he died."

In a way, she understood that. Granny Kay had said the same thing, that she had loved Grandpa John so much, she couldn't ever see herself married to another man.

Once they returned to the garage, Dak took her hand. "You need to decide what you plan to do, Amelia. I'm flying to Bali in the morning, with or without you," he said.

Well, that was putting it bluntly. "I will go with you, Dak," she said. "But..."

He lifted a brow. "But what?"

"I'll be going for some R&R, not to be at your beck and call."

He chuckled. "You think not?"

She met his gaze. "I know not."

A smile spread across his lips. "Then this trip ought to be rather interesting."

• • •

That night Dak couldn't sleep, so he got up and went downstairs to the sunroom to stare out at the waterfall. He was beginning to think he had made a mistake by inviting Amelia on this trip. Already, she'd become more firmly embedded under his skin. Once they reached Bali, it would take some work to get her out...and he knew just how to do it. In his experience, once he'd managed to seduce his woman of choice, the thrill of the chase was over. And so far, it had always been about the chase, nothing more.

He wasn't the type who thought about a woman constantly, nor did he analyze the kisses they shared. After all, kisses weren't all that different. If you tasted one woman, you'd tasted them all. Even their scent was forgettable.

Unfortunately, that wasn't true when it came to Amelia.

There was something about her taste that was addictive, making him want more of it. And her scent was unforgettable. What was more unnerving was the fact that he knew it wasn't just the cologne she wore—it was her. She had a scent all her own.

Something else that was different was that he actually enjoyed spending time with her. She didn't go out of her way to impress him, hanging on to his every word or showering him with compliments. She asked questions, he answered, she listened. Like a sponge, she'd absorbed every word he'd said about his father. And he hadn't seen the expected look of horror in her eyes when he'd told her about how he and Michael had met. Most women believed he'd been born with a silver spoon in his mouth, and he'd never done anything to correct them. After all, he'd seen so many of his companions talk down to people they considered less than they were. It would remind him of the way he'd been treated when he was sixteen, at his first job working as a valet. And as bad as those women's opinions were, in a way, he was glad to see that side of them. Their words and actions revealed just what type of person they truly were.

It was obvious that Amelia was headstrong, which was probably the reason Stonewall had warned him about her. After all, Stonewall knew Dak preferred docile women, ones that were more eager to please. He didn't want to waste time arguing with them, or having them question his motives—especially when he made those motives clear. So, what the hell did Amelia mean when she'd said she wouldn't be at his beck and call?

He never said that he wanted her at his beck and call... but he did want her in his bed. And he was sure that once he got her there, she would enjoy it as much as he would.

He'd figured that after their tour of the house and yard, she'd have headed off to her bedroom. He'd needed the distance. Being around her for so long had shaken him to the core. So, he'd escaped to his office. He hadn't had anything in particular he'd needed to do there, but he'd *had* to get away from her. Her looks, her scent...everything about her was a temptation he couldn't deal with until they reached Bali.

When he had come out of his office hours later, he'd been told that she'd gone into town to shop. He should have been happy about that. Except, he'd figured she would have returned by dinner time. She hadn't. In fact, she hadn't returned until after dark. He'd been just about to send out a search party when she'd waltzed into his home, laden down with a number of shopping bags. There were so many, that Silas had to help her to bring them in.

He'd been about to give her hell until he'd seen the look of sheer happiness on her face. That's when she'd told him she'd had the best time, and she couldn't recall the last time she'd spent a day out, shopping without a care in the world. Without worrying about getting paged to come into the hospital.

And then she had done something he never expected—something he was learning she did a lot. She had tossed her bags aside and raced into his arms, kissing him on the cheek and thanking him for making it possible. Women had thanked him *after* going shopping, right before handing his charge card back to him. But Amelia hadn't used his money, hadn't asked for his card.

After that quick kiss, she had grabbed her bags and raced up the stairs, making two trips to get them all. And all he could do was stand there and watch her. In just one day, she'd driven him mad. Mad with desire.

Not even the sound of the waterfall could calm the need raging within him. He'd never wanted a woman the way he wanted her. And that was the crux of his problem. He didn't want to desire *any* woman this much. But he couldn't dismiss the way he'd felt seeing that happy look on her face. There was something really sexy about a woman with dimples. And when that woman grinned from ear to ear and all but did a happy dance in front of him. It was enough to make any man come apart. While she'd been upstairs with all her packages, he'd gone down to the entertainment room for a much-needed drink.

Through the intercom, he'd told her that he'd kept dinner warm, then he'd gone upstairs to his own bedroom, where he'd intended to stay sequestered for the entire night. And he had showered and gone to bed. Only now, after tossing and turning for more than an hour, he was back in his favorite spot—the sunroom. But even here, he couldn't escape thoughts of her.

How on earth would he survive being with her for seven days? He drew in a deep breath and somehow caught her scent into his nostrils. That meant she was near. He turned and saw the light on in the kitchen. It was after midnight. Finishing up his drink, he decided to go see what Amelia was up to.

# Chapter 8

MELLIE HAD JUST FINISHED the last of her packing and glanced at her watch. It was after midnight in Vermont but was three hours earlier in California. She picked up her phone, knowing Whitney would be expecting a call. Her best friend had called Mellie when she'd been out shopping, and Mellie had promised to call her back.

"About time you called, Mel."

Mellie threw her head back and laughed. "Aren't we impatient."

"Never mind about that. And before you give me the scoop on Dakota Navarro, I want to know if the Defenders were at the wedding."

Mellie shook her head. The 'Defenders' was the nickname Whitney had given Stonewall's three good friends—former convicts who were now top-notch attorneys in Oregon—Locke Dangerfield, Shogun Duke and Macayle Wasilla. The three men had made names for themselves as defenders of the law. And they were the best-dressed lawyers Mellie had ever seen.

Whitney had met the three men at Stonewall and Joy's wedding but had refused to say which one of them she had a thing for. Mellie had an idea, though Whitney had never confirmed her suspicion. And just to keep Mellie guessing, Whitney always asked about all three of them.

"Yes, they were in the wedding party. But that should be no surprise to you. I told you how close they are with Drew."

"I should have been there," Whitney said in a pouty voice.

"I invited you to go as my plus-one."

"I know, but I was tied up with that case from hell."

Mellie nodded. "And how did it go?"

"I won!"

Mellie jumped up, happy for her friend. "That's great! And you're just telling me now?"

"Calm down, Mel. The trial ended yesterday, and I just got the verdict an hour ago. I'm happy about it."

"You should be. You kept an innocent woman from going to prison. I'm proud of you."

"Thanks. Now I'm home alone, celebrating with my bottle of wine. My girl Stella Rosa never disappoints."

Mellie smiled. Stella Rosa had always been Whitney's favorite wine. "Go light on Stella. She can sneak up on you."

"She eventually will, but not before you tell me about Dak."

Mellie told her about his reaction to her showing up unannounced and about their game of pool. Then she'd regaled her friend about the way he had prepared breakfast for her, and about the beauty of Dak's home. She'd even confessed to their kiss last night.

"Are you ready for him, Mel?"

"The question is, is he ready for me?" Mellie said, sliding down in a chair.

"Stop trying to be a badass and just enjoy the moment. Do you know what it means to be chosen to share Dak Navarro's world for a week?"

"Only because you told me."

Whitney had overheard a woman—some fashion model—at the spa in LA, whispering to another woman about how she'd shared Dak's world a few years ago. The woman claimed he was generous with his money, loved buying her gifts and was more than fantastic in bed. The woman had sworn it had been the best seven days of her life. Unfortunately, once it was over, that was it. He didn't do repeats.

"Are you getting excited?" Whitney asked.

Mellie thought about that. "I guess I am. I've never been to Bali."

"Bali? Wow! I heard it's a beautiful place."

"I Googled it, and it looks incredible. I can't wait to see everything."

"Mellie, you should be concentrating on what you're going to do with Dak, not what you're going to see of the country. You and I both know what he wants—you in his bed. Stop acting like you don't realize that."

Mellie rolled her eyes. "Nothing will happen unless I want it to."

"Then trade places with me. If everything I've heard about his expertise in the bedroom is true, then I'm all in."

In a way, Mellie knew she was all in as well. Just being around Dak got her worked up. But she only gave herself to a man on her terms, no matter who the man was. She wouldn't make an exception with Dak. "I'm restless. I think I'll walk around and stretch my legs a bit."

"You're horny, hon. Admit it."

Whitney was probably right. It had been a long time since she'd been with a man and spending time with Dak hadn't done anything to keep her hormones in check. "I won't admit anything. Since you won't tell me which of the Defenders rocked your world, I'm going to keep some secrets, too."

"Umm, one day I'll tell you everything."

*Everything*? How much did she have to tell? "Now you've made me curious."

"I will tell you...sometime later. In the meantime, I'll expect a call from you when you get back. And please have fun."

"I intend to. Bye, Whit."

She clicked off the phone, wondering why Whitney was being so secretive. All three men—Locke, Shogun and Macayle—were handsome as sin. But because Mellie had gotten to know them as her brother's friends, she'd never considered them as anything other than older brothers. And they'd never treated her as anything more than a kid sister.

Standing and stretching, she realized she felt a little hungry for something sweet. Then she recalled seeing ice cream in the refrigerator earlier, both chocolate and vanilla. It was after midnight, but she was used to eating at odd hours, thanks to getting stuck working the night shift so often. Surely, Dak wouldn't mind if she helped herself to a bowl of chocolate ice cream, which was her favorite.

Slipping on a robe, she tiptoed down the stairs. Even though Dak's bedroom was on the other side of the house, she didn't want to chance waking him. There were no lights on downstairs, but she knew how to find her way to the kitchen. Once there, she flipped the light switch, then went to the freezer. Yes! There it was. She pulled out the carton of ice cream, and was just reaching into one of the cupboards to get a bowl when a deep, husky voice behind her said, "What are you doing up?"

She quickly turned to find Dak standing a few feet in front of her wearing just his pajama bottoms. *Oh my.*

• • •

Dak's gaze roamed over Amelia. She was wearing a sexy lace nightie with a matching sheer robe which left little to the imagination. When his gaze moved to her chest, he watched as the nipples pressed against the soft material seemed to harden right before his eyes. And he had no doubt his erection was hardening right before hers. There were certain things that were beyond their control. And a deep physical attraction was one of them.

She placed her arms across her chest, seemingly to shield her breasts from his eyes more than anything. But the gesture only made her already short nighty and robe raise up, exposing her delectable thighs. His gaze automatically moved to them. When she realized what she was doing, she dropped her hands and tugged on her robe, trying to cover more of herself. It didn't help. She finally gave up and glared at him.

"Do you have to look at me like that, Dak?"

He cocked a brow. Look at her? If only she knew how hard it was not to cross the floor and take her in his arms, right there and then. She would never believe how long it'd been since he had a woman in his bed. And it was all her fault. Since meeting her, he just couldn't work up the interest to find another bed partner. She had literally crushed his desire for other women. And she was concerned with the look he was giving her?

"Why are you up?" he asked again, instead of answering her question. More than likely, she would not have liked his answer.

"I got hungry. Then I remembered seeing ice cream in the freezer earlier today. And it's my favorite flavor. I figured you wouldn't mind."

Dak should mind. Not that she was eating his ice cream, but that she was standing there, looking good enough to eat. The thought made him unconsciously lick his lips.

"Well, do you mind?" she said, when he didn't say anything.

"No. In fact I'll join you."

Dak knew he was only asking for trouble, given what she was wearing and how he was feeling. But then, he was half-dressed himself. This was his house and he wouldn't make any excuses for being comfortable. Still, he couldn't help but notice the way she was checking him out, especially below the waist.

"You want to join me?" she asked.

He heard the wariness in her voice and knew joining her was probably the last thing she wanted. Too bad. If she only knew what he really wanted to do with her, she would probably run back to her room. But he'd control himself and wait until they were in Bali to touch her the way he wanted to. He had already broken a sacred house rule by letting her spend the night in his home. He wasn't going to break another by making love to her here.

"Do you have a problem with that, Amelia?"

She shrugged. "Why should I? It's your ice cream." She turned to get the bowls from the cupboard and when she once again got on her tiptoes, his gaze couldn't help but focus on the new skin revealed as her already short robe and nightie got even shorter. When she realized it, she quickly turned around. "Maybe you ought to get the bowls. You're taller."

"No problem."

Amelia quickly skirted out of his way, stopping to stand at the end of the counter when he went to the cupboard for the bowls. "Is anything wrong?" he asked.

She shook her head. "No, nothing is wrong."

He smiled, wondering if she was thinking the same thing he was—nothing was wrong that a little roll between the sheets wouldn't cure. He effortlessly opened the cupboard, pulled out two bowls and sat them on the counter. "Are you going to fill them or do you want me to do it?" he asked, when she seemed determined to stay where she was.

"You can do it. I think I'll go and put on more clothes."

Dak smiled at her. "If you feel the need, go ahead. But I don't intend to put on any more. You do know we'll be spending a whole week together, right? That time also includes nights."

"Why are you mentioning that?"

*Did she really have to ask?* "No reason," he said, filling both bowls to the top—hers with chocolate, his with vanilla.

"Do you want to sit in here or in the sunroom?" he asked her.

"Is it well-lit out there?"

*Was she asking because she was hesitant about being in the dark with him*? He nodded. "There's a full moon tonight, and it will offer a lot of light. And the yard is lit. But if that's not enough, there are lamps, too." He put the ice cream cartons back in the freezer, stuck spoons in the bowls and headed toward the sunroom, aware that after a brief hesitation, she was following.

She looked around. "It's beautiful out here at night, Dak."

He placed the bowls on the table. "That's the way I planned it when I designed this place. No matter the time of day or night, you can clearly see the waterfall, as well as hear it."

"I like the way the boulders, gravel, and shrubs around the waterfall are lit up as well. It's so beautiful. I bet you come out here when you can't sleep. This place is so peaceful and calming."

"It is certainly that," he said, sitting down and watching as she slid into the chair across from him. After she said grace, he watched, enraptured, as she took a spoonful of ice cream and slid it into her mouth. His already aroused body got even harder at the thought of her taking him in her mouth the same way.

"Umm...this is so delicious," she said.

For him, it was just chocolate ice cream. She was the delicious one. Her kisses had proven that much. Now he couldn't help wondering how she tasted intimately.

"Aren't you going to eat yours? It's melting." It was on the tip of his tongue to say he'd rather eat her instead, but figured she wouldn't appreciate his candor—at least, not yet. "Right. I like to let it soften a bit." Then he proceeded to take a spoonful. "All packed?"

"Yes. I'm so excited."

He cocked a brow at her. She hadn't even been sure if she was going, and now she was excited? "Why?"

"Because I'm going somewhere I've never been before. This is an adventure for me, Dak."

Hopefully, it'd end up being more of an affair to remember for her. Granted, things might be a little awkward whenever they saw each other again at functions, but they were adults. They'd handle it.

"I hope you see it as more than just an adventure, Amelia."

"We'll see."

Yes, they would. And she would discover that once his jet took off, his entire attitude would change, right along with the plane's altitude. He'd go into predator mode. After all, he'd wanted her, and only her, for two solid years. That's a long time to go without female companionship. The only good thing about it was that he'd been too busy to worry about it. However, the nights had been long and when he'd slept, Amelia had been who he'd dreamed of. And even though he wanted her more than he'd ever wanted another woman, he expected her to leave once their time was up. He wasn't about to change for any woman...not even Amelia.

"How long is the flight?" she asked.

"First, we'll fly to London, which will take about seven hours. We will spend the night there and fly out to Bali the next day. That will be an additional sixteen hours, with one stop in between to refuel."

"So, we're looking at total air-time of twenty-three hours?" At his nod, she said. "That's an hour short of a day."

"Yes, but we'll be traveling on my luxury jet, not a commercial airline. I think you're going to like it."

"I heard about your jet. You let Joy and Stonewall use it for their first date."

"That was a different jet. I've gotten a new one since then."

"Oh. I can't wait to see it, Dak."

"And I can't wait to show it to you."

They continued eating ice cream, making casual chit-chat. He kept glancing over at her, amazed at her beauty. He could understand how she'd won so many beauty contests. She was definitely the most gorgeous woman he'd ever seen. That was one of the reasons he'd found it hard to believe she wasn't taken. A woman with her looks didn't usually stay single for long.

"Why don't you have a man?" he finally asked when curiosity got the best of him.

She looked at him. "I thought we covered that last night."

"No, you said you weren't seriously involved with someone. Now I want to know why."

"What if I said that it's none of your business?"

"You have that right."

"Good. I intend to use it. It's none of your business, Dak. All you need to know is that I am happily single—not the reason why."

"That makes me think things, Amelia."

"What sort of things?"

"That maybe you're a tough woman to satisfy."

She lifted a questioning brow. "Satisfy in what way?"

"Any number of them."

A smile spread across her lips. "Does the possibility that you won't be able to satisfy me either make you, umm...I don't know...nervous?"

He returned her smile. "Nope. Not to sound cocky, but I'm confident in my abilities."

She didn't say anything for a moment as their gazes held. Then she added, "And what if I told you that I'm confident in my abilities, as well?"

"Then I would say, bring it on."

She broke eye contact with him and finished off the last of her ice cream. Standing, she glanced over at him. "Be careful what you ask for. You might just get it."

Then without saying another word, she took her bowl and spoon and headed into the kitchen, sashaying a very delectable ass in the cutest nightie set he'd ever seen. But then, he really hadn't seen many women's nightclothes since most of the ones he'd entertained got naked the minute they entered his bedroom. It was nice to see a woman in sexy lingerie for a change. It was definitely different.

But then, Dak had a feeling that spending time with Amelia would be different than anything he'd ever experienced. And he couldn't wait.

# Chapter 9

NOT WANTING TO KEEP Dak waiting, Mellie made sure she was packed and ready to go before he made it downstairs. He blinked when he saw her. "Good morning, Amelia. What time did you get up? Or did you even go to bed last night?"

She thought he looked good. He was casually dressed but looked impeccable in a pair of dark brown slacks and a beige buttoned-down shirt. The man was lean with well-defined muscles and his abs were downright perfect. There was no way she could ever deny that Dakota Navarro was truly a fine specimen of a man.

"I went to bed after satisfying my sweet tooth and slept like a baby." She hadn't, really. No baby would have had the risqué dreams she'd had last night.

"That's good to hear." He glanced around, and then asked, "Where's your luggage?"

"I've taken it out to the car already."

"Which car?"

She thought his question odd. "The car I drove here from the airport."

“We’re taking my car, so I’ll move your luggage...”

“Hold up,” she said, gesturing time-out with her hands. “I need to return my rental car to the airport.”

“No, you don’t. Silas will return it for you.”

She scrunched her brow, trying to figure out how that made sense. “We are going to the airport, right?”

“Of course.”

“Then why can’t I drive my own car there and return it myself?”

He crossed the room to stand in front of her, and her head swam. Not only did he look good, but he smelled good, too. “Because our time together officially starts today, and I want you with me.”

Mellie didn’t want to admit it, but she liked the sound of that. She couldn’t recall the last time a man had said something like that to her. She was pretty sure nobody ever had. “I never took you for the clingy type, Dak.”

He leaned in, so close she could feel the warmth of his breath on her face. “Not clingy, Amelia, but consumed. Like you, I tend to work hard. But when I play, I play even harder.”

She scrunched her brow. “By being consumed with a woman?”

“By being consumed with you.”

Mellie decided this back-and-forth banter wasn’t getting them anywhere. She was about to take a step back when he reached out and wrapped his arms around her waist. “You rushed off last night,” he said in a husky voice.

“No, I didn’t. I’d finished my ice cream and I felt we had nothing else to talk about.”

“Who said anything about talking?”

She drew in a deep breath. Dak Navarro didn't miss a beat when it came to flirtation, but she wasn't exactly a wallflower. She knew the drill—there were always new single doctors hired by the hospital who were anxious to prove their bedside manners. She'd always managed to handle them with ease, but she had a feeling Dak would be another matter, especially when he stared intently into her eyes.

Deciding to change the subject, she took a step back and asked, "Are you packed?"

"Yes."

"Where is your luggage?" she asked.

"In my room. I'll bring it down in a minute. I've arranged to have breakfast served on my jet. However, if you're hungry now, I can certainly prepare something for you."

"I'm fine. And please don't think you have to take care of me. I can prepare something for myself."

"I don't mind taking care of you."

A part of her believed him. Before going to bed, she scoured the internet for information about him. She'd found numerous articles where women had complimented him on the way they'd been treated in his care. Whitney had overheard a woman saying the same thing—that Dak had been attuned to their every need, solicitous to their wants and had made them feel as if they were the most important person in his world...only for that one week. Some had admitted to taking full advantage of everything he offered, since they knew that one week was all they'd get.

Mellie didn't want anyone to take care of her. She looked after and could certainly take care of herself. After all, for years, it had been just her and Granny Kay, and they'd cared for each other. Even when Stonewall had come back into their lives again, she and Granny Kay had quickly let him know they weren't defenseless, nor did they need to be protected and coddled. They were strong women who could manage quite well by themselves. And any man in their lives had better let them do it.

Mellie read a little farther, not thrilled with what she'd found. How could those other women be so mercenary? She had no intention of taking advantage of his kindness—or his wealth—no matter what he said.

One thing she'd noticed in a lot of the articles about Dak was that there was a common complaint among Dak's week-long flings—he never let any of them get too close. One woman claimed there was an invisible line he refused to cross about how much he shared of himself. Mellie shook her head. That was odd. He'd shared a lot of things with her already. He'd told her about his father—how close their relationship was, how much the man had meant to him. Of course, maybe he felt more comfortable with her because of his relationship with Stonewall. It wasn't as if she was a stranger to him. Through Stonewall, they'd both known about each other for years. That had to be it.

"Amelia?"

"Yes," she said, returning to the present, to the man still standing in front of her. Too close. He was no longer holding her waist, so she took a step back.

"Do you want breakfast now or can you wait? It'll be another couple of hours."

"I can wait. But I would like a cup of coffee. I could put on a pot, if you'd like."

"Coffee sounds great. I'll go back upstairs and grab my luggage. The car that will be taking us to the airport will arrive in half an hour."

She watched him stride back up the stairs and appreciated how good he looked doing it. The sheer masculinity that radiated off him was mind-blowing. And the scent of his aftershave lingered in the hall, surrounding her in a sensual warmth.

No man had ever gotten to her this way before, and she wasn't going to let Dak be the first. She could appreciate a gorgeous man as much as the next woman, but she wasn't about to let him override her common sense.

Drawing in a deep breath, she headed into the kitchen to make a strong pot of coffee. She was going to need all the fortification she could get.

• • •

Dak closed his bedroom door, then leaned against it. Drawing in a deep breath, he rubbed a hand down his face while his heart pounded like crazy in his chest. Why did he have such an extreme reaction every time he saw Amelia? And how did she manage to keep surprising him?

He'd dated lots of beautiful women in his lifetime—actresses, models, businesswomen, heiresses....Gorgeous women who looked stunning in anything they wore...and even more stunning wearing nothing at all. So, what was it about Amelia Courson that rattled him so badly?

The moment she'd turned the most beautiful pair of brown eyes on him, he'd been dazed. They were sultry brown, and had a way of drawing a man in, mesmerizing the hell out of him and filling him with fantasies that were out of this world. Out of this damn universe. And worse, she was just as desirable first thing in the morning as she was late at night. But he'd already realized there was much more than just sex appeal at play in his attraction for Amelia. And he intended to find out just what the hell that 'much more' was, over the next seven days.

"Get a grip, Navarro," he muttered, moving away from the door. "You haven't met a woman you couldn't handle. You'll manage to walk away when the time comes. You always do."

*Yet*, his inner thoughts then grudgingly reminded him, *you walked away from her two years ago, and she's been on your mind ever since. And you haven't been able to get lost in another woman since that dance. Hell, you haven't even tried.*

No, he hadn't, he thought, gripping the handle of his luggage. That's why this trip with her was so important to him. He needed to get Amelia Courson out of his system once and for all, and a full week with her, in and out of his bed, ought to do it. Damn, he hoped so.

But what if a week with her wasn't enough? What if it had the opposite effect, allowing her to burrow even deeper under his skin? He shook his head. No, that was impossible. Such a thing hadn't happened before and he couldn't see it happening now. On the other hand, he'd never wanted a woman as badly as he wanted Amelia.

Last night, when he'd walked in on her in the kitchen, and saw that she was dressed in that sexy nightie and matching robe, he'd almost swallowed his tongue.

He paused at his bedroom door when his cell phone rang. Recognizing the ringtone, he pulled it out of his pocket. "Yes, Syl?"

Sylvester Wright had been a good friend of Dak's father. Michael had taken Syl under his wing at the police academy when Syl had been hired on with the force. At the time, Michael had been an instructor with the Coachella Police Department. Syl and Michael had had an instant connection, and over the years the two had become the best of friends. Before he died, Michael had made Syl promise to look after Dak, and he'd kept that promise.

Syl had been part of the air rescue squad and had flown choppers for most of his police career. There was only a five-year difference in their ages, but there were times when Syl acted as if he had more than twenty years on Dak, trying to act like a surrogate father for Dak because of the promise he'd made to Michael.

Dak constantly reminded Syl that he didn't need a keeper. Syl's response was that Dak deserved it for luring him away from the police department and making him his personal pilot.

Syl was in top physical shape and had women throwing themselves at him all the time. He claimed it was the 'man in the uniform thing' and refused to take any of it seriously. A divorce ten years ago had left a bad taste in Syl's mouth, and he'd sworn he'd never marry again. But Dak knew it was only a matter of time before a certain woman, Peggy Henderson, changed Syl's mind about that. Syl had taken the bait and hadn't yet realized he'd been caught.

"I was just taking a look at the information Jefferson forwarded to me, Dak."

Dak already knew where this conversation was about to go. "And?"

"I see the other passenger is Amelia Courson."

Dak rolled his eyes. "And?"

"Please tell me she's not the Amelia Courson who is Stonewall's sister."

"Sorry. That's exactly who she is."

He held his phone away from his ear when he heard the expletives flowing from Syl's end. The man had put in a few years with the Navy before becoming a cop and could 'curse like a sailor' better than anyone Dak knew. "Calm down, Syl."

"Calm down, my ass. Are you crazy? Does Stonewall know you're sniffing behind his sister? A better question to ask is whether Stonewall knows she's going with you for one of your 'Dak's world' flights?"

"He knows."

"And you're still alive?"

"Stonewall's my bodyguard. He's supposed to protect me, not kill me, Syl."

"He used to be your bodyguard, Dak. Now he's a friend—a *good* friend. And you know better than anyone what his sister means to him. He'd talk about her all the time."

"So?"

"Just so you know...When Stonewall kicks your ass, I won't lift a finger to help you. In fact, I'll be cheering him on."

Dak felt a gigantic headache coming on. "Stonewall will not be kicking my ass. He knows Amelia is here and she knows the score. She's not a kid and can make her own decisions about what she wants to do."

"Okay, then. But don't say I didn't warn you." And with that, Syl hung up on him.

Dak placed his phone back in his pocket, trying to ignore the fact that Stonewall had told him the same thing.

# Chapter 10

"AMELIA, I'D LIKE YOU to meet my pilot, Sylvester Wright."

Mellie smiled as she gazed into the man's sparkling blue eyes and knew immediately that she would like him. He was taller than Stonewall and Dak, but was just as handsome, in a ruggedly sexy sort of way. "Nice meeting you, Mr. Wright."

"Just call me Syl," he said, taking her hand. "And how are Stonewall and Joy?"

"They're fine," she said, studying the man. "I remember you now. You were at their wedding."

He nodded. "I got to know Stonewall when he was Dak's bodyguard. And when Stonewall took Joy on their first date in Dak's plane, I was their pilot. I think we bonded because we were both cops at one time."

She remembered that Dak had loaned Stonewall his plane and pilot to fly Joy to Martha's Vineyard for the evening. It was the date that had officially kicked off what Mellie thought of as a perfect love match.

"They're expecting a baby in January," she said, smiling.

"That's great news. Tell them congratulations," Syl responded.

"I will."

Moments later Dak was leading her up the steps of the plane. The moment she stepped inside, she couldn't believe her eyes. She'd expected it to be luxurious, but this was stunning. "It's...gorgeous," she said, glancing around.

"Thank you. I've only had it a year and had it specially designed and built by Granger Aeronautics. It's faster than a normal luxury jet and has many state-of-the-art elements. Come, let me show you around. Then we'll make ourselves comfortable."

She gasped in awe as he led her through each room of the jet. The first cabin was spacious, with two cubicles of four seats that faced each other. She liked that there was a lot of leg room between the seats. Even a man as tall as Syl could stretch out in comfort. There was even a loveseat on the opposite side. She loved the sky-blue interior and the matching shade of carpeting looked rich and plush.

They passed a bathroom that was larger and more elegant than the one at her house. Next, they walked into what she figured to be a meeting room with a long conference table. There was a big screen television and, in addition to the lights in the ceiling, there were several lamps lined up against one wall. The other wall provided a floor to ceiling window that ran the length of the room. She couldn't imagine trying to conduct business in this room while knowing you were at least thirty-five thousand feet.

After showing her around the meeting room, they passed another bathroom that was even larger than the last one, before coming to what he said was his dining suite, which was separated into three sections.

The first dining area looked like it could be used for up to ten guests. The next one seemed to be a little cozier, with a round table and swivel chairs that seated four. Then, finally, they came to an area that was obviously meant for more intimate dining. There were only two seats, but the area was just as spacious as the section that seated ten. There was a wet bar off to the side, and a wine-rack filled with close to twelve bottles. When Dak told her to look up, she found that the entire ceiling was made of glass.

"It's beautiful in here at night, when you can see all the stars," he said.

She could just imagine. Well, honestly, she really couldn't. This was all too much for her imagination right now.

They then entered the area he called his entertainment suite. It even had a pool table. There were more tables where he said he often sat and worked on puzzles or did word games during long flights to keep his mind sharp.

There was also a television that was so large, it filled one of the walls. There were plenty of windows in this room and she could tell it had been designed with Dak's likes in mind. This room even had its own private bath.

Finally, they walked through a set of double doors to the bedroom suite. Mellie was convinced she'd never seen a bedroom so elegant. There were wall-to-wall windows and a ceiling made of glass. Mellie wondered what it would be like to sleep among the clouds. And the bathroom was as spacious as one you'd find in a five-star hotel.

"This suite is simply beautiful, Dak."

"Thanks. Now I want you to meet Peggy."

She lifted a brow. "Peggy?"

"Yes. My flight hostess. Come on, our breakfast should be ready by now."

When they reached the dining suite, Mellie saw breakfast had already been set in the dining area for two. A very attractive woman, who appeared to be about her age, smiled at her when Dak made the introductions. "Amelia, this is Peggy. If you ever need anything, just let her know."

"It's nice to meet you, Peggy," she said to the blond-haired, blue-eyed woman dressed in a professional flight attendant uniform.

"Same here, Ms. Courson."

"Please call me Mellie."

She nodded. "It's nice meeting you, too, Mellie. If you need anything, please let me know."

"Thanks."

"Breakfast is ready, Dak."

Although the woman was smiling, Mellie didn't detect any chemistry between Peggy and Dak. But still, she wondered if he and Peggy had ever been involved. After all, she was a very attractive woman.

"This way, please," Dak said, taking her hand and leading her to the table. The platters were covered but whatever was in them smelled good. When he slid into the seat across from her, she realized just what an intimate fit it was. She took a deep breath and was immediately sorry she had. A woman could get drunk on his scent alone. Everything about him threw a woman's hormones out of whack.

It hadn't been easy to stay in that bedroom with him. When he'd moved to stand by the bed, she couldn't help imagining what it would be like to roll around in the sheets with him, with the stars all around them and the moon as a backdrop.

"Excuse me for a minute. I need to talk to Syl about something. Go ahead and get started with your meal."

When he got up and walked off, she let out a long breath and wished he wasn't such an impossibly sexy man. Although he'd told her to go ahead, she decided not to start eating until he returned. Besides, she could use this time to gather her wits, because she'd definitely lost them, the minute she'd walked into Dak's bedroom.

Pulling out her phone, she decided to text her grandmother to let her know of their destination and sent Joy a text as well. Mellie figured Granny Kay or Joy would let Stonewall know if he asked. And knowing her brother, he would ask.

"You're not eating?" Dak said, sliding back into the seat across from her.

She'd just put her phone away. She glanced at him and smiled. "I was waiting for you."

"You didn't have to do that," he said.

"I wanted to."

During this trip, Mellie was sure that Dak would discover a lot of new things about her. Specifically, things she did not because she felt she had to, but because she wanted to. Why did she have a feeling sharing a bed with him would be one of those things.

• • •

"Syl mentioned he used to be a cop. Has he been your pilot long?"

Dak glanced over at Mellie as he buttered his toast. She wouldn't be the first of his female guests to ask about Syl. Before, he'd found it amusing, but right now, he wasn't laughing. "Why do you want to know?"

"Just curious."

He couldn't help wondering just how deep that curiosity went. "He's been with me right from the start. He and my dad were good friends."

"And Peggy?"

He looked at her, quizzically. He'd been around enough women to know when they were asking about another woman out of curiosity...or for another reason. He had a feeling Mellie had another reason. "Peggy wasn't a friend of Dad's, if that's what you're asking," he replied, knowing it wasn't.

When she didn't say anything, he decided to add, "She was recommended by one of my clients. She'd worked for him, and he told me she had a pleasing personality and would be good as a flight hostess."

Amelia shrugged. "Then why didn't he keep her?"

Dak smiled. "He married a much younger woman who saw Peggy as a threat."

"She *is* gorgeous."

"Yes, and eventually Syl will start noticing."

He watched Amelia raise a brow. "Is there something going on between them?"

Dak chuckled. "Not that I know of, but Peggy is convinced she belongs with him. Unfortunately, I don't think Syl got that same email."

Amelia smiled broadly, and Dak couldn't help but wonder if that was relief he saw in her eyes. Had she seen

Peggy as a threat? No reason why she should. He didn't belong to any woman...not even Amelia.

"Like I said, she's gorgeous," Amelia said. "Syl doesn't come across as someone who's slow."

Dak took a sip of his coffee. "He's not slow, just determined. He was married before, and it ended badly. He's sworn he's never going through that again. Peggy, on the other hand, has never been married. But Syl feels she's the marrying kind, so he's determined to keep his distance. And I must say, he's been doing a pretty good job of it for almost a year now."

"That's how long she's been working for you?"

"Yes."

She shook her head. "All I can say is that, typically, men don't realize a good thing until it's too late. I hope he's not one of them."

Dak didn't like the personal implications of what she'd said, so he decided to change the subject. "We'll take off once we've finished eating and are buckled into our seats."

"My goodness," she said, wiping her mouth. "I wasn't aware we were holding things up."

"We're not, so there's no need to rush. Besides, I enjoy sharing meals with you."

And that was the truth. Normally, he ate alone. Even when he'd invited a woman to go away with him, he made sure they weren't together every single minute. He usually needed at least some time alone, especially if the woman began getting too clingy. However, as usual, with Amelia, things were different. He didn't want any solo time, and he damn sure hoped she got clingy. Real soon.

"This meal is delicious," Amelia said, intruding into his thoughts.

“Glad you like it.” He took another sip of his coffee. “Tell me something I don’t know about you, Amelia.”

She glanced up with those sultry brown eyes and pushed a lock of hair away from her face. His heart rate accelerated. God, she was beautiful. “Would you believe that I was squeamish when I was growing up? I totally freaked out at the sight of blood, even my own.”

He found that hard to believe, given her current profession. “Yet you wanted to become a doctor?”

“Not at first. I wanted to be an astronaut.”

He leaned back in his chair. They were still sitting on the tarmac and other planes were flying in and flying out around them. “So how did you go from wanting to be an astronaut to becoming a doctor?”

She leaned back in her seat as well. “During that time, it was just me and Granny Kay. My grandmother has always been involved with the church committee that looked after the sick and the shut-in’s. One of the things she did often was visit the sick, either in the hospital or in nursing homes. And she usually took me with her.”

“That had to be rather depressing for you,” he said.

She took a sip of her coffee, then shook her head. “It wasn’t so bad. And I grew up admiring the doctors and nurses. Their sole purpose was to make people better. One day I decided that I’d make more of a difference if I stayed on earth and helped heal the sick, instead of flying off into space, chasing a new frontier.”

“How did you get over your problem with blood?”

She smiled broadly, and he forced back a groan at seeing those two dimples. “Granny Kay struck again. When I told her about it, she said the best way for a person to conquer their fears was to never let those fears conquer them. So, she began taking me to see a lot of horror flicks. Although I knew we weren't seeing real blood, it helped me get past my problem with it."

Dak couldn't help thinking that Amelia was very lucky to have a grandmother like Granny Kay. Unfortunately, the advice she'd given Amelia—to not let her fears conquer her—wouldn't work for everyone. Not everyone could get past their fears that easily.

Larry Smalls had preached to his young son the dangers of falling in love and letting a woman become a permanent part of your life. And Dak had seen those issues become a major problem with Michael Navarro, who had taken a chance on love, and lost her. The fear of losing another loved one was a fear so deeply rooted within him, he doubted he'd ever conquer it. And so, he found it easier not to let anyone get too close. He liked his life just the way it was. No permanent woman. No worries. No grief. He only had himself to be concerned about, and no one else.

"Now it's your turn."

He glanced over at Amelia. "To do what?"

"To tell me something about Dakota Navarro that I don't know."

"There is too much to tell."

She shrugged. "I have a week."

He chuckled. "Even if you had years, you would never know the real me. I don't share myself with others."

She met his gaze and held it, as if appraising him. Finally, she tilted her head. "What if I told you that I'm determined to learn all about you this week, Dak?"

"Then I would advise you to spend your time doing something you won't fail at, Amelia."

"Such as?"

"Satisfying me in the bedroom."

• • •

"Are you sure, Miguel?" the man with the South American accent asked.

"I'm sure. I'd know that face anywhere," Miguel said, glancing around to make sure he wasn't overheard. He was sitting in a café at the airport. People were coming and going, but no one seemed to be paying any attention to him, and that was good. Their leader had been in a foul mood lately. Miguel figured that hiding out for years with a price on his head, eluding the authorities, could do that to someone. Hopefully, this news would brighten his day.

There was a pause and then the person on the other end said, "What's the aircraft's final destination?" Miguel could hear the excitement in his voice—more excitement than he'd heard in years. At least not since he'd received news of his father's death, and was informed that he, himself, was suddenly a wanted man.

"Final destination is Bali."

There was another pause, then he said, "Get some of your men together and fly to Bali. You know what to do. I have a score to settle, and I want you to make sure it's done."

# Chapter 11

A SHORT WHILE LATER, Mellie sat fiddling with her seatbelt, doing her best to avoid looking at Dak. He was sitting in the seat directly across from her. It was better than if he'd been sitting beside her, but it was still too close for her peace of mind.

She couldn't stop thinking about what he'd said about satisfying him in the bedroom. Of course, he would consider that to be her only role on this trip.

"Do you need help over there?"

She glanced over at him. "Help with what?"

"Your seatbelt. You've yet to snap it in place."

The moment he said that, she stopped playing with the belt. A loud click sounded in the cabin. "Happy now?"

"I think Syl and Peggy are the ones who are happy."

His words made Mellie realize she'd been holding everyone up. He'd told her that during breakfast, but she'd forgotten. "I owe them an apology."

"No need. They'll assume you're merely nervous."

"I'm not nervous. I've flown before, lots of times," she said.

"I wasn't talking about flying, Amelia. I meant about flying away with me."

She lifted a questioning brow. "Do they know something about you that I should be concerned about?"

Dak shifted in his seat, and Mellie wished she hadn't noticed the way the material of his slacks stretched across his muscular thighs. Thighs she had yet to see but had dreamed of often enough.

"Not that I'm aware of."

She moved her gaze from his thighs to his face. "Excuse me?"

He smiled and she had the feeling he'd noticed just where her eyes had been focused. "You asked if Sly and Peggy knew something about me that you should be concerned about. I merely answered that there wasn't anything I was aware of."

His casual reply made Mellie even more determined to discover the real Dak for herself. "You know, Dak, I'm not as naive as you seem to think I am."

He chuckled. "Trust me, Amelia, not for one minute did I ever believe you were naive. I know you are a highly intelligent woman. However..."

She tilted her head. "Yes?"

"I think you'll be wasting your time trying to figure me out, if that's your plan. I told you what I'd like you to do."

"Satisfy you in bed?"

"Yes, among other things."

*Among other things*? Wouldn't rocking his world be enough? Still, curiosity made her ask, "What other things?"

His smile widened even more. "When the time comes, I will show you."

She rolled her eyes. "You know, I never did like show and tell."

He laughed. "That's good to know. But don't worry. My take on it is show and do."

She was about to offer a flippant comeback when Syl's voice came over the intercom. "We're about to take off. Please keep your seatbelt fastened until we reach our cruising altitude. Enjoy the flight."

Mellie drew in a deep breath. What she'd told Dak earlier was true. Flying didn't necessarily make her nervous, take-offs and landings did make her sort of anxious. It was the sensation of first leaving the ground and then returning to it abruptly that made her stomach queasy. However, once the plane leveled off, she was fine.

"Are you okay over there?"

She looked at Dak. "Why wouldn't I be?"

"Just asking."

She decided to ignore him for the time being, and just sit quietly, trying not to look out the window. That only made her anxiousness worse. Unfortunately, the only other place to look was at him, which meant she couldn't ignore him after all.

When she glanced over, she found him looking at her. So now they were looking at each other. It wouldn't be the first time they'd done that.

She recalled the way he'd walked into the hall where Joy and Stonewall were having their rehearsal dinner, wearing a pair of dark slacks and a white shirt with the first two buttons undone. He'd looked as if he had stepped off the cover of a magazine.

Mellie had known his identity immediately. He'd been featured in several tabloids and magazines, so everyone knew who he was. Heck, she'd even seen him featured on a television show about the rich and famous. However, none of the images she'd seen had done him justice. His chiseled features were classic, and so delicious that even a diabetic patient who'd been warned off sugar would be tempted to take a lick. Even a woman who would never dream of having a one-night stand would suddenly be tempted to do just that...with him.

When he'd walked in, a sudden buzz had filled the room. Mellie had seen one woman actually drooling. Others were fanning themselves, and several were licking their lips. One older married woman had caught Mellie's attention when she'd made the sign of the cross on her chest, obviously asking forgiveness for her sinful thoughts. Mellie could understand all the females' reactions.

Dak had given a cursory glance around the room at every woman who looked his way. But it had been Mellie whose gaze he'd latched onto and held with an intensity that had made her panties damp. Even before Stonewall officially introduced them, it had been quite obvious they were attracted to each other.

"What are you thinking about, Amelia?"

She answered without thinking. "I was remembering the day we met."

• • •

It wasn't often that a woman could throw Dak for a loop, but Dr. Amelia Courson seemed to do it almost regularly. Those were the last words he'd expected her to say... mainly because, while he'd been looking at her, he'd been remembering the same thing.

He could clearly remember the moment he'd first seen her—a uniquely beautiful flower seated among others. But she'd been the one who'd stood out, pushing the others effortlessly into the background. He'd had no idea at the time that she was Stonewall's sister, and once introductions had been made, it hadn't mattered. He was too far gone. Desire, as thick as it could be, had already settled in his veins.

"Why was that on your mind?" he asked.

"The way you're looking at me now reminded me of the way you looked at me then. Like you could eat me alive."

There was no need to tell her that was exactly what he'd been thinking. "Isn't that a coincidence? I was reliving the same moment. It was the night of Stonewall and Joy's rehearsal dinner. I wanted you."

She nodded. "And I wanted you. Honestly, I had expected you to make your move at the reception after Joy and Stonewall took off for their honeymoon. Instead, you left."

Was that disappointment he heard in her voice? "Trust me. It was best that I did."

Amelia leaned forward slightly, as if she didn't want to miss any part of his answer to her next question. "Why?"

She was still holding his gaze, but the desire he was certain he'd seen moments ago in her eyes wasn't quite as obvious now. And those lips he was dying to kiss again were now in a tight thin line. Whether she realized it or not, her body language was telling him a story he didn't want to hear.

Had she been disappointed that he'd left? Or had she felt rejected? Knowing the sooner he cleared things up, the better, he decided to set her straight. "Had I stayed, Amelia, I would have seduced the hell out of you, in ways you can't even imagine."

What was it about her that made him open up and tell her things he'd never admit to other women? He watched as her tight lips eased into a smile, and then, finally, he saw a twinkle of desire return to her gaze. "And you don't think I could have handled you, Dak?"

Now he was the one leaning forward in his seat. "For once, I wasn't sure I'd be able to handle *you*."

God knows that had been the truth. He had wanted her so badly that night, that the depth of his desire had outright scared the shit out of him.

And that wasn't like him. He never showed his emotions. He went through life as a businessman who handled everything that came his way like a deal to be made. Yet when he had met her gaze, she hadn't flinched. Her sultry brown eyes had studied him with the same intensity that he'd watched her. Neither of their gazes had wavered.

He was known for being in control at all times, yet around Amelia, he'd found things reversed. Nothing he did or said could change it. That night, even from across the room, she'd slipped into his system, become embedded under his skin, claimed his penis, branded his tongue and built a need within him that he couldn't shake...or deny.

There was no way one night with her would have been enough—he just knew it. So, he'd done the one thing he'd never done before when it came to a woman—he'd hauled ass.

For months afterwards, he'd tried to convince himself that his intense attraction to her had been nothing but a figment of his imagination. But his growing desire for her—and his decreased desire for any other woman—finally made him accept that their connection that night had not been a fluke.

Whatever she'd been about to say was lost when Syl's voice came on the intercom. "We are now cruising at forty-thousand feet. You're free to move around."

Thank God! Those were the words he'd needed to hear. Unsnapping his seatbelt, he stood. Then, never releasing her gaze, he crossed over to her, leaned down and unsnapped her seatbelt as well.

"I could have done that myself, Dak."

He straightened. "You weren't quick enough for what I need to do."

She looked up at him. "And just what is that?"

Since he seemed unable to hold his tongue around her, he decided to put it to better use. "Kiss the hell out of you, Amelia."

• • •

Mellie knew she should put Dak in his place but liked the way he was thinking. He wanted her in his arms. And she wanted to be there. So why argue?

While they had been sitting there, looking at each other, something had changed. She'd been attracted to him before, but somehow, it was different now. Her desire for him was deeper, more complex. And it was rushing through her body in a way that was intense, hypnotic...and downright terrifying.

Yet...

When he held out his hand to her, she took it. And in the warmth of his skin, she felt his need, too, the same one she was feeling. Even though they had kissed a couple of times before, and she had enjoyed it each time, she couldn't wait to find out what it was like to have someone kiss the hell out of her. Once they took this step, would she ever be able to go back? And would she want to? It looked like she was about to find out.

But first...

"What about Peggy?"

"She'll only come if I call for her."

He gave her hand a gentle tug and pulled her up to stand in front of him. Too close. Yet not close enough. Remedying that quickly, he placed his hands at her waist and pulled her to him, letting her feel every hard inch of him. He was aroused. Then again, so was she. A man couldn't hide his arousal but a woman could. At least most of the time.

"Do you recall the last time we kissed?" he asked, bringing his mouth close enough to hers that she could feel the warmth of his breath on her lips. "And I don't mean that quick smack on the lips you gave me when you returned from shopping."

She smiled, remembering the excitement she'd felt then. "Do you?" she countered.

"Yes," he said, inching his mouth even closer. "It was the night you arrived. I had wanted to continue our sensual exploration last night, but you left as soon as you finished your ice cream. So now I have to make up for lost time."

She frowned up at him. "Only if I let you."

He moved his mouth closer. "You will let me, Amelia. Deny it all you want, but I know you want me as much as I want you."

He sounded rather cocky. Mellie knew she should protest, but why waste time when all he'd done was state the truth. She did want him, maybe even more than he wanted her. She'd gone without having a man in her bed for a long time—ever since Ivan had proven what an ass a man could be.

"Whoever you're thinking about right now? I know it isn't me."

She blinked and met Dak's gaze. "What makes you so sure?"

"You were frowning. And the thought of our mouths locking, our tongues twisting, tangling and tasting would have made you smile. However, one day you'll need to tell me about him."

Mellie lifted her chin. "I'll tell you about him, the day you tell me about her."

She saw a flash of something appear in his eyes, then it was gone. "There's no her and never was."

"If you say so."

"And," he said, as if her comment was of no significance, "there never will be one. No woman will ever become a permanent part of my life."

"So you say."

"So I know."

And before she could reply, he captured her mouth with his.

• • •

Dak needed her more than he had a right to. More than he should. But there was something about Amelia that brought him to his knees and made him love every moment of it.

She tasted like the sweetest apple pie his dad used to bake, sweeter than the cotton candy Dak would look for at the county fair. No woman's lips should taste this good. Hell, she was taking the art of kissing—the glorious twisting, tangling and tasting—to an unprecedented level. And he couldn't get enough.

A shot of desire hit, stronger than any he'd ever felt, racing up his legs and ending straight in the groin. He felt the moment his erection jumped, and knew she had, too. Going with it, he pulled her even closer to him. He wished she hadn't decided to wear jeans for the trip. If she'd worn a dress, his hands would have been all under it by now.

She arched into him and his erection hardened even more. And when she began grinding her hips against him, he tightened his arms around her, letting her feel exactly what she did to him.

This was the woman he had fantasized about for two years. The woman who'd put a cap on his desire for any other woman. The woman he needed...desperately. And the woman who, although she wished otherwise, wanted him as much as he wanted her.

Right now, all he could think about was this kiss—a kiss he didn't want to end...ever. But what he really wanted to do was sweep her into his arms and take her to the bedroom. If Amelia had been any other woman, he would have done that by now. And they would not have come out from behind those closed doors for hours. But Amelia deserved more than that. Not just because she was Stonewall's sister, but because she was different. He'd known, right from their first meeting, that Amelia was special. And he'd have to make sure to treat her that way.

When he finally released her mouth, she said, "Wow. Now I know how it feels to get the hell kissed out of me," she said, running her tongue over the lips he'd just tasted.

Watching her just aroused him all over again. "I need a drink, Amelia. What about you? Would you like a glass of wine?" he asked, needing to do something with his hands—something other than pulling her back into his arms.

"A glass of wine sounds nice."

"Then come with me, Amelia."

Taking her hand, he led her toward the back to the entertainment room. She glanced around. "It's hard to believe we're flying among the clouds," she said, standing by a window to look out.

"It's beautiful, isn't it?"

"Don't you ever get nervous, Dak?"

He glanced over at her while he poured their wine. "Nope. I love flying. When it's just me and Syl, I sometimes take over as pilot."

She lifted a brow. "I didn't know you could fly a plane. Stonewall never told me that."

"Do you think your brother tells you everything?"

"Hardly. Most of the time, I only find out stuff by eavesdropping on him, Striker and Quasar. Unfortunately, they've caught on to me, so now, they talk in code whenever I'm around."

"So, you're one of those nosey sisters, are you?" he asked, handing her the glass of wine he'd poured.

"Not intentionally. However, when I overhear something interesting, who could blame me for trying to find out more?"

He took a sip of his wine. "And now my friend is going to be a father."

She smiled. “Yes, and I can’t wait. She took a sip of her wine. “How long before we arrive in London?”

“About six hours. Once we land, we’ll spend the night at a hotel. Flight restrictions require that Syl not fly more than a certain number of hours a day.”

She nodded and glanced at the pool table. “What about a game?”

He’d prefer to haul her off to the bedroom to play another sort of game, but he was a patient man. His goal was to learn everything about her, get to know her body, discover her erogenous zones and cherish every part of her. In the next week, he had to know everything about her, inside and out. It was the only way he could think of to get her totally and completely out of his system. Once he knew her secrets, he could move on.

“My sexy doctor, you’re on.”

# Chapter 12

*MY SEXY DOCTOR...*

Why did Dak calling her that make her feel good all over? Probably because when she was working at the hospital—something she did all the time, lately—she had to wear scrubs, little or no makeup, flat shoes for comfort, and kept her hair in a ponytail. She didn't worry about impressing anyone with her looks. Her job was to heal. Looking good while doing it never crossed her mind. Evidently, Dak thought differently.

They played pool, and she could feel his eyes on her the whole time, ramping up the sexual tension between them, and raising her body temperature.

"I won again," he said, taking the pool cue from her hand. "What do I get?"

There was no need to ask what he wanted. She knew. He'd made it clear the instant she stepped on his plane. And, in all honesty, even before then. "You get lunch," she said with a teasing smile. "It's that time, isn't it?"

He glanced at his watch. "No. When we crossed the Atlantic, we raced forward in time. Now it's dinner time.

I'll let Peggy know we're ready for it." He leaned in and placed a soft kiss on her lips. "Just so you know, food isn't all I want."

She smiled up at him. "I hear you loud and clear, Stak Dak."

"Stak Dak?"

"Yes. If you can give me a cute handle, I can do the same for you. The breakdown for Stak is this—S is for sexy, T is for tantalizing, A is for attractive, and K is for kissable."

He wrapped his arms around her and placed another kiss on her lips. "Are you saying you find me all those things, Amelia?"

Mellie didn't have any reason not to be honest. "I do. And I'm sure a lot of other women—the ones who've shared this jet with you—did too." She mentally chided herself for bringing them up. She didn't want to think about those other women, who like her, had accepted his invitation.

Instead of releasing her, he held her gaze and when she turned her head away, he touched her chin with his fingertip to bring it back. "If you recall, I told you this is a new jet. Not even two years old."

"I remember." She wondered why he was telling her that.

"You're the only woman who's ever been on this jet with me, Amelia."

She forced herself not to smile, refusing to acknowledge how much knowing she was the first meant to her. "You didn't have to tell me that, but thanks for letting me know."

At that moment, there was a knock on the door. He released her and turned slightly. "Come in, Peggy."

The woman entered with a smile on her face. "Dinner is ready."

"Thanks, we'll be right out."

When Peggy closed the door behind her, he glanced back at Mellie. "We should be landing in London in a couple of hours. I've made arrangements for us to stay at one of my hotels."

She lifted a surprised brow. "You own more than one hotel?"

"I am in a conglomerate with four other businessmen. We own equal shares."

"I see." She noticed that Dak didn't say anything about their sleeping arrangements once they got to the hotel. Did he assume they would be sharing a bed? Should she let him know now that wouldn't be the case? Then again, it might be best for her not to jump to conclusions. He could very well have made arrangements for her to have her own room.

"Are you ready?" he asked.

"Definitely."

They headed toward the dining area. When they got there, Mellie stopped. Dak, who'd been walking by her side with his arm around her shoulders, stopped as well. "What's wrong, Amelia?"

She gestured toward the beautifully decorated table. Dinner for two by candlelight. She could tell from looking out the windows that daylight was fading, and night was setting in. However, she hadn't expected anything so formal, so...romantic. "This is so beautiful. I feel like I'm terribly underdressed."

"You look fine. Besides, I'm not dressed up, either."

He wasn't. But Dak looked sophisticated, no matter what clothes he wore.

"Whatever the chef prepared smells good, doesn't it?" he said, pulling out a chair for her.

"You have a chef on board?"

"Yes. He'll come out and say hello after dinner. I didn't have a traveling chef on my last jet because all I had was a galley. But this jet has an operational kitchen."

"Where?" Mellie thought she'd seen all of the plane.

"At the front. There are sleeping cabins for the staff there, as well."

Dinner was delicious and at the end of the meal, an Asian man appeared. Dak introduced him as Chef Malow. They had just finished dinner and the table cleared when Syl came on the intercom and told everyone to buckle up. The jet would be starting its descent into London. They'd be on the ground in less than thirty minutes.

"Have you ever been to London before?" Dak asked her once they were buckled up again in their seats.

"Yes, but it's been years. I came one year for spring break with a friend."

Dak nodded. "It was nice of him to bring you here."

She started to look away, letting him think her friend had been a guy. But then she thought back to the way she'd felt when she'd assumed other women had been on this jet with him. "It was a 'she'. My best friend Whitney was my roommate in college. We had a blast."

"I'm sure you did." Then he asked her about the places she'd seen.

She and Whitney had hit every tourist trap in the city—and every nightclub. "We wanted to see the changing of the guards at Buckingham Palace, but we were never at the right time."

"That must have been disappointing."

Dak kept her talking so much that Mellie didn't realize the plane was landing until it touched ground. Somehow, he had sensed her anxiousness and had intentionally engaged her in conversation.

"We're here," he said, unsnapping his seatbelt.

She smiled as she unsnapped hers. "Yes, we're here."

A short while later, Dak took her by the hand and walked her out of the airport to a private car that was waiting for them. It seemed that when you arrived on a private jet, you didn't have to go through the regular procedures with Customs. An airport representative had appeared on the plane after it landed and cleared everyone.

Moments later, they were being whisked off to the hotel. It was nighttime in London, yet the streets were well-lit, so Mellie could recognize several landmarks she'd seen when she had visited before. Dak was sitting beside her in the backseat of the car, with his arms wrapped around her shoulders. It was rather cozy, and she had to admit she liked being snuggled close to him.

"Jet-lag gotten to you yet?" he asked.

"Not yet," she said, truthfully. "But I'm used to going without sleep. I often end up working double shifts at the hospital."

"Why? Are they *that* under-staffed?"

"Afraid so." She wondered if he knew how good he smelled. Whatever cologne he was wearing needed to be bottled, with his name on it.

"Stonewall once mentioned to me that it was your dream to open a private practice, one that specialized in internal medicine."

"It's still my dream...but I don't see it happening anytime soon. Hopefully, things will come together, though."

"Have you ever thought of collaborating with other doctors? I understand sometimes doctors pool their resources and form a partnership."

She managed to keep a straight face, as memories of the partnership she'd planned with Ivan overwhelmed her. She cleared her throat, to stop from choking on the rage she still felt. But it was done, and Ivan was history. She wasn't going to ruin her time with Dak thinking about that low-life. "I considered it, at one point. But it's not that easy to find a group of doctors who all get along, have the same vision...and are trustworthy."

"It's the same thing in the business world," he said. "There are people I refuse to do business with because of their lack of ethics. No matter what I do in life, I will never forget that I am Michael Navarro's son."

She tilted her head to look at him. "Meaning?"

"My father was a decent man and treated people with respect. As a cop, he was the best. It was standing room only at his funeral, and everybody had a Mike Navarro story to tell."

Mellie always heard the love in his voice whenever Dak spoke of his father. It was very much like when she heard Stonewall speak about their father and grandfather. "I am sure your father is very proud of you, Dak. You've accomplished a lot in your life, and I have a feeling you've only just begun."

He didn't say anything, but merely acknowledged her words by tightening his arm around her shoulders. Instinctively, she cuddled closer to him.

• • •

"This hotel is simply beautiful, Dak."

"I like it." There was no need to tell her that the first time he'd seen the Winchester Hotel—once a famous landmark in London—it had been a disaster, left to fall into disrepair after the death of the last Winchester family member. So Dak, along with several international businessmen got together and decided it would be a worthwhile—and profitable—venture to restore the hotel to its original grandeur. Now the Winchester Plaza Hotel was one of the most majestic in London and had a five-star rating.

The hotel was busy, but the clerk had recognized Dak as one of the owners and had made sure he and Amelia were given VIP treatment. In no time at all, they were shown to a lavish suite. He was surprised she hadn't questioned their sleeping arrangements yet. Did that mean she was ready to share his bed? Just in case that assumption was wrong, he made sure the suite had two bedrooms.

The bellhop escorted them to their room with their luggage. Once he brought their bags inside, Dak tipped the guy and closed the door. He leaned against it, watching as Amelia looked around taking in the elegance of their suite. "I hope this meets with your approval, Amelia."

She turned to him. "Are you kidding me? This suite is fit for a queen."

*Then we have the perfect suite,* he thought, watching her move through the room. Her walk was majestic, and her posture was perfect, and he figured both were the result of years of training while competing in those pageants.

"I take that to mean you like it," he said, moving away from the door.

"Yes, and I appreciate the extra bedroom."

He shoved his hands into his slacks, coming to a stop in front of her. "Do you? Just because it's here, that doesn't mean you have to use it."

"But I will," she said, tipping her head back to look at him. They were alone. Really alone. And their bodies knew it, if the sexual energy sizzling between them was any indication.

She took a step closer and placed her hands on his chest. "We will sleep together, Dak. I think we both know that. But when we do, I'd like it to be my decision."

He didn't say anything. All he could do was watch her, all the while thinking he would never get tired of looking at her. She had the most beautiful brown eyes he'd ever seen. He got lost in those eyes...and never wanted to be found.

Dak knew he needed to take a step back when he felt his control starting to slip. Still, with her hands on his chest, generating a heat that was spreading south quickly, it wasn't that easy to do. "I just hope you don't make me wait too long, Amelia."

What appeared to be an understanding smile touched her lips. "I won't, Dak. I promise."

"I intend to hold you to that." Then he lowered his mouth to hers.

• • •

Hours later, Dak stood naked at the window in his bedroom, looking out into the London night. He figured it was way past midnight, but he wasn't able to sleep. How could he, when the most beautiful woman in the world was sleeping in the bedroom next to his, and all he could think of was crawling into that bed with her.

Amelia had promised she wouldn't keep him waiting long and he hoped like hell she kept her word. He thought back to the way she had snuggled up to him on the car ride to the hotel. He wasn't the cuddly type, but he had sure enjoyed having her so close.

Knowing he needed his sleep—or at least some of it—he went back to the bed and slid between the sheets. Soon enough, he'd enjoy breakfast with her tomorrow morning. And since they wouldn't leave until after the noon hour, he'd make sure she finally saw the changing of the guard. It was the least he could do, considering they were right here.

After he made a couple of calls, everything was set. And he had another surprise in store for her tomorrow. Not only would they see the changing of the guards, but he had arranged a private tour of the palace. Hopefully she would be happy about that.

Dak adjusted his head on his pillow, not sure why making Amelia happy was important to him. For the time being, he would just accept that it was. He was about to close his eyes, anxious to dream about her and the moment he would slide into her body when his cell phone rang. He recognized the caller immediately. Reaching for his phone, he clicked it on. "Syl? What's up?"

"Did you know Peggy is occupying the hotel room next door to mine?"

Pulling himself up in bed, Dak asked, "How am I supposed to know something like that? Jefferson is in charge of making hotel arrangements." Syl, Peggy and the chef always stayed at a hotel adjacent to the airport. "Is there a problem, Syl?"

His pilot didn't say anything for a minute. Finally, he said, "Nope. No problem." And then there was a resounding click in Dak's ear.

Dak placed his phone back on the nightstand. Obviously, Syl did have a problem. Otherwise, Syl wouldn't have wasted his time calling him. It seemed as if having Peggy so close was a bit uncomfortable for his friend.

Dak slid back down in bed. He knew exactly how Syl felt.

• • •

Syl looked at the clock on the nightstand. It was past midnight, and he could hear music coming from the room next door—the one Peggy was occupying. Why wasn't she asleep at this hour? He needed to be on his game tomorrow, and he knew she did, too.

The music wasn't loud enough to be disruptive, but for him, someone with acute hearing, it was still disturbing. He could call the front desk and complain. It might be a good idea to request another room—one on another floor would be best. However, if he did that, he'd be admitting weakness on his part. And he refused to be vulnerable to any woman again.

He shifted, trying to get into a more comfortable position. Actually, the soft music was somewhat relaxing. Maybe that was the reason Peggy was playing it. She must have it on her phone's playlist. More than once, he'd noticed her with a Bluetooth connection in her ear as she went about her work on the jet. It wasn't her fault he could hear it in his room. The walls of this hotel were paper thin, and their beds probably rested against that same wall.

Thinking of her that close, in bed, didn't help him relax. Hell, he could almost smell her luscious scent filtering through the walls. Every time he got a whiff of it, he got hard. And trying to sleep with a boner was no fun.

There had been strong sexual attraction between them from the beginning. He'd chosen to ignore it...but not her. The woman had done just about everything she could think of to get his attention...except dance naked in front of him. If it got that far, he might actually have to give in. But that hadn't happened yet.

It wasn't that Peggy was pushy. Nor was she aggressive, by any means. She carried herself like a professional...yet the message was there in her eyes whenever their gazes connected. Her invitation was pretty damn clear. She wouldn't seduce him, but she had no problem with him seducing her. And she was willing to wait for that to happen.

He intended for her to wait a very long time. Sylvester Wright didn't chase women. They made themselves available and if he was interested, he would let them know.

*So why wasn't he interested in Peggy?*

He *was* interested. Every glimpse he caught of her curvy ass, as she moved about the plane getting it ready for Dak to board and preparing for take-off, drove him crazy.

But he recognized something about Peggy. She was a keeper. While she might indulge in a casual affair now, over time, she'd expect more. And that wasn't something he was willing to give anyone again. Relationships didn't last. Even the ones that seemed the most solid.

He shifted in bed again, acknowledging his problem was definitely a physical one. He needed to get laid. It had been over a year since a woman had shared his bed.

When they reached Bali, he would see if any of the island girls would be interested in spending the night in bed for a night. Hell, maybe two nights.

He smiled at the thought of that and settled deeper into his pillow. Now he had something to look forward to....

• • •

Peggy moaned in her sleep and opened her thighs wider. Syl's hands were inching up her legs, his tongue following in their wake. They were alone in a cabin, though she wasn't sure where. Not that she cared right now. All that mattered was that they were alone and naked in bed together. This would be the night. He was still licking his way up her thigh to her center. Her clit was throbbing at what was to come and—

She jerked up in bed at the sound of her alarm, and almost cried. Another interruption. She had yet to finish a lovemaking dream with Syl. It wasn't fair. But even more unfair was the fact that she had to settle for a dream, when the object of her obsession was right next door. This should have been Chef's room, but somehow there'd been a mix-up. There had to be. She and Syl never had rooms this close. He and Chef were usually on the same floor, while she was on another. It was unnerving. And she could tell Syl felt the same way when they'd been given their room keys. He had ignored her on the elevator ride up. She was grateful that Chef had conversed with her. But then she and Syl had gotten off on the same floor. Although they'd walked down the corridor to their rooms together, he hadn't said anything until she got to her door. And then, all he had said was that he would see her in the morning.

Just knowing he occupied the room next door and was sleeping in a bed that was big enough for both of them nearly made her weep with need. This was ridiculous. They were attracted to each other. She was thirty-five and although she'd never been married, she had come close. On the day of her wedding close to ten years ago, she had refused to say "I do" once she'd found out that he'd had an affair. The other woman had felt she'd had a right to know.

At the time, her parents had felt it was something she and Neil could deal with *after* the wedding. They'd nearly convinced her, but when she stood before the minister and faced Neil, she just couldn't go through with it. All she could see in her mind were the pictures that had been texted to her that morning.

Instead of saying, "I do," she had slapped him and told the church full of people what a low-life he was before walking out. It was something she didn't regret doing, especially after finding out later that the woman who'd sent her the pictures hadn't been the only one.

Rubbing a hand down her face, Peggy tried to wake up. They would be flying out again in a few hours. As she eased out of bed, she realized it was time to make a decision. She was tired of unfinished dreams.

It was time Captain Sylvester Wright faced the attraction between them. Once they were in Bali, she was going to force his hand. He could either give in to the chemistry between them or reject her. The decision would be his to make. But whatever he decided, the consequences would be final.

# Chapter 13

"THANKS FOR ARRANGING EVERYTHING today, Dak. I loved finally seeing the changing of the guards, and the tour of Buckingham Palace was awesome," Mellie said, snapping on her seatbelt.

They were back on the jet and headed for Bali. She was still bubbling over with excitement from the day's activities. On the tours, she'd even met one of the Queen's grandsons—Princess Anne's son. On the drive back to the hotel, Dak had told her he'd met the royal through a number of business dealings.

"I'm glad you enjoyed yourself," he said, snapping his seatbelt as well.

The man was amazing. He was sitting there, acting as if a private tour of Buckingham Palace and meeting someone in the royal family was no big deal. She couldn't wait to tell Whitney about it.

"So, Amelia, on this leg of the trip, we'll be going through another time warp. There is a six-hour difference between Bali and London."

"I guess I'll have some real serious jet-lag by the time we land," she said.

Just then, Sylvester's voice came over the intercom, telling them to prepare for take-off. A funny feeling settled in her stomach. "Do I need to talk you through it?" Dak asked.

Just as she'd suspected, he'd picked up her pre-flight anxious state. "If you want to."

"To be honest, I prefer to do something else." Unsnapping his seatbelt, he got up and took the seat beside her. "I didn't like being that far away from you anyway," he said, buckling up again.

Mellie had to admit, she liked having him closer, too. "How are you going to help me get rid of the butterflies in my stomach?" she asked. "Will you hold my hand?"

"No. I plan to kiss you until we level off."

The thought of him doing that made something else—desire—flutter in her stomach. "Do you honestly think that will work?" she asked, already leaning in toward him. She always enjoyed his kisses.

"I intend to give it my best shot," he said, leaning toward her and capturing her mouth.

Their seatbelts made it a bit awkward, but they still managed to get their arms around each other. Pleasure filled her senses and when his tongue delved deeper, she could actually feel the heat radiating from him. Why did he have to taste so good? And why was she so quickly becoming addicted to it? He changed the angle of his mouth to deepen the kiss and she released a deep moan. Dak had told her that Peggy wouldn't come unless they needed her, but if this part of the plane wasn't soundproofed, there was no way the woman would have missed the sound of pleasure she'd just made.

If kissing her this way was a strategic move of his to heighten her desire and lower her resistance, she had to admit that it was working. Her hands slid over his shoulders and then spread across his back. The feel of his muscles, combined with the heat radiating off him, was wreaking havoc with her self-control. She'd always wanted him. Now, she *needed* him.

"We've just hit forty-thousand feet. You're free to move around the cabin."

At the sound of Syl's voice, Dak released her mouth, then reached out and gently caressed her face with the pad of his thumb. "I guess I can let you go now," he said in a husky tone.

"Why stop now?" she asked softly.

"Good question." He unsnapped both their seatbelts, pulled her onto his lap, then captured her mouth again.

• • •

Never had kissing a woman left Dak this breathless, this urgent for more. He was putting everything he had into this kiss, and she was returning it, ten-fold. The intensity, the *intimacy*, of tangling his tongue with hers was almost more than he could handle. He'd always been able to maintain control when he was with a woman. But with Amelia, he was losing it fast.

He should be berating himself for letting her burrow even deeper under his skin. What he should do was end the kiss and make some damn excuse to put some distance between them, even if only for a minute. Just until he recouped his senses. But the thought of stopping, of ending this sensual play of their tongues, was just too hard. He'd reached the point of no return.

Dak loved hearing her moan, which let him know she was enjoying this interlude as much as he was. Finally, when the need to breathe overruled the need to kiss, he released her mouth. "Did you want to continue this in the bedroom? We could even take things further."

She looked at him with swollen lips. "Further how?"

"Without any clothes on sounds pretty damn nice."

Throwing her head back she laughed and slid out of his lap. "Is sex all men think about?"

"No. We also think about business deals and try to figure out ways to increase our profit margins. However, when I do think of sex, it's usually when I know I want it." There was no reason to lie about it. Women served a purpose in his life but not the most important purpose. Although, if anyone was to change that, he had a feeling it could be Amelia. That is, if he let her. And he had no intention of doing that. "Do you want to watch a movie?"

"Depends on what kind of movie it is. Just because I can tolerate blood and guts, that doesn't necessarily mean I want to watch it."

He tried to hide his smile. "Anything else?"

"Yes. I prefer not watching anything that deals with doctors. We don't act the way we're often portrayed."

He stood. "Then maybe you should select something. Even if it's not something I'd normally watch, I think I can suffer through it—for you."

"You shouldn't have to do that. This is your plane, after all."

"And you're my guest." Soon to be his lover. Anticipation sent shudders of arousal through him.

"What brought *that* on?"

He knew exactly what she was asking. Her gaze was focused below his belt.

"It's been there since our kiss," he said.

"Maybe. But now, it's much bigger."

Were they actually discussing the size of his erection? "Possibly. You are a very desirable woman, Amelia. And I want you. I've made that fact known several times." He rubbed his chin thoughtfully. "But you're far too observant when it comes to my anatomy."

"That's a big part of my job, Dak."

"Then hopefully, you'll see what's happening with me as an acute condition, one I don't intend to let become a chronic one."

"And you don't think that it might?" she asked, holding his gaze.

"Nope, my sexy doctor. I plan to remedy the condition long before it comes to that. Now, let's go watch that movie."

• • •

Mellie should have known Dak would want to cuddle. When they were seated in front of the big screen, he lifted her from her seat and into his lap. He seemed to like having her there and she had to admit, she liked being there. She had never cuddled with a man...not even Ivan. Though, she could now truthfully say that Ivan didn't have a romantic bone in his body. He definitely hadn't made her feel the way Dak does. There hadn't been the strong sexual chemistry between them that she shared with Dak, but at the time, she'd thought sex wasn't that important. They had shared a love of medicine and that was enough. Of course, she had been wrong.

"Do you like cop shows?" Dak asked, breaking into her thoughts.

"A lot better than doctor shows."

Dak smiled. "Good. Have you ever seen the movie, *City of Lies*, with Johnny Depp and Forest Whitaker?"

"No, but I like both of those actors."

"Then I think you'll like this movie."

He was right. She did like it. And what she liked even more was the way Dak held her in his arms, gently caressing her skin. Sometimes, he would even pause the movie to kiss her.

Although they'd only been in flight a few hours, it was already dark, and the stars sprinkled in the sky made the night even more beautiful. Mellie couldn't describe how it felt to watch a movie forty-thousand feet above the earth's surface. She might have changed her mind about being an astronaut, but for her, this was the next best thing. Over lunch, he'd told her that his jet felt like his second home, and she believed him. It certainly had all the comforts of one.

"It's dinner time," Dak said, checking his watch. "I understand Chef has prepared a really special meal for us tonight."

She looked at him. "What's the special occasion?"

"You, Amelia. You are special."

She wondered if he said that to all the women who he invited to share his world. Probably. There was no reason she should be any different. She was nothing more than his flavor for the year. For some reason, that didn't bother her as much as it had before. Because she intended to get the same thing out of this week that Dak did. When this trip with Dak ended, that would be it. He would return her to Charlottesville, and there would be no follow-up calls, no additional dates. Chances were, he would not see her again...until the next wedding, or obligatory visit to Stonewall and Joy when their baby was born.

"We can look at another movie after dinner, if you'd like," he said, easing up with her in his arms and then letting her slide against him to stand on the floor. She'd been very aware of his erection the entire time she'd been sitting in his lap, and it was still going strong. Evidently, it didn't take much to turn him on.

He led her to the dining area and just like the night before, the table was set for two, with a beautiful white tablecloth, fine china that looked better than the set she had at home, and crystal wine glasses. She sniffed the air. Whatever the chef had prepared smelled good.

"Everything looks beautiful."

"You are beautiful."

She smiled over at him. "Thank you."

"Never thank me for telling the truth," he said, pulling the chair out for her.

"Thanks, Dak."

He leaned in and whispered close to her ear, "You're welcome, Amelia." He then brushed a kiss along the side of her face.

She wondered if he had any idea what he was doing to her with his kisses, his compliments, the way he looked at her? Was this all part of his plan, to seduce her within an inch of her life? If so, it was working. She could feel her control slipping, but she knew it was only because she was letting it. Dak had that effect on her.

A half hour later, she sat back in her chair, stuffed. Dinner had been delicious. The chef had definitely outdone himself, creating a culinary masterpiece of chicken marsala over white rice that was fluffier than even what Granny Kay made, with the best tasting yeast rolls, braised green beans and carrots and roasted brussels sprouts. Chocolate cake that literally melted in her mouth had been saved for last.

"Did you tell the chef how much I like chocolate cake?" she asked, smiling as she slid her fork with the last piece of cake on it, into her mouth.

"Yes."

"And how did you know that?"

"From the wedding. Both of them."

She threw her head back and laughed. He had sat beside her at Stonewall and Joy's reception, where chocolate cake had been served. She recalled switching their slices, since his had been bigger than hers. She'd done the same thing at Drew and Toni's wedding.

"I guess my lack of manners wasn't something you'd easily forget," she said.

"It had nothing to do with manners, Amelia. You knew what you wanted, and you went after it. There's nothing wrong with that. I do it all the time."

She just bet he did and couldn't imagine him handling his business any other way...even his personal business. "I'm sure you can be ruthless when you want to be."

A smile curved the corners of his lips. "Yes, when it calls for it. I'm not one to let anyone get the better of me. In the world of business, only the strong survives."

"And in your personal life?"

He held her gaze as he took a sip of his wine. "In my personal life, I have no reason to be ruthless. I prefer another approach."

"Which is?"

"Persuasion."

She arched a brow. "And does that usually work?"

A small chuckle escaped his lips. "It hasn't failed me yet. Want me to prove it?"

Sensations began stirring in her stomach with his question. Did she? He'd shown his flirtatious side a number of times, and now he was proudly claiming to be a pro at seduction as well. How in the world would she handle him? But then, did she *want* to handle him?

They were both adults and she knew where an affair with him would and would not lead. Mellie had come on this trip with Dak with her eyes wide open. She had also come on this trip with something else—a need to do more than just relax. She needed to let go and experience everything life had to offer—everything *Dak* had to offer. After all, she'd never get a chance like this again. And she intended to take advantage of it.

Ever since that fiasco with Ivan, she'd held herself back, not wanting to get involved with someone who could turn out to be Mr. Wrong. She didn't have the time or energy for that. Instead, she played it safe, not bothering to date at all, except for those social functions she attended with her friend Craig.

Now, she was faced with a real, living, breathing, masculine man, who wanted her, no holds barred. So why was she holding back? Dak had already introduced her to things beyond her wildest dreams. Flying high above the clouds in his jet was just one of them. From the moment she'd stepped onboard, he had given her his full absolute attention.

"Amelia?"

She stared back up at him. "Yes?"

"You didn't answer me. Did you want me to prove how persuasive I can be?"

There was no need to put off the inevitable. Just by the way he was looking at her, heat was stirring in her blood, moving through her veins and settling between her legs.

It would have been nice if they'd waited until they reached Bali to share a bed, but she couldn't think of anything more perfect than being made love to among the stars. She had a feeling it would be an experience she would never forget.

She slid her chair back, stood up and walked around the table to him. When he stood, she leaned in and wrapped her arms around his neck. "Yes, Dak. I want you to prove it."

# Chapter 14

WITHOUT ANOTHER WORD, DAK swept Amelia into his arms, and took her to his bedroom. After placing her on the bed, he began removing his clothes, and watched as she removed hers, sliding out of her slacks and tossing them aside. "Am I about to get initiated into the mile-high club?" she asked, pulling her blouse over her head.

He tilted his head. "And what do you know about the mile-high club?" He wondered if she had any idea just how sexy she looked, sitting in the middle of his bed in just her panties and bra? Black lace had never looked that good on any other woman. Maybe one day he would confess that he'd managed to get a hold of the film footage for every pageant she'd been in. He'd locked the discs away in the safe in his bedroom at home, but not before watching the contests over and over again. Whether it had been the swimsuit, evening gown or talent competitions, she'd been the best in his book.

"Not much. But I'm ready to find out."

He studied her, wondering what had made her change her mind about waiting for them to become intimate. Not that he had any complaints. He knew as well as anyone, that a person could hold desire back for only so long. Maybe Amelia had hit that threshold. He hoped so. They were both mature enough to know kisses were a short-term satisfier, one that fueled the growing need within them—a need they were finally ready to do something about.

He was down to his boxers and could feel the heat of her gaze on his groin. In response, his penis twitched. Her eyes widened. "Did you make it do that?"

Dak chuckled. "No, you made it do that, my sexy doctor. Even without physical contact, I respond to you."

And he could see that she was responding to him as well. His experienced eye could make out the hardening of the nipples that pressed against her bra, and her feminine scent was giving her away as well. He couldn't wait to taste her.

She glanced around to look out the window. "We seem so close to the stars."

"We're closer up here than if we were on the ground, but they're still millions of miles away. Still, it is beautiful to be surrounded by them, isn't it?"

"Yes." She let her gaze travel over his body. "You're beautiful, too. I can't wait to see all of you."

He had no problem with that. Not wanting to keep her waiting any longer, he tucked his fingers in the waistband of his briefs and peeled them down his thighs. He was actually getting turned on from her reaction at seeing him naked. "Is this what you wanted to see, Amelia?"

"Definitely. I love what you're packing. But you're so very big."

Dak threw his head back and laughed. One thing he'd discovered about Amelia was that, like Stonewall, she didn't mince words. "Oh, I think you can handle me."

She let out a breath. "I hope so."

"And now, for you," he said moving toward the bed. Reaching out, he slowly slid his hands up her legs, loving the feel of her silky skin. When he reached her panties, he traced a finger along the lace panties. "Ready for these to come off, Amelia?"

Holding his gaze, she replied, "I'm ready when you are."

Taking that as a yes, he said, "Lift up for me." When she did as she asked, he eased her panties down her hips and off her legs and tossed them aside to join the rest of her discarded clothes. Then, finally, he turned his attention to what he had revealed.

The sight of her womanly mound made him groan. She was beautiful there, just as he'd known she would be. "You are beautiful. Natural is always my preference."

She lifted a brow. "Why?"

"It serves a purpose."

"Sounds like a man who knows."

He chuckled. "Let's just say that I've done a fair amount of research on the topic. And now for this," he said, reaching up to undo her bra. Once it was off, he tossed it away as well.

Dak released a long, satisfied breath. She was beautiful and her body was gorgeous. He couldn't wait to get his hands on her, inside of her. He suddenly felt the need to taste her, using his mouth in ways that were guaranteed to make her scream. It was a good thing he'd had this bedroom soundproofed.

"Did you notice, Amelia, that at dinner, I didn't dive into the chocolate cake the way you did?"

She nodded. "I thought you might have been saving it for me, since you know it's a weakness of mine." She grinned.

"No, I had a craving for a different type of dessert," he said, lowering his gaze to her womanly mound and licking his lips. "And I can assure you that you will enjoy it as much as I will."

She lifted a brow. "More than chocolate?"

He crouched down by the bed to face her, placing his hands on either side of her thighs. This close to her, her scent was even more potent, and he inhaled deeply, pulling it in through his nostrils. "Even more than chocolate."

"I'm not sure about this, Dak."

Obviously, this was something that was new to her. That meant one of two things. Either she'd never had a man go down on her before...or the ones who had, had done a damn lousy job of it. In either case, it was time for Dak to right a wrong.

• • •

The moment Dak's hands made contact with Mellie's skin, her thighs began to tremble. And when his fingers slid down to touch the very center of her, she threw her head back and moaned, clutching the bedspread as if her life depended on it.

"Dak..." She needed to let him know he was going where no man had gone before, that she'd never let anyone get this close to her. And if what Whitney had told her about this was true, Mellie wasn't sure she could handle having her mind blown. It was a huge first step, one she'd never get back.

"Umm?" he said, flicking his tongue out to lick the side of her inner thigh.

Mellie moaned again at the delicious sensation. "I...I've never...," she said, barely getting the words out.

He licked the other side of her inner thigh, then asked, "You've never what?"

She tried to calm her breathing, but she couldn't. Her heart was racing too fast. "I've never done this before."

He paused and glanced up at her. "What? Had sex?"

Of course, she'd had sex. But not like this. "I've never done this," she said softly.

He just went back to her other thigh and began lightly nibbling on it, then laved up one side, coming close to her center. Not missing a beat, he tilted his head slightly to look up at her. "You couldn't do this to yourself, Amelia. Are you implying this has never been done *to you*?"

"Yes." That was what she meant, but couldn't say, because the slow strokes of Dak's tongue were making her almost incoherent.

"Do you know what that means, Amelia?"

His thumb had replaced his tongue and she didn't have to glance down to know his mouth was close, very close to her sex. "What does it mean?"

"Let me show you."

Dak gently eased her thighs apart and after glancing up at her with a wide smile, he winked before lowering his head and taking her with his mouth. She would have shot off the bed the moment he inserted his tongue inside of her, if he hadn't been holding tight to her hips. All she could do was sit back, with her legs open and his face buried between them, and writhe in pleasure.

And then he went on the attack, kissing, licking, and swirling his tongue inside of her, making her feel as if it was about to explode. She'd never, ever felt anything like this before. And when he nibbled on her clit, she couldn't sit still any longer. She fell back on the bed, thrashing her head back and forth and gripping the covers for dear life.

That didn't seem to bother him any, and he shifted her legs to his shoulders and pressed his tongue even deeper inside of her, claiming her clit like it belonged to him. And at that moment, it did. A sudden rush of vulnerability hit her. She'd sworn, after Ivan, that she'd never risk being so exposed with a man again. Then again, a part of her had known she would eventually succumb to Dak's brand of persuasiveness. It was hard to walk on the wild side without letting go. So why did this make her feel so out of control? And would she be able to reclaim her composure when it was over?

What Dak was doing with his tongue should have been illegal. When it reached the point where she couldn't take anymore, she reached down and grabbed hold of his head. But instead of pushing him away, she held there, and bucked her lower body against his mouth.

That made him sink in even deeper, and then, after an unusual flick of his tongue, she lost it. Literally. She screamed out her release, feeling as if all the stars in the sky were shining bright all around her. Her scream turned into a cry and then little whimpers, as spasms churned through her body.

Dak lowered her legs from his shoulders, and through eyes glazed with passion, she watched as he grabbed a condom out of the nightstand. Her heart skipped a beat as she watched him skillfully roll it on. She had seen a man put on a condom, but it had never made her drool before. But that was what Dak did to her.

"Do you still like chocolate better than what was just served to you, Amelia?" he asked, returning to the bed.

"Chocolate is chocolate, but that was chocolate with a cherry on top."

He chuckled. "You definitely have a way with words."

She was about to ask what he meant when she realized her position. She was laying at the edge of the bed, with her feet dangling and her legs wide open, giving Dak a full view of her center, as if inviting him for another round. But before she could close her legs, he pulled her into the middle of the bed, then slid between her open legs as if that's where he belonged.

She looked up at him. "I screamed. Now everyone will know what we're doing in here."

Dak was smiling down at her. "And I'm about to make you scream again. But don't worry about anyone hearing. This bedroom has been soundproofed."

Relief washed through her. "Thank goodness."

"Chocolate with a cherry on top is a good description of this."

When she got his meaning, she grinned. "You're awful."

"And you're delicious and hot, my sexy doctor. Now that I know what you taste like, I'm bound to crave it. I think you should know that."

Mellie couldn't believe they were laying here, talking about oral sex so openly. But it had been incredible, almost life-changing, and she was glad Dak had been her first. She couldn't imagine allowing anyone else to do something like that to her. It was as if he'd been cherishing her with his tongue.

Okay, so she needed to put a romantic spin on it, even if there hadn't been one. There was no harm in that, was there?

"Ready?"

She smiled as she placed her hands on his shoulders. She loved touching him and now that he was straddling her, she could feel his huge erection between her legs. "I hope so."

She stared into his eyes and saw intense desire. And that was fine. She recognized it for the lust that it was. She'd seen desire in other men's eyes before, but on Dak, it looked different. His was so potent and powerful that it stole her breath and made her nipples pucker.

The air surrounding them seemed electrified, as if soaring through the heavens was making the atmosphere crackle with passion. Their passion.

As if sensing her wonder, he lowered his mouth and kissed her, claiming her mouth at the same time he began easing inside her, stretching her.

Her center, the same place where pleasure had erupted earlier, was on fire again. She wasn't sure what was more powerful—the way his mouth was devouring hers, or the sensation of having his penis slide inside her, making her body writhe in pleasure all over again.

She decided they were equal—both working together to bring about the best results. And the only ones that mattered.

He continued pushing his way inside of her, going deeper still. And the farther he went, the hotter she became.

When he suddenly released her mouth, she cried out, "Dak..."

Moving, slow at first then faster, he thrust in and out of her, each time making a connection to her throbbing clitoris. It was as if he was performing to music, and only the two of them knew the melody and the rhythm. No man had shared himself with her the way he was doing and she wasn't sure how much more her body could take. But it was taking him—all of him—trembling in response to the way he was stroking her inside and out. New sensations began to build up inside her, making her whimper and dig her nails into his shoulders.

Mellie knew this was just the beginning. Dak wasn't playing. He was serious in giving her body the attention it had never had before. And she'd needed it, more than she'd even known. She had come on this trip to take care of herself, after taking care of others day in and day out. But now, she realized that taking care of herself also meant taking care of this—sexual needs she had ignored for too long.

"I've wanted this since meeting you," Dak said in a low, guttural tone. "No other woman would do. It was you or no one. I've waited for you, Amelia."

And then he kissed her again, as his words played around in her mind. *I've waited for you Amelia.* Had he just admitted to not sleeping with anyone else since meeting her? No, she must have misunderstood. Men often said things in the throes of passion that they didn't mean and wouldn't remember afterwards. This had to be one of those times.

Thoughts of anything but him fled her mind when he caught her mouth in a deep, drugging kiss. She was powerless to do anything but return it. And that, in turn, seemed to ignite something fierce within him. He released her mouth and began thrusting harder and harder into her. She felt him in every part of her body, every single pore.

He was riding her hard, making love to her like she'd never been made love to before. All of the fantasies she'd had about him came rushing back with a vengeance, and she matched his rhythm, grinding her body against his in an erotic dance as old as time.

Suddenly, something exploded inside of her. And as he continued to thrust deeper and harder, her orgasm went on and on, blowing her mind, and taking over her body. Just as she went over the edge, she screamed his name, her voice hoarse, her body trembling.

Seconds later, she heard him holler her name in a deep, guttural voice, and she could feel the muscles of his shoulders tighten beneath her hands. Throwing his head back, he gave himself over to his own orgasm, then laid down beside her and pulled her close.

Tonight, forty-five thousand feet above the earth, in a luxury jet bound for Bali, Indonesia, Mellie had learned what real lovemaking was all about. And she had a feeling her life would never be the same again.

# Chapter 15

DAK EASED OUT OF bed, leaving Amelia sleeping, and got up to get a drink. Slipping into his robe he left the room. Using the stars that lit the sky and the full moon as light, he made his way to the entertainment room.

Walking over to the bar, he grabbed a bottle of bourbon and poured himself a glass. Then, taking a sip, he drew in a deep breath. He wasn't sure what the hell had happened in that bedroom but making love with Amelia had changed him. Sex had never, *ever*, been that good. The last few hours with Amelia had been profound, overpowering and totally, undeniably exceptional.

Sliding onto a stool at the bar, he tried to pull himself together. Amelia didn't have the experience many women had when it came to sex, yet making love to her had affected him deeply. Every time they'd made love was more pleasurable than the last. It seemed hard to believe that a woman who'd never engaged in oral sex could be the person he'd most enjoyed in bed...ever. It was amazingly true.

Was it because he'd gone two years without a woman? Or because she'd been his fantasy woman for that time?

Maybe, but he doubted it. And he was even fairly certain it had nothing to do with her performance in bed—not that he had any complaints.

So what was it about her that made him, even at this very minute, want so badly to go wake her up so he could make love to her again? It was as if now that they'd been intimate, he'd developed a hunger for her that could only be satisfied by sliding inside her body every chance he got. He had never felt such a connection to any woman, nor had he ever wanted to.

And yet, he couldn't wait to hear her scream his name again, to see her come in his arms while her inner muscles clenched him as if she didn't ever want to let him go, and drive him right over the edge with her? If they'd been on land, he'd have found a way to put some distance between them, just until he'd figured this out.

That in itself was something he'd never done before—put space between himself and any woman. There had never been one who made a difference.

*Amelia did. But she shouldn't. He couldn't let her.*

Dak rubbed his hand down his face, then finished his drink. He had to make some sense of what he was feeling or he'd be in trouble. He'd invited her to join him, in the hopes that one week would be enough to get her out of his system, and not push her more deeply into it. He needed to get a grip.

"Dak?"

He looked up when he heard his name. The sound of Amelia's voice was an automatic erection-maker. Standing in the doorway, wearing his shirt, she looked sexier than any woman should. Her body glowed in the light from the stars in the sky. Even the mass of tousled hair didn't distract from her beauty. She looked as if she'd just been made love to—soft, swollen, irresistible—and his body sprang to attention, ready to do it again.

He forced his heartrate to slow down. "You want me, my sexy doctor?"

She held his gaze, and he recognized the vulnerability in the dark depths looking at him. "I shouldn't, but I do."

It was the same way he didn't want to want her, but he did. And the sad thing about it was that he couldn't fight it. Easing off the stool, he strode toward her, his erection growing with every step he took. And from her expression, he could tell she'd noticed...and liked it.

Dak always considered himself a pretty smart man, but now, he wasn't so sure. If he had any brains—any that hadn't gone south—he'd have gone straight to the cockpit and told Syl to turn the plane around. They'd head back to the States, first to Charlottesville to drop Amelia off and then straight on to Vermont. After all, there was only so much temptation a man could take.

So why hadn't he done that? Why was he, instead, walking towards her with a boner the size of Asia?

As he came to a stop in front of her, he caught wind of her scent. It was reaching out to him, drawing him in, changing his definition of desire. Never in his life had desire been this keen, this potent, this obsessive. "Are you sure you want me?" he asked, taking her hands and sliding them to his chest where his heart was beating.

"Yes."

He brought her hands down to her side. Then he took hold of her around the waist and lifted her up. She automatically wrapped her legs around him. Holding her close, he strolled over to the glass wall and pressed her back against it.

Then he kissed her.

The moment his tongue entered her mouth, it was like coming home. As their tongues mated, he gave up trying to figure out why this one woman had such an effect on him.

The kiss they were sharing was so different, in so many ways, for him. Yes, it was erotic, sensual and intense. But it was also highly addictive. Her scent alone made his head swim. And now that he'd had her, in every possible way, he wasn't sure he'd ever be able to manage without her. She was creating a hunger in him, one only she could satisfy. And though he hated to admit it, he suddenly realized that seven days with her might not be enough.

Having her pinned up against the wall like this was creating all kinds of caveman urges to spring forward. Jesus! He knew he needed to release her mouth so they could breathe, but he honestly wasn't ready.

She might want him, but deep down, he knew that he wanted her more.

• • •

When Dak finally released Mellie's mouth, she felt weak in the knees and was glad he still had her pinned to the glass wall of the plane. She hoped it was as strong as it looked. But that was the last thing on her mind right now. Just seeing the way he was looking at her right now was making her a little lightheaded.

She hadn't bothered to button up the shirt she was wearing and he hadn't belted his robe, so they were skin-to-skin. The only part of them not touching at the moment were their mouths, and that was only because they'd needed air. She felt every hard inch of him, and now that she knew how it felt to have him inside of her, she wanted more.

Without lowering her to the floor, he reached over and opened the table drawer, then pulled out a condom. After ripping it open with his teeth, he sheathed himself with one hand, still keeping her propped against the glass wall with the other. And then he was back at her mouth while both hands caressed her womanly folds, spreading them apart. When she felt his erection unerringly find its mark, she tightened her legs around him as he eased inside, and her body stretched, once again, to accommodate him.

And then, gripping her hips tight, he began pounding into her—hard. He released her mouth and stared into her eyes, showing her exactly what he was feeling. When her inner muscles began milking him, he threw his head back and let out a deep growl. She saw the muscles of his neck tighten, and sweat form on his forehead.

"You have the most luscious scent," he said, in a deep, husky voice. "This, *this* is where I belong, Amelia. Look at us."

She glanced down and saw them. Even with all his pounding, he never fully pulled out of her. Just seeing their bodies intimately joined and the way he thrusted and out of her sent a shiver through her. Feeling him moving inside her was one thing, but actually seeing them? What a turn-on.

"I'm coming, Amelia..."

And so was she. It was as if his words unleashed a tsunami of passion, and she did what she always did when he brought her to a climax. She screamed.

He continued pounding hard into her, rocking her world, her universe. Then he leaned in to kiss her again, and the way his tongue claimed her mouth had her coming again. Being with him was like being on a rollercoaster that never stopped.

If anyone had ever told her this much pleasure was possible, she would not have believed them. Lucky for her, Dak didn't seem to know the word impossible.

• • •

A few hours later, Dak and Amelia were buckled in their seats as the plane made its descent into the Ngurah Rai International Airport. From there, a private car would be taking them to his home that was an hour away.

After making love against the wall of the plane, he had gathered her in his arms, then taken her back to bed to make love to her again. They had just finished taking a shower together—where they'd made love again—when Syl announced it was time for them to prepare for landing.

He glanced over at Amelia. They were sitting side by side, her head on his shoulder as she slept. When they'd first boarded the plane, he'd sat in the seat across from her, but he liked this better. He needed to be close to her.

She had slept through the landing and now it was time to wake her up. What was he going to do with his Amelia? Funny, the thought of claiming her felt, somehow, right. And for the next six days, she would be all his.

He glanced up when the airport officials from Customs boarded the plane. He relaxed when he saw it was Wayan, the head Customs official. Because of the trips he often made to Bali, he had come to know Wayan, and he smiled as the man walked over to him.

"You're planning on getting off, Dak?" the man asked him in his native Indonesian tongue.

Dak answered him in kind. "Yes. I just need to wake her up."

Wayan nodded. "She looks like an angel."

Dak glanced down at her and had to agree with Wayan's assessment. Even in sleep, Amelia was breathtaking. Right now, she looked peaceful and innocent—nothing at all like the woman whose sexual appetite seemed as great as his. Unbuckling her seatbelt, and not caring that they had an audience, he kissed her awake. She roused, returning his kiss with enthusiasm.

"Maybe I should step outside," Wayan said, this time in English, although the words were spoken with a strong Indonesian accent.

Amelia turned around so fast, she almost fell from the seat. "Careful, Amelia," Dak whispered, placing his hand on her knee. "It's just Wayan."

"Wayan?" she asked.

"Yes. He's an official from Customs, and he's here to see our passports."

She nodded and reached for her purse from the bin beside her, then pulled out her passport and handed it to Wayan, while Dak flashed his own. Wayan smiled. "Welcome to Bali, Miss Courson." He then glanced over at Dak, who read the unspoken question in the man's eyes.

Dak nodded, letting Wayan know that yes, Amelia was Stonewall's sister. Wayan had met Stonewall during the time he'd been Dak's bodyguard. Dak had forgotten all about that until now. Standing, he said, "Come on, Amelia. Our car is waiting."

Then, taking her hand, he led her into paradise.

• • •

"Slide closer to me, Amelia," Dak whispered, once Mellie was settled in the backseat of the private car.

She could barely keep her eyes open. Jetlag was hitting her hard, and she was absolutely exhausted. All she wanted to do was sleep, and at the moment, she couldn't think of a better place to be than in Dak's arms.

She eased closer to him, and he surprised her by lifting her into his lap, then tightening his arms around her. She lowered her head to his chest and breathed in the manly scent that was Dakota Navarro. He'd told her it would take an hour to reach his home, and she was just where she wanted to be. She smiled, happy she had him for the next six days.

"What are you smiling about?"

She eased her eyes open and looked up at him. Deciding to be honest, she said, "I have you all to myself for an entire week."

He chuckled. "You like that, do you?"

Mellie nodded then whispered, "After last night, how could I not? But first, I need to sleep for a long time. Okay?"

He smiled down at her. "Okay. I'll wake you up when we get home."

She closed her eyes, thinking that he made it sound as if they were a married couple, who were on their way home from a trip abroad, or a party, or just a night out on the town. It didn't matter. She knew he hadn't meant the words to mean anything. They were here to enjoy the moment. And she would.

Mellie let her mind wander to all the things he'd done with her, to her, in his bed, against the glass wall, then back in his bed again. Oh, and she couldn't forget the shower. Dak was one virile man. No wonder women stood in line to spend time with him.

She wasn't sure how long she slept. She didn't remember the car ever coming to a stop, and she certainly didn't recall Dak carrying her inside his home in his arms. And she only roused a little when she felt herself being undressed and placed under the covers.

Then a naked male body drew her into his warmth and held her close to him. She felt his hands slowly running through her hair and the kisses he placed close to her lips.

She cuddled closer to Dak, and let sleep take her. At that moment, she couldn't think of anywhere else she'd rather be.

# Chapter 16

MELLIE OPENED HER EYES to the sound of heavy rain beating against the window. Shifting in bed, she discovered that she was alone. Yawning, she sat up, and glanced around, remembering where she was. She recalled the plane landing in Bali, but very little else. Glancing down at herself, she saw she was naked, but didn't remember taking off her clothes.

"I undressed you."

She snatched her head up and looked at the man standing in the doorway, wearing a pair of jeans and nothing else. And just like that, her mouth started to water.

"You undressed me?"

"Yes. You were absolutely exhausted, so I took care of it for you."

"Thank you." There was no need to ask if they'd slept together last night, because she could smell his scent on her pillow. "How many hours have I slept?"

"Twelve. I figured you would wake up to eat, or at the least go to the bathroom, but you didn't."

She rubbed a hand down her face. "Jetlag always does me in."

"That's understandable. You've traveled through three times zones."

And she'd felt it. "Thanks for letting me sleep it off."

"What else was I supposed to do, Amelia?"

Deciding not to tell him to give him any ideas, she changed the subject. "It's storming outside."

"It rains a lot here. Good thing most of our activities will be inside."

She wondered if that was his way of letting her know what he expected of her. Funny enough, that didn't bother her anymore. She might not remember what happened after they arrived in Bali, but she did remember every single thing they'd done together on his jet. Not only had he awakened parts of her body that she hadn't realized had been asleep, but he'd shown her just how mind-blowing an orgasm could be. Evidently, there were different degrees of it. Before Dak, she'd only experienced climaxes on the low end of the scale. But Dak... Dak had taken her as high as she could go. To the stars, literally.

"Are you hungry?" he asked.

She nodded. "What time is it here?"

"Six p.m. Back in the States, it would be seven in the morning. That's probably why you're awake."

"Yes, but after I eat, won't it be time to go back to bed again here? I probably won't be able to sleep."

"I'm glad to hear that," he said smiling.

She'd just bet he was. Glancing around, she said, "This is a beautiful bedroom."

"Thanks. Once you're up and about, I'll show you the rest of the house. Wayan was here earlier and prepared dinner for us."

She recalled that name. "Wayan? The guy from Customs who came aboard the plane to check our passports?"

"Same name but different person. In Indonesia, parents have a unique way of naming their kids. There are only four names they can use—Wayan, Made, Nyoman or Ketut. And believe it or not, the names apply to both men and women."

"You're kidding, right?"

"Not at all. Regardless of the family, the first child will always be Wayan, the second child Made, the third child Nyoman and the fourth, Ketut. So Wayan, the Customs agent you met, is the oldest in his family. And Wayan, my cook, who is female, is the oldest in her family. The only distinction for gender is that because she is female, Wayan can use Ni in front of her name. That means Miss, in our language."

"Interesting."

"I thought so, too. It took me a while to familiarize myself with the local language and customs, but it was worth it. I'll set our dinner while you shower and dress."

"Thanks."

As she watched him leave, she couldn't help thinking that he was one beautiful man. From the front view, or the back, Dak was sexy as hell—in his looks, in the way he moved, in his confident, slightly cocky attitude. She drew in a deep breath and shivered as she remembered all the things that body had done to hers last night...or whenever it was. The time change had her a bit confused as to what day it was. She still couldn't believe she had actually slept for twelve hours straight.

She got up and walked around the room, taking it all in. The walls of the bedroom were solid glass, from top to bottom. The rain had stopped, and when she looked outside, she was amazed at the gorgeous view of the Java Sea. Dak had said his home had originally been in a compound with one other house. To ensure the privacy he wanted, he'd later bought the entire compound. Everything she could see belonged to him—the gardens, the waterways. She could hardly wait for a tour.

And maybe she'd get one soon. She certainly felt well rested, and after a shower, she'd feel even better. Of course, the thought of showering conjured up images of her and Dak on the plane, last night. And she realized she might want to save her energy for more satisfying pursuits.

• • •

Dak glanced up when Amelia walked into the kitchen. She had changed into a beautiful sundress that flowed around her ankles and she looked as relaxed and beautiful as ever. He could tell she had washed her hair, and he loved the way the silky looking strands fell in waves around her shoulders.

"You look nice," he said, trying not to stare at the way the hem of the dress swished around her legs as she walked.

"Thanks. I've only seen the bedroom and kitchen, but so far, I'm impressed. This place is beautiful. I've never seen a house made of glass before."

"What better way to enjoy the beauty of the countryside? Come sit down. I'll give you a complete tour after we eat. We'll need the exercise to walk off dinner. Ni Wayan prepared a feast for us."

"Whatever she cooked smells wonderful. Will she be coming by every day?"

"No. Only when I call her. Most of the time, I prefer to put together my own meals when I'm here. I can't wait to make a few of my favorite dishes for you."

"That sounds awesome." She glanced around. "Do you need any help?"

"No. Everything is ready. The dining room is through that area. Just have a seat and I'll bring everything out."

"Okay."

Moments later, Dak brought in all the dishes and placed them on the table. Amelia was standing at one of the windows, and when she heard him, she turned around. "I don't remember seeing any of this last night. The grounds are simply gorgeous."

"You were sleeping when we arrived. Besides, it was dark and you would not have been able to see much of anything, anyway."

She moved away from the window and joined him at the table. "Ni Wayan is a wonderful cook. I'm sure you'll agree," he said, pulling the chair out for her.

"Thank you. I'm sure I will."

He sat across from her, and for the first time, he realized how large the table was. She seemed so far away, and he was surprised by how much that bothered him. After she said grace, he lifted the tops off the platters and the aroma made him moan. "She prepared my favorite."

"What?"

"Ayam goreng. It's the Indonesian equivalent of fried chicken, but the whole chicken is cooked in oil after being marinated with spices grown right here in the compound. I wasn't sure how spicy you'd want your meal, so I asked her to tone it down a little for you."

She chuckled. "I'm Stonewall's sister, remember? I like my food spicy, just the way he does."

Dak smiled. "I wasn't sure, and didn't want to take any chances. But next time, I will remember that."

Too late, he recalled there would not be a next time for them. There was never a next time for the women he invited to share his world for a week.

But if she'd noticed his misstep, she didn't let on. Instead, she was focused on the task in front of her—deciding which piece of chicken to take. He was pleased to see her choose the white meat. That meant he wouldn't have to share any of the dark pieces.

Dak took the top off a second platter, this one containing an assortment of vegetables. There was also a separate platter of botok—a mixture of vegetables, dried fish, chili and shredded coconut steamed in banana leaves.

"Umm, everything looks delicious," she said, licking her lips.

He wished she hadn't done that. Desire kicked him in the gut, and he cleared his throat, trying to get a hold of himself. "I can't wait for you to try everything."

He was glad she wasn't a finicky eater. It was a pleasure to watch Amelia put a little of each dish on her plate to try. He needed to stop comparing her to the other women he'd spent time with. She was definitely in a class by herself.

"This is absolutely delicious," she said, after taking a taste of everything on her plate.

"For dessert, she made a batch of pineapple cookies. You're going to love them."

She smiled at that, and then they both sat back to enjoy their meal. Over dinner, she told him more about her work at the hospital. He could definitely understand why she needed a break. "Doesn't the medical team have a union?" he asked. It was quite apparent to him that doctors at her hospital were overworked.

"Not in the real sense of what a union is supposed to do. We don't consider ourselves workers, per se. We're professionals. Lifesavers. The thought of a doctor going on strike is unheard of. Lives could be lost."

"So who's fighting for you?"

She licked her lips again and he felt another pull in his groin. "We have to fight for ourselves, but lately, that hasn't got us very far. The only way I was able to get thirty days off was to outright demand them. I was getting burnt out. An exhausted doctor makes mistakes. The hospital just settled a huge lawsuit last year and that opened the eyes of the administration to the situation."

But not wide enough obviously, he thought, if that was last year, and she still had to fight to get time off. "You think you'll be able to last another ten years? You'd mentioned that you doubted you'd be able to open your own private practice before then."

"Unfortunately, I don't have a choice. I made a foolish mistake."

He glanced across the table at her. "Oh? And what mistake was that?"

• • •

Mellie looked over at Dak. Why had she said anything about that? She should have known she couldn't slip anything past him. At any other time, she would be happy to spend time with a man who hung on to her every word, and who gave her his undivided attention. But in this case, it wasn't so great.

Not wanting to discuss Ivan and the fool she'd been, she said, "Trust me, you don't want to know. And I'd rather not talk about it."

Not taking his eyes off her, he said, "Trust me, I do want to know. But for the time being, I will respect your wishes and we won't talk about it. But be forewarned, Amelia. I can tell by the look in your eyes that whatever it is bothers you. And if it bothers you, it bothers me."

Why would it matter to him? It was one thing to be curious about what she'd said, but it seemed to have another sort of an effect on him. She hadn't thought he was the possessive type, but maybe he was. And that was fine, as long as he knew how far he could take it, and for how long. Should she remind him that all they had together was a week? Actually, less than that now. When they returned to the States, she had no doubt that he would happily go his own way and she would go hers.

Deciding it was best to change the subject, she asked, "So, what's planned for tomorrow?"

"I want to show you all around Bali. It's a beautiful island."

She believed it. "How long have you owned this place?" She still couldn't get over staying in a glass house. The only way you could discern the walls from the windows was by shape—the windows were arched. The architecture was definitely modern, and the décor inside was just as modern. Dak's Bali home was extraordinarily beautiful.

"I've had it for six years. When I first came here, an Italian businessman and his wife owned the main house in the compound. I made them an offer for their home and they sold it to me. I moved into their place while this house was being built."

She nodded. "But wasn't there another house? What did you do with it?"

"That one is a lot smaller, just a third of the size of this one, so I use it as a guest cottage. Whenever I come here for a long period of time, that's where my flight crew normally stays. In this case, Syl. I've added a few other cottages as well, for some of the house staff."

"What about Chef and Peggy?" she asked.

"They usually go elsewhere, visiting friends, or touring other islands."

After they had finished dinner, he brought out dessert. The pineapple cookies Wayan had left for them were delicious. "Ready for me to show you around?"

"Absolutely," she said, standing.

During the tour, it didn't take long for Mellie to realize that Dak's home was as state-of-the-art as his jet. It had every modern technological device imaginable, all set in motion with the use of a remote, voice command or the flick of a finger. He told her that most Balinese homes combined the indoors with the outdoors. Instead of walls, some rooms had curtains, ones that were thick enough to protect against the wind and rain.

He kept those curtained walls drawn during the day. And for security, those same curtained walls would be replaced by glass at night, with a single voice command. He showed her how the glass walls seamlessly slid into place over every opening, in just a few moments. She noticed that in some rooms, those that faced the beautifully designed courtyard, the interior walls were completely glassed. When she mentioned the gorgeous gardens, Dak explained, "I've added several small cottages on the compound. Ni Wayan lives in one and the family whose job it is to take care of the grounds lives in one of the others," he said.

"The grounds are incredible, Dak."

"Thanks. There are over two hundred species of flowers here."

She glanced up at him. "You like flowers that much?"

"No, but Dad did, and I wanted this to honor him."

Mellie admired how Dak did things to keep his father's memory alive. She often thought of her parents and what they must have gone through during their final hours.

Her parents, who'd rarely taken a vacation without her and Stonewall, had decided to fly to Miami to meet up with friends. While they were there, Hurricane Andrew hit hard, and they'd been unable to evacuate in time. Their beach hotel had been demolished, killing everyone left inside. She'd only been five and Stonewall nine, at the time. Then, shortly after they moved in with their grandparents, her granddaddy passed away too. She had lost the two most important men in her life in the same year.

She'd been devastated and had clung to Stonewall to the point where he had to have found it somewhat annoying. But he'd never complained. Then one day, he was gone. He'd been sent to prison and she'd been devastated all over again.

It was then that she'd decided that she never wanted to have to rely on a man again. And thanks to Granny Kay, she'd learned how to look after herself. Still, that didn't mean she wouldn't like to have a man in her life, now and then. But after Ivan, she'd learned to be very careful who she shared herself with. She'd taken a chance on him and it had cost her.

Dak, however, seemed different. And because their affair had an end date, she could relax and just enjoy the time she had with him in this beautiful place.

Dak's home had three levels. There were five bedrooms and six bathrooms. His bedroom was on the third floor and took up an entire side of the house. He showed her how, with just a voice command, he could arrange to have music play throughout the entire house or just in those rooms he wanted.

After seeing the house, they took a tour of the courtyard. She'd never seen so many flower gardens. Granny Kay was the one with a green thumb in their family, and Amelia could just imagine her grandmother's reaction if she were to see the various species of flowers. On the other side of the courtyard was Ni Wayan's vegetable garden. Dak told her that they used what they harvested in the kitchen. And there were so many spices! Amelia didn't recognize them all—there were so many of them—but she did recognize the ones that were common in this region, like nutmeg, ginger and turmeric.

By the time they returned to the house, it was starting to get dark. "I know it's getting late, but I'm not the least bit sleepy," she said.

He glanced over at her. "If you're trying to tell me that you'd like to stay up late tonight, I don't have a problem with that, Amelia." Placing his arms around her shoulders they walked up the stairs. "I'm sure we can think of something to do."

• • •

The man sitting in the parked car wasn't happy. "Just as I suspected, the house is in a secured compound. There are probably alarm systems set up around the perimeter. There's no way in that I can see."

The man on the other end released a series of expletives. "I don't care what you have to do, Miguel, I want my orders followed. Don't call me back unless it's to tell me that you've succeeded."

Then the phone clicked in Miguel's ear.

# Chapter 17

THE MOMENT DAK PUSHED open the double doors to his bedroom, he wondered if he was doing the right thing. He glanced over at the woman whose hand he was still holding. She was different, and he was discovering he liked that. Other women had traveled with him before, but none of them had felt like they belonged. Amelia did.

He would question why he felt that way later. After closing the doors behind them, he pulled her to him, wrapping his arms around her waist. "I guess we can get ready for bed, and then talk until you fall asleep," he suggested, though that was the last thing he wanted to do right now.

The moment she had walked into the kitchen earlier, looking more radiant than a woman who'd slept for twelve hours should look, he hadn't been able to stop thinking about making love to her again. They'd made love several times already among the clouds. Now he wanted to give land a try. And then another...

"Is that what you really want to do?"

"No," he said, being totally honest. "Our feet are on the ground now. I want to see how it feels to be inside you down here."

Amelia chuckled and he liked the sound. "I'm curious to see the way it feels as well."

Glad they were on the same page, he lowered his mouth to hers, kissing her gently yet thoroughly. This time, they weren't in a hurry. Before they'd been in a race against time, getting in as much as they could before Syl came on the intercom to announce it was time to buckle up. Now, they didn't have to worry about any intrusions.

The kiss might have started out slow and drugging, but now it was greedy. He loved her taste and not for the first time, feared he was becoming addicted to her. It was as if her taste, her essence was flowing right into his bloodstream. She broke off the kiss and took a step back from him, licking her lips. Did she know that was a total turn-on for him? His breathing got heavier, as he thought of how that tongue would feel licking on a certain part of his anatomy.

"You have a real serious look on your face, Dak. What are you thinking?" she asked in a voice that sounded as sexy as she looked.

There was no way he would tell her the truth, so he gave her the watered-down version. "I was thinking how much I love your mouth. And your tongue..."

When he didn't finish what he was saying, she asked, "What about my tongue?"

He wondered what he could say that wouldn't sound too raw. "I like the look of it."

She grinned. "Are you serious?"

"Very much so."

She stuck out her tongue, as if to see for herself how it looked. Quickly leaning down, he captured it into his mouth and began sucking on it. He was greedier than before and could tell by the way she rolled her hips against him, that she was too.

Releasing her mouth, he swept her into his arms and carried her over to the bed, feeling a hundred times more aroused than before. In a matter of seconds, he'd undressed her, undressed himself and sheathed a condom.

Dak heard Amelia moan and he looked over at her. "What's that for? I haven't touched you yet."

"Doesn't matter. Your kiss left me hot."

He had news for her. Just seeing her naked on that bed, *his* bed, had him on fire. He remembered one moment in particular, when they'd made love on the jet. He'd caressed her lower back, and it seemed as if that touch had triggered one of her hot spots. Since that discovery, he'd made a point to touch her there often, just to watch her become a wildcat between the sheets.

Moving back to Amelia, he reached for her legs and tugged her toward him, wanting to pull her to the edge of the bed. Then he grabbed one of the large pillows, and lifting her hips, he tucked it beneath her and then spread her legs apart. He liked this position since it afforded deeper penetration.

"Are you deliberately being slow, Dak?" she asked when he stood there staring down at her.

Dak couldn't help it—he loved looking at the area between her legs. "I've been called many things, but slow isn't one of them," he said, and without further ado, he planted his hands on the sides of her. Then staring into her eyes, he lowered his body and began easing inside of her.

"Okay," he said through clenched teeth, as he slowly tunneled his way through her wet womanly folds. "I confess that I am slow with this. But that's only because I like where I'm going, but I'm not in a rush to get there."

Amelia moaned as he slowly increased the pressure. "What if I said I needed you to pick up the pace a bit?"

"Then I'd tell you to be patient. This particular visit will be worth the wait."

She moaned again as he settled deep inside her, and when he felt her inner muscles clench him, his eyes nearly rolled to the back of his head. He doubted she had any idea just how good that felt. It was as if she was trying to drain him.

"Stop that," he said, knowing she wouldn't...and hoping she didn't.

"What are you going to do if I don't?"

Since she'd asked, he decided to show her—his sexy doctor—and he thrust hard. He only hoped she realized what a dangerous game she was playing...for both of them.

• • •

Mellie shuddered in pleasure, as Dak finally penetrated her as far as he could. Once there, he didn't move, and their gazes locked...just like their bodies were at that moment. To retaliate, she rolled her hips against him, urging him on. And when a slow smile spread across his lips, she'd known that she was done for.

"I need to teach you some patience," he said, taking her hands, raising them above her head, then holding them there. That made her breasts move higher, tempting his eager mouth.

It didn't take Mellie long to figure out that Dak was a breast man. He took a nipple into his mouth, and went at it as if he'd never tasted a breast before—slowly, thoroughly—and it was driving her close to the edge. It felt so good, she almost forgot he was still inside her, until he began moving down there as well. OMG! Was he trying to kill her? With every pull on her nipple, his lean hips and taut thighs thrust inside her. It felt almost too good to bear, and her head started to swim.

He pulled his mouth from her breast and stared down at her. "Now, what were you saying earlier, my impatient Amelia?"

Did he honestly expect her to answer? She couldn't, even if she'd wanted to. The pace of his strokes, the way he was drawing the whole length of his shaft in and out of her, was with a precision and expertise that was blowing her mind.

With each thrust, she felt his erection touch her clit and it was driving her insane with need. Her nerve endings were frazzled, and was that music playing somewhere in the background? A musical beat that matched each one of his thrusts? Deciding to get back at him, she focused on using her inner muscles to clamp down on him again...at least, when she could manage to do it. His powerful thrusts were making it nearly impossible to concentrate. And after a few unsuccessful attempts, she decided to give up trying. She was enjoying this too much.

"Now to teach you a lesson for toying with me, Amelia."

Without missing a beat, he let go of her hands and lifted her up a little, then began to caress her back with his fingertips. Fire shot right through her. It hadn't taken him long to figure out that part of her back was her biggest erogenous zone. Hell, she had dated Ivan an entire year and he'd *never* figured it out. She was about to ask Dak how he had known about it, when suddenly, she could barely breathe. Her body felt like it was exploding in a prism of passion so profound, it had snatched the breath right from her lungs.

Then, as if he was experiencing the same amazing sensations, his body started to buck and thrust wildly inside of her. Then he threw his head back, and she couldn't resist reaching up and skimming her fingertips along his neck.

As if her touch was some sensual force, he clenched his jaw and jerked hard, not once or twice, but three times, then hollered her name at the same time she screamed his.

She grabbed his head to bring him down for a kiss, but he was shuddering so hard, the entire bed seemed to shake. And he was still working her clit like it was the key to his pleasure, making her climax yet again, this time, more powerfully than the last. He might have discovered the erogenous spot on her back, but it seemed she'd found one too, when she'd touched his neck.

Finally, he pulled himself out of her and eased them both up in the middle of the bed. She had no strength left, and was content to lay there, her body still trembling from orgasmic aftershocks. As if determined not to let her go, he threw one of his legs over hers and struggled to regulate his breathing.

"If only you knew what you do to me, Amelia," he said, pulling her closer.

If only he knew what he did to her, too. She didn't have enough air in her lungs to tell him. One day, maybe tomorrow, she might show him. And with that thought in mind, she drifted off to sleep.

• • •

Dak suddenly came awake when he heard a sound outside. Shifting, he glanced down at Amelia. Their limbs were so entwined, there was no way he could leave the bed without disengaging their bodies, which would likely wake her. But he had to get up and investigate where the noise had come from.

As he slowly went through the process of separating their bodies, her drowsy eyes opened. She smiled at him and said in a groggy voice, "Hi."

"Hi, sweetheart. Go back to sleep. I just need to check on something."

"Okay." She turned over and buried her head in the pillow as he eased from the bed and slid into his pants. The house had automatically gone into secure mode when it got dark, and he was glad for that.

What he'd heard was probably nothing more than some sort of wildlife. Maybe it had been one of those giant lizards—the Komodo dragon. They were comparable in size to alligators back in the States. But Komodo dragons were even more deadly. Their shark-like teeth and poisonous venom could kill a person within hours of a bite. He'd only ever seen one on his property before. But since then, the man who took care of his yards regularly put a certain kind of sand around the perimeter that kept them at bay. While he'd never had a problem, he'd heard of other people who'd protected their property the same way he did, and every now and then, they'd come across a badass dragon that trespassed anyway.

He went into his walk-in closet, where he'd installed a concealed door. Behind it was a room he referred to as "command central". Numerous screens filled the walls and sitting on a desk was a monitor that connected to all the others. At any point and time, he could see the entire perimeter of his property, with just a glance. No one knew about his secret room but Syl. And Dak intended to keep it that way.

He often wondered what had driven him to take such security measures when he'd built this place. Yes, he'd been in the USN, but that part of his life was over. Still, he couldn't discount the fact that he'd made a number of enemies, especially on that assignment in South America when he and his team had ruined a terrorist plot to assassinate the president of Argentina and take over the government. That had been years ago, and even though he was pretty sure most of the insurrectionists were dead now, he didn't like taking chances. So, yeah, maybe he was a little paranoid. He still occasionally had bad dreams, but for the most part, his past with the USN was behind him. Still, it never hurts to be careful.

He knew nothing was ever that simple—and not all threats came from the same direction.

A few years ago, Dak had found that out the hard way. One of his past business associates had had a bone to pick with him over some past business dealings that hadn't gone his way, and had decided to do something about it. The result had been an attempt on Dak's life. That was when Dak had hired Stonewall to be his bodyguard.

Watching the monitors, Dak walked over to the portable bar and poured himself a glass of bourbon. Where had that noise come from? He did a quick scan of the compound's perimeters to make sure nothing was amiss, so he could return to Amelia. He missed her already.

He was about to go back to bed when suddenly saw some movement. Zooming in the camera, he relaxed when he saw it was only Syl. He and Peggy were staying at the other house on the compound for the rest of the week.

Syl probably wasn't too happy about that, especially since Chef had caught a flight out yesterday to go visit his family in India. Normally Peggy would have gone somewhere else, too, usually visiting a neighboring island. Apparently, she had decided not to do that this time.

That meant Syl was alone in that house with Peggy. Umm...interesting. Was that why Syl was out walking the grounds at this hour? Working off sexual tension? Hell, if Syl had been uptight about having Peggy occupying the hotel room next to his in London, Dak could only imagine how worked up Syl was, now that they were both under the same roof.

Dak felt for his friend. Lusting after a woman was a bitch if you couldn't do anything about it. *Couldn't or wouldn't*? Dak took another sip of bourbon and shook his head wondering how long Syl would be able to hold out. Peggy was wearing him down. Dak could see it, but poor Syl didn't seem to have a clue. This was going to be fun to watch.

*Speaking of fun...* Finishing off the last of his bourbon, Dak left the room, too anxious for his own good to return to a woman he couldn't seem to get enough of.

# Chapter 18

PEGGY KNEW THE MOMENT Syl had returned to the cottage. He hadn't been thrilled when he'd discovered she had not left the island after all. But it was his problem, and he'd have to figure out a way to deal with it.

He walked into the kitchen and immediately stopped when he saw her standing there, pouring a glass of wine. "You're still up?" he asked in a brisk voice.

She glanced over at him, recorking the wine bottle. Not surprisingly, he was being his usual glowering self. At least, that was the way he usually acted around her. "Was I supposed to be in bed or something?"

"I figured you would be."

She tilted her head. "Sorry to disappoint you, Syl. Is that why you were gone for nearly two hours?"

Instead of answering, he turned to leave the room, and finally, she snapped. "Yes, by all means walk out on me. Why don't you avoid me for the rest of the week, too? That way, you don't have to deal with your problem."

He turned back around, frowning. "Problem? I don't have a problem."

"Don't you?" she said, placing the wine glass on the counter with a thump and crossing the room to stand in front of him. She was tired of the way Syl acted whenever he was around her—as if she had some contagious disease.

"No, I don't."

"I think you do."

He crossed his arms over his chest, his very massive chest was accentuated by perfect shoulders and a trim waistline. She'd always thought he looked sharp in his pilot's uniform but the way he looked now, standing in front of her, wearing a pair of jeans and a t-shirt? He was drop dead gorgeous. "I beg to differ, Peggy."

What was it about Sylvester Wright that got to her so badly? She'd never experienced anything like the irresistible sexual energy that surged between them anytime they got close. And she knew he felt it too. She'd seen it in the way he reacted to her—his dilated pupils, his erratic breathing. They could be so good together. So why was he fighting it?

"And I beg you to choose, Syl."

"Choose what?"

"You want me, I know that. Just like you know that I want you. We're not kids anymore. I'm thirty-five and you're thirty-nine. Don't you think we're too old to play games? Especially when we're here, all alone. Why not see where this heat between us can lead?"

He dropped his hands to his sides and took a step toward her. "You think I'm playing games? What about you? Can you stand here and say you don't get a kick out of strutting your ass around me so I can look at it? Make me want it? And what about the way you lick your lips before you take a drink. Do you have any idea what that does to me? Do you not think that I know when you're looking at me?"

"I said I wanted you too, Syl" she snapped, getting in his face. "It's time for you to make a choice, here and now. Take me or leave me. I'll only ask once."

For the longest time, he just stared at her, his breathing erratic. And then when she was certain he was about to take a step back and turn to leave, he reached out and pulled her to him, snarling, "Dammit, I'm taking you." He lifted her off her feet and planted her backside right on the kitchen table. Then his hands went to his shirt...

• • •

Syl tore off his t-shirt and then he hurriedly removed his briefs and jeans. He felt totally out of control, but there was no stopping him now. He reached out to undress her, but she'd already pulled her sundress over her head. Underneath, she was naked.

Jesus! Had she planned this? Had she intentionally pushed his last button on purpose? He should get dressed, then walk out and leave her ass right there, sitting naked on the table. But he couldn't do it. Damn, she looked even better without clothes than she did with them. More than anything, he wanted to grab that ass, fondle those perfect shaped breasts and discover the secrets she kept hidden between those long legs.

"Take me, Syl. I need you to take me."

He heard the words and this time, he listened. There was an urgency in her voice, and he recognized the sound. She needed to get laid just as badly as he did. He wondered how long it had been for her. It didn't matter, her body needed a man's attention—right now. He'd do his best to make sure the first time would be totally satisfying for her. But the second time...

Hell, was he actually thinking about a second time? Yes, he was. It would follow right after the first. And the second time would belong to him. Picking his pants up off the floor, he dug inside his wallet for a condom and wasted no time sheathing himself. Then he reached out and wrapped his arms around her waist.

"Open your legs for me, Peggy."

She did as he asked, and he quickly moved between them. When she linked her arms around his neck, the feeling of having her hardened nipples press into his chest almost made him shudder in pleasure. Her mouth was right there and the lips that he'd wanted for so long were within reach. He intended to take them when he took her.

His engorged shaft entered her the same exact time his mouth claimed hers. Her body felt tight but so damn good. When he began thrusting inside of her, she lifted her hips off the table to meet every one of his strokes. Every thrust was hard, urgent...and hitting the mark, if the moans she was making were anything to go by. He loved the sounds she made, and they drove him on, making him pick up speed.

Syl tried to avoid thinking about how good they were together. If anyone had told him he would be taking a woman on a kitchen table, he would not have believed them. He'd always preferred a slow seduction in a bed. At least, he had, until now. This wild, reckless coupling was the best sex he'd ever had. He'd happily take Peggy wherever she wanted it—on the couch, the floor, a wall... Hell, he would even bang her against the refrigerator. The thought of doing that made him throb, and a throbbing erection made him a greedy bastard.

She pulled her mouth away from his and threw her head back, releasing a deep moan. He knew what was coming. His thrusts didn't stop as he rode out her orgasm with her, making sure she got everything she needed from him. When he was certain she had, he'd intended to pull out of her, but she tightened her legs around him, keeping him locked in place.

"This time, I want to take you, Syl."

He was game. "Where?" he asked.

"On the sofa."

Lifting her off the table, her legs wrapped around him, and with him still fully embedded in her, he moved to the living room. When he went to place her back on the sofa, she protested, "No, I want to be on top."

He didn't have a problem with that. He untangled their bodies, then stretched out on the sofa, leaving room for her to straddle him. When her center was directly over his erection, she eased down and he pushed upward. He never felt such pleasure sliding inside a woman. At least, he hadn't...until she began riding him hard, clenching her inner muscles with each stroke.

God help him, where had she learned to do this? He was barely able to control himself. And he needed this to last. Opening his eyes, he saw those delectable breasts in his face, so he took a nipple into his mouth. Maybe, if he distracted her, she'd slow her wild ride—it was pushing him over the edge far too quickly. Unfortunately, his actions had the opposite effect, and she rode him even harder.

Suddenly, he could feel it happening. He released her breasts and looked up into her dazed eyes that were staring back at him. His hands grasped her hips as he felt the muscles in his back tighten along with the veins in his neck. He drew in a sharp breath just seconds before he climaxed, with her name on his lips. Moments later, she collapsed on top of him and he quickly switched positions, giving her everything he had.

Three orgasms later, they were both drenched in sweat after giving the sofa—and each other—off-the-charts workouts. "What do you say we take this to the bedroom?" she asked, kissing his face.

"I thought you'd never ask," he said, standing with her in his arms.

As he moved toward the stairs, it suddenly struck him that although he'd tried everything, he could think of to avoid this situation, he was ultimately very glad it had happened. He had taken her—several times in fact—and he intended to keep her. And even though he had issues to work out, the bottom line was that Peggy was now his.

# Chapter 19

"THIS TOWN IS SO interesting, Dak," Mellie said as she and Dak walked through the courtyards on his compound that afternoon. "I'd never heard of Kuta Square before. It's a really busy place."

That morning, they had made love again, before they got up, showered and got ready for the day. Over a breakfast he'd prepared, Dak told her about Syl and Peggy occupying the other house, so she wouldn't be surprised if she saw them on the grounds.

Then they had driven into town to check out the shopping district, which was made up of several fashion boutiques and numerous dining outlets. Dak had been patient while she'd looked for souvenirs for Stonewall, Joy, Granny Kay and Whitney. And when she'd tried on a few outfits, he'd been happy to offer his opinion. He'd told her she looked good in them all, but not as good as she'd look without them.

They had lunch at one of the cafes where she'd had a chance to experience even more Balinese food. Dak had already asked Ni Wayan to prepare dinner that evening, but Mellie had been afraid she'd still be too full to appreciate it. She needn't have worried.

She liked Ni Wayan immediately. The older woman spoke little English, but Mellie was impressed to discover Dak spoke Indonesian well. He told her learning the language had made sense for him. He had a lot of business interests here.

"This is so very beautiful, Dak." They had come to the area where his property met the Java Sea. With all the beautiful flower gardens and low hanging trees, the place looked good enough to be on a postcard.

As they slid onto a bench that faced the sea, Mellie realized that Bali already ranked high on the list of her favorite places. The town was nice and the people friendly, but she knew it was Dak's company that made this place special.

"Are you ready to tell me now, Amelia."

His question seemed to have floated along with the breeze off the sea. Tilting her head, she glanced over at him. "Tell you what?"

"What foolish mistake you made that is stopping you from opening your own practice sooner rather than later?"

Did he never forget anything? Obviously not. She could put him off again, but she figured he would only bring it back up later. And she could tell him it wasn't any of his business, which was true. But somehow, she couldn't bring herself to do that, not when she was sitting there, feeling more relaxed than she had in years, surrounded by remarkable beauty...and it was all thanks to him.

"It's not exactly a 'what', but a 'who'," she finally said.

"Okay then. Who was your foolish mistake?"

She leaned back against the bench and stared out at the sea. "I will tell you, but first, you have to promise that you won't share this conversation with Stonewall. Granny Kay and my best friend Whitney are the only ones who know about it."

He didn't say anything. It was as if he wasn't sure he should make such a promise, but when she frowned at him, he relented. "Okay, I promise."

She drew in a deep breath, then let it out slowly. "His name was Dr. Ivan McIntosh. We met when I was doing my residency in St. Louis. He'd been working at the hospital a good five years already and was a regular physician on staff. We began dating, and soon found out that we shared the same dream about one day opening our own practice. We went out for a year, and I thought the relationship was going somewhere. Too late I discovered it meant much more to me than it did to him. He had his own agenda—one that didn't include me."

She glanced away from the sea to look over at Dak. "I only had a half-year left before I completed my residency, and we began discussing the possibility of becoming partners. In the end, we decided to open a practice together."

She swallowed. Even though it had been years, Ivan's betrayal still hurt. "One day he came to me all excited, saying that he had found the perfect location. I went to see it and agreed it was ideal. It even had the potential for growth in later years."

"The two of you were going to get married?" Dak asked.

She shrugged. "The subject of marriage never came up. But I figured, once we got our practice up and running, it would be the next step. And I trusted him enough to believe that."

"What happened?"

"Together, we had fifty thousand dollars saved to start up the practice. I gave him my part, but the day we were to sign the papers, he called to tell me he'd decided to operate the practice alone. When I asked for my money back, he said he'd had to use it to close the deal, but would give it back to me in six months."

"Did he?"

"No. Every time I called to collect, he'd ask for six more months. In the end, he never gave me my money back. Ivan began blocking my calls and then his attorney wrote me a letter stating I had *given* Ivan money, that it hadn't been a loan. The letter further stated that unless I could prove otherwise, I was not to harass his client or they would make sure I lost my medical license."

When Dak let out a stream of expletives, she smiled. It felt good to have someone outraged on her behalf. She'd been outraged herself.

"I could have taken him to court but his attorney was right," she continued. "I had no proof it hadn't been a gift. But I knew that if Stonewall found out about it, he would have taken the money out of Ivan's hide. And I couldn't let that happen. I couldn't let him get into trouble again, risk jail again, because of a stupid mistake I'd made."

She chuckled. "Granny Kay put Ivan on her prayer list. She believes that one day, he will see the light and eventually pay me back. I am not holding my breath, waiting for that to happen. Trust me."

Dak didn't say anything for the longest time, and she got worried. Did he think less of her? Finally, he said, "I'm not a religious man, so I won't hold my breath, waiting for that to happen, either. All I can say, Amelia, is that there is one certain thing about life—we all make mistakes, and if we're smart, we learn from them."

She nodded. She'd never again allow herself to be fooled by someone like Ivan. She'd pushed aside all her doubts about him, and they'd come back to bite her in the ass. Now, she was more careful, learning the true nature of the men she spent time with. With the exception of Dak, she hadn't been impressed.

The last she'd heard, Ivan was doing well for himself and had extended the facilities. There was no reason he couldn't pay her back now, but he hadn't and probably never intended to.

Dak got up and extended his hand. "Dinner should be ready about now. Let's head back."

• • •

Dak glanced across the room at the beautiful woman sitting curled up in the chair, sipping the glass of wine he had poured for her. He actually regretted that he only had two more days with her. Typically, by now he'd be more than ready for his time with a woman to end, but not with Amelia. He had even considered inviting her to stay an additional week. He'd never done that before, but there was no reason he couldn't. He wasn't ready to end his time with her. One week just hadn't been enough.

She was quite a woman, one who had the ability to not only stimulate him in the bedroom but out of it, as well. They took walks every day and would engage in stimulating conversations, even broaching a number of controversial topics. They didn't always agree but she could hold her own against him, and he appreciated that. He was used to women giving in too easily, not wanting to oppose his thoughts, for fear he wouldn't want to see them again. He didn't know why they'd bothered. He'd made sure they all knew that he wouldn't be seeing them again anyway.

But Amelia... Amelia was totally different. He could see himself spending a lot more time with her, playing a game of pool, engaging in stimulating conversation...and of course, sharing his bed. Dak took a sip of his wine, trying to figure out how he felt about that. Why was he thinking of making her an exception to his usual rules? Yes, she was beautiful, intelligent, energetic...but so were several other women he'd shared his time with. But there was something about Amelia that set her apart from the others. He had to give her that. However, that was all he would give her.

Nothing had changed, as far as he was concerned. He didn't need a permanent woman in his life, now or ever. Marriage was not in his future. Eventually, he would adopt a child, the way his father had done. But he didn't need a Mrs. Dak Navarro to accomplish that.

"That's odd."

He lifted a brow. "What?"

"You said Syl and Peggy were in the compound, but I haven't seen them. It's been three days."

Neither had he, but he had a good idea why his two crew members were MIA. But instead of telling her, he asked, "Would you like more wine?"

"Nope. I'm fine. I can't believe our week is winding down, Dak. I'm going to miss this place."

*And I'm going to miss you*, he thought. "I'm glad you're enjoying yourself."

"What's not to enjoy," she said, placing her wine glass down and easing out of her chair, intentionally or otherwise, flashing him a nice view of her thighs. The sundress she was wearing was short and sexy as hell.

"I've visited someplace I've never been before," she said, slowly strolling toward him. "I have seen the most beautiful views, eaten the most delicious meals, and been introduced to a wonderful new culture."

Coming to a stop in front of him, she reached up and wrapped her arms around his neck. "But most importantly, I've had the company of a very handsome, attentive, and absolutely wonderful man."

She then moved closer and took his mouth with hers. He was ready for her, wrapping his arms around her tight as their mouths mated as if this would be the last time. He could tell her need tonight was just as fierce as his own, and using his body language, he let her know he approved.

Her moan told him that she understood every stroke of his tongue, every nudge of his erection against her center. He wanted her and would always want her.

She suddenly broke the kiss and pressed her forehead against his. "You're hot," she said breathlessly.

In a voice as calm and as steady as he could make it, he said, "Baby, you're hotter." And then he swept her into his arms and carried her up the stairs.

• • •

Dak immediately came awake and sat up in bed, recognizing the sound. Gunshots. And they were hitting his bedroom window. "What the hell!"

Amelia was now awake as well, and in the dark, she reached out for him. "Dak!"

"I'm here, baby. Someone is shooting at us."

"Shouldn't we get down on the floor," she asked in a panicked voice.

He drew her closer to him. "No, we're fine just where we are."

"How can you say that? This bed is so close to the window!"

"We're fine, trust me," he said, pulling her tighter into his arms. "The glass is bulletproof."

At that moment his phone rang, and he recognized Syl's ringtone. He grabbed the phone off the nightstand, while still holding Amelia. "Syl? Yes, we're okay. What about you and Peggy?"

"We're okay. What the hell is going on, Dak?" Syl asked.

"I don't know. Hopefully one of the assholes remains alive long enough to tell us," Dak said as anger flowed through his body.

"I've called the police. They're on their way," Syl said.

"Okay. Stay put until they get here." Dak disconnected the call and placed the phone back on the nightstand.

"Are Syl and Peggy okay?" Amelia asked, concern obvious in her voice.

"They're fine. Their cottage has the same type of security in place that I have here."

With the sound of gunshots still hitting the windows, Dak got out of bed. After sliding into his pants, he tossed Amelia the dress he'd taken off her earlier. Once she was dressed, Dak held out his hand. "Come with me."

Once she took his hand, he led her out of the bedroom, to his walk-in closet. "Where are we going?" she asked, holding tight to his hand.

"You'll see."

He pushed the door open, and then using his other hand, he touched the inside wall. She gasped when it opened into another room.

"Is this your security room?" she asked, glancing all around.

"You could call it that. I generally refer to it as my command center. Every single device and security equipment that you see here was created by my company."

She followed him over to look at the huge monitor on the desk. Bright security lights were on, giving him a clear picture of the area around his home. Several men were down on the ground—some of them, not moving. Dak counted six men in all.

*Who were they and why had they attacked his compound?*

Amelia shivered. "I can't believe this is happening, Dak. Stonewall told me that your business is an electrical and mechanical engineering firm that specialized in advanced technology, and created high-tech security devices."

"Yes, that's some of what we do, although we are now developing other things as well," he said.

"But who are those men? And who returned fire on them? Your guys?"

He turned to look at Amelia, lifting a brow. "My guys?"

"Don't you have people protecting your compound at night?"

He turned back to the screen. "No."

"Then who shot those men?" she asked.

He glanced over at her. "They shot themselves. The windows in this house are not only bulletproof, but they're reflective. In fact, they acted like a ricochet. Every bullet those men shot at the windows came right back at them. And they managed to get close enough to the house that they wouldn't have stood much of a chance."

Amelia's jaw dropped, and she stared at him as if she couldn't quite believe what he was telling her. She was about to ask him something but stopped when the police sirens filled the air.

"Come on, let's get decent. We have to go meet with the police."

# Chapter 20

NOW STANDING OUT IN the yard of Dak's compound, Mellie couldn't stop looking at the glass windows surrounding his home. There wasn't even a dent. Then she looked at the bodies still scattered on the ground. She had heard of bulletproof glass, but she had never heard of bullets ricocheting off it before. But the proof was right in front of her.

Who were the men shooting at Dak's home? And why had they decided to attack? Had they been home invaders, thinking to catch him unaware...or someone else?

Dak was still talking to several policemen, but she couldn't understand what they were saying, so she walked around, looking to see if any clues had been left behind. Watching Dak interact with the police, she realized that he was no stranger to this kind of thing. In fact, it had been because of a situation like this, a few years ago, that Stonewall had become his bodyguard. But the man responsible for the attempts on Dak's life then had been caught and was now serving time. Were there others? Dak had certainly been prepared for such a thing. When she'd first seen his home, she'd thought it was *extraordinarily* beautiful. She hadn't been wrong. His glass house was a fortress.

She saw Peggy standing alone, so she crossed the yard to go to her. She could tell the woman was shaken at seeing the bodies. As a doctor, Mellie was no stranger to death, but she'd never seen it like this. The place looked like a combat zone. She could certainly understand why Peggy would be upset.

"Are you okay, Peggy?" Mellie asked, touching her arm.

Peggy drew in a deep breath and nodded. "Yes. But this is horrifying. Who were these men? Why did they come here?"

"I have no idea," Mellie said. She glanced around. "Where is Syl?"

"He left to go check the plane, to make sure it's okay. It's in a secured place at the airport but after what happened here, he's not taking any chances."

The thought that someone might have tampered with Dak's jet sent chills down Mellie's spine. "Was there any damage to the house where you and Syl are staying?"

"No, that house wasn't the target, apparently. It was as if they were intentionally spraying bullets into Dak's home, as if they knew he was there. Syl said they probably expected Dak to be in bed, so they focused most of their firepower at his bedroom window."

"Only to have those bullets come back at them," Mellie said, shaking her head. If Dak had had regular windows, there was no way they could have survived such an attack.

When the coroner arrived to collect the bodies, Peggy asked, "Do you want to come back to the other house and join me in a drink?"

"A glass of wine would definitely help right now," Mellie said. "Just give me a minute to let Dak know where I'll be."

Moments later, she returned with a police escort. At Peggy's questioning look, she said, "Dak's orders," explaining the presence of the two-armed officers. "Although he's had the grounds searched, he's not taking any chances."

"I'm glad he is not," Peggy said as they began walking to the cottage, with the officers following close behind them. Although it was dark, the grounds were well-lit, and from the number of police officers mulling about, Mellie could tell that they were taking the attack on Dak's compound seriously.

When she mentioned it to Peggy, the other woman said, "That's understandable. Tourists, and those who own homes here, are good for the island's economy. I'm sure the authorities want them to feel safe."

At any other time, Mellie would have thought it the perfect night for a stroll, with the combined scents of the sea and flowers filling the air. But tonight, the breeze contained the stench of death. "I've never been so afraid in my life," Peggy said, breaking the silence.

Mellie knew how she felt. She'd been terrified as well, but Dak had helped her through it.

Before she could say anything, Peggy added, "Had I not been with Syl, I don't know what I would have done."

Mellie nodded, not sure if Peggy was insinuating that she'd been with Syl, the way Mellie had been with Dak, or that she was glad they'd been in the same house at the time. She remembered Dak saying that Peggy was interested in Syl, but the man was fighting the attraction. Had he finally given in?

When they reached the house, one of the officers turned to them. In English, thank God, he instructed them to stay outside with the other officer while he went inside to check the building. A few minutes later, he returned and gave the okay for them to go inside. The officers then stood outside and guarded the door.

"I hope they find the people responsible. Syl said the men weren't local," Peggy said, leading Mellie into the kitchen.

Although the house was a lot smaller than Dak's, Mellie liked it. Like the main house, it was made of glass, but it could be reverted into to an open-air home, if desired. "I wonder where they came from?"

"I'm sure Dak will get to the bottom of it," Peggy said, uncorking the wine and pouring them both a glass. "I don't want to think about what could have happened if Dak hadn't had the foresight to install state-of-the-art security measures in this compound. That was a lifesaver."

"It definitely was," Mellie said, taking a seat at the table.

"Do you like being a doctor?" Peggy asked, walking over to join her.

Mellie wondered if the other woman really wanted to know the answer or if she simply needed to engage in conversation to get her mind off of what had happened outside these walls. It really didn't matter, since Mellie honestly wanted to do the same thing. "I love being a doctor." She was about to tell Peggy how stressed she'd been, and how this was the ideal place to rest and relax... and then she thought about what had just happened and couldn't say anymore.

"What about you, Peggy? Do you like being a flight hostess?"

Peggy nodded. "Definitely. It's all I've ever done. I became a flight attendant for a commercial airline just after I finished college, mostly flying international routes. I loved it. On one of those flights, I met a businessman and his wife—a lovely couple. He was in the process of buying his own private plane and asked if I would consider coming to work for him, as a flight hostess. Although I told him yes, I figured I'd never hear from him again. But his wife called me one day, nearly six months later, and offered me the job. I worked for them for five years and had the best time of my life. Unfortunately, when Mrs. Pennington got sick and died of cancer, Mr. Pennington remarried less than a year later. His new wife was a woman young enough to be his granddaughter. She took one look at me and said I had to go."

Peggy took a sip of her wine. "At least he referred me to Dak. He's a great employer."

"I can believe that," Mellie said.

"I understand your brother was his bodyguard at one time."

Mellie wondered how she knew that, and figured Syl must have told her. "Yes, he was, a few years ago."

"Chef mentioned it to me. Chef liked him and said he was a really nice guy."

Mellie smiled. "Yes, I have to say I have a wonderful big brother. He's definitely a keeper. Do you have any siblings?"

"No, I was an only child. My parents wanted other kids but the doctor advised against it."

"Are your parents still living?"

"Yes. They have a horse ranch in Utah. Dad's been talking about selling it for years, but hasn't done anything about it. I call them every week and try to get home at least two to three times a year. Even more often if Dak doesn't have a lot of international travel lined up."

Mellie wondered how often Dak travelled overseas—and if that would always be a way of life for him. They suddenly heard voices, and when they turned around, both Dak and Syl were entering the kitchen.

Mellie immediately went to Dak. "Are you okay?"

"I'm fine. Let's go home."

She wondered if Dak realized what he'd said, referring to his home as hers. "I'm ready."

She glanced over to where Syl and Peggy were standing. Syl's arm was around her waist. That left no doubt in Mellie's mind that their relationship had definitely moved to another level. "Thanks for the wine, Peggy."

"Thanks for talking me down."

Dak turned to Syl. "We'll talk tomorrow. I'll have a better idea of my plans after I make a few calls."

"Roger that," Syl said.

Then Dak took her by the hand and led her out of the house. Once outside, Mellie noticed that several armed guards were still there. "Are they staying?"

"For the time being. None of the men who attacked the compound were Indonesian. As far as we know. All of the dead are from South America. The authorities figured no more than three or four men managed to get away. They are scanning the area, looking for them. What has them confused, though, is how the South American men got into this country, when there is no record of them coming in through Customs."

She glanced up at Dak. "So how did they get in?"

"I'm not sure. But in order to bypass Customs, they would have needed some inside help."

She nodded. "Do you have any idea why they attacked the compound, Dak?"

He tightened his grip on her hand. "I'm not sure. But you can bet I intend to find out."

As they walked back, she saw the bodies had been removed and men were hosing the area down to remove any bloodstains left behind. When they reached the house, he opened the door for her. And once he shut it behind them, he swept her into his arms and carried her up the stairs.

• • •

They made love for hours, thanks to the adrenaline still surging through their systems. Now, fairly certain that an exhausted Mellie had fallen asleep, Dak got out of bed and went into his command center. He made a phone call to the one person he knew could provide some answers.

The man who picked up didn't waste time saying hello. "It's been a while, Raven."

During his time in the USN, Dak had been a part of the In-flight Unit. Each team member's code name was that of a bird. Dak had been named Raven because like a Raven, he didn't attack unless provoked. And the complexity of a Raven's chatter was similar to Dak's ability to speak so many different languages.

Not wasting time on pleasantries, he said, "My compound in Bali was attacked tonight, Sparrow." Marcus Lancaster, code name Sparrow, was the only one of Dak's teammates still in the USN organization. The other agents, like Dak, had settled into a normal life. Or, at least as normal a life that they could manage. Marcus had been given the name Sparrow because of his mane of red hair, as well as for his diligence, productivity, and persistence—all the things a sparrow was known for.

"What the hell! Are you okay?" Sparrow asked.

"Yeah, I'm fine. My place has ricochet windows, so you can guess how things played out."

Sparrow laughed. "Served their asses right. They got what they deserved. Who were they?"

"Men from South America. A few got away."

He could hear cursing on the other end. "That's not good, Raven. That means there's still a threat."

"I know, and I'm taking every precaution. I've learned that the men were able to get inside my compound without setting off the alarm because it was an inside job."

"How?"

"I checked footage from my security video. It appears that on yesterday, one of the men who normally comes to assist my gardener was replaced by someone else. That man, a local Indonesian, opened one of the gates to allow someone else to tamper with that part of my security system."

"Do you know who it was?"

"Now we do. He's being picked up and questioned."

"Good luck with that. I doubt he's still alive. You know how it works. Cutthroats pay someone a lot of money to be their patsy, and then they kill them before they can spend it. No way in hell will they let him live to talk. It's too much of a risk."

Dak figured that much as well. "I need to know something, Sparrow. Is the USN absolutely sure Kovalenko is dead, or is it just damn wishful thinking on their part?"

There was a pause on the other end that lasted almost too long to suit Dak. He was about to say as much when Sparrow spoke. "I'm sorry I didn't tell you the last time you asked me about it, back when that last attempt was made on your life, but it's time I address your concerns. Kovalenko is dead, Raven. I put a bullet in him myself."

The one thing Dak was certain about was that if Sparrow admitted to killing Kovalenko, the man was definitely dead.

It had taken years for Dak to stop looking over his shoulder, and he would admit to getting spooked when that attempt was made on his life a few years ago. That's when he'd hired Stonewall as his bodyguard. The USN had quickly proven there was no connection between the murder attempt and Dak's former life as an agent with them. He'd pissed someone else off.

"I need some answers, Sparrow, so I'll know what my next move should be." But he had already decided what that move would be. He'd told Syl earlier to get the jet ready to take off for South America.

"I'll do what I can. But I'll need the names of those people who were in the compound with you. We need to check them out, too."

Dak knew there was no need to tell Sparrow not to waste his time, even though he'd trust Amelia, Syl and Peggy with his life. When Sparrow went looking for something, he checked under every rock. It was part of the reason he was so good at what he did. "My houseguest was Dr. Amelia Courson. My pilot, Sylvester Wright and my flight hostess, Peggy Henderson were in the other cottage." As an afterthought he added, "My flight chef, Aryan Reyansh, never made it to the compound. He took off to visit his family in India the day after we arrived."

"Interesting."

Dak didn't say anything more, deciding to let Sparrow think whatever he liked. He was certain the man's investigation would prove the chef was just as clean as the others.

"What about your household staff, or anyone having access to your home or the compound?"

After Dak provided Sparrow that information, he said, "I'm flying to South America."

"I don't think that's wise, Raven. Just sit tight until I call you back. Give me at least forty-eight hours."

As far as Dak was concerned, that was too damn long. There was no reason to think whoever was behind the attack on the compound wouldn't try again. And from the kind of ammunition those men had used, Dak knew they'd wanted him dead. But that wasn't going to happen. Nor would he allow anything to happen to Amelia.

Since he'd be flying off to South America, the best thing for him to do was to get her out of harm's way, as soon as possible. There was no way around it—she would have to go home. He would contact Jefferson for him to find the next available commercial flight headed back to the States. And he'd make sure Amelia got on it. Afterwards, he would head to South America.

"I'll expect your call, Sparrow," Dak said, ending the call.

There was no way Sparrow hadn't caught on that Dak wasn't going to wait on his call. Sparrow knew him better than that. Dak believed in being proactive.

A raven didn't attack unless provoked. He *had* been provoked and now it was time for the prey to become the hunter.

# Chapter 21

THE NEXT MORNING, MELLIE had awakened to find Dak kissing his way down her body. Using his mouth he had given her one hell of an orgasm before he'd made love to her, giving her several more before the sun appeared in the sky above the sea. Not to be outdone, she had turned the tables, taking the dominant role by straddling Dak and riding him until he'd yelled out her name. The mere sound of that made her come yet again. Finally, she collapsed on his chest from sheer exhaustion.

She was still on top of him, their bodies joined. Even now, she could feel his hardness throbbing inside of her, as if he was getting ready for another round. She was, too. And she was about to tell him so. Only his next words stopped her.

"Because of what happened last night, Amelia, I can't let you remain here. I'm sorry, but I've made arrangements for you to go back home. Today."

*What?* His words caught her completely off guard, and she looked down at him, into the depths of his beautiful dark eyes, seeking understanding. "You're sending me away?"

Reaching up, he gently pushed back a strand of hair that had fallen in her face. "Trust me, sweetheart, I don't want you to leave. But until I find out who's behind last night's attack, it's not safe for you to be here with me."

She caught herself before she could confess that there was no other place she'd rather be, but instead, she said, "I'm not afraid. I know how to use a firearm, Dak."

The smile that appeared on his face caught her breath. That smile, along with his sharp cheekbones, chiseled jaw and gorgeous eyes always did something to her. Even now, though their conversation was anything but sexy, she couldn't help but notice that his erection hadn't gone down any.

"I'd heard you were good with a firearm," he said, softly rubbing her back. "Stonewall told me how you and Granny Kay took classes, as well as self-defense training, when he was away all those years. But I refuse to put your skill to the test on my watch. If anything were to happen to you, I'd have Stonewall to deal with." He pretended to shudder, and she released a small laugh despite the seriousness of the situation.

"Then come back with me. Let the Indonesian authorities handle it. Surely, they could handle finding out who's behind an attempted home invasion, couldn't they?"

He held her gaze for a moment then said, "I don't know who or what I'm dealing with, Amelia, but I doubt that last night's events had anything to do with a home invasion. What last night proved is that I have an enemy out there.

And I don't want to put you in danger by keeping you with me, just in case he decides to try again."

"An enemy? What? Another disgruntled former business associate?"

"I'm not sure, but I intend to find out."

Why did she feel there was more to this? Something he was keeping from her? "What is it, Dak? What aren't you telling me?"

"Let me worry about things, okay, my sexy doctor? Like I said, if anything ever happened to you, I'd have Stonewall to deal with. And nobody wants that."

Mellie eased her body off of him, already missing the connection. As she gazed up at the ceiling, she asked, "Is that all that matters to you? Stonewall's anger?"

He shifted positions, moving to loom over her. "No, that's not all that matters. You matter. I'd never forgive myself if I placed you in danger. Besides, tomorrow was our last day here anyway."

"I see." Was that his way of saying he was tired of her? "When is Syl flying me home?"

"He's not. I'm putting you on a commercial flight. It's safer that way. It will be a direct flight to New York with a stop in London to refuel. Arrangements have already been made. Peggy will fly as far as London with you, then she'll visit friends she has there. It's not good for her to stay here, either."

Mellie didn't say anything. She didn't want to leave him, knowing his life was in danger, but he was sending her away and there was nothing she could do about it. Didn't he know that she would worry about him? She fought back tears, suddenly realizing that she'd done the one thing she'd promised herself she wouldn't do—fall in love with Dak.

He didn't want a woman's love. He'd made that abundantly clear. But he now had hers, although she would never tell him how she felt. She had more pride than to confess her love to a man who didn't want it. She'd done that before. The only difference was that Ivan had pretended he had wanted her love, when all he'd wanted was her money.

Reaching up, she wrapped her arms around his neck. "What time does my plane leave, Dak?"

"At four."

"Then make love to me until it's time for me to leave."

A smile touched his lips. "There's nothing else I'd rather do, Amelia."

And then he lowered his mouth to hers.

• • •

"Tearing off to South America isn't a good idea, Dak."

Dak glanced over at Syl but continued moving around his bedroom, packing. "Even if Kovalenko is dead, there's still a possibility that I have a price on my head. It's unlikely that all of his men died with him. They could have regrouped. And before attempting another coup, it would make sense that they'd want to get the man who thwarted their last attempt out of the way—me."

"If that's true, don't you think flying to their turf is playing right into their hands? At least let me go with you. I promised Mike that I—"

"I know what you promised Dad, Syl. But I'm a grown-ass man, and I can take care of myself."

"Not when you're rushing out and putting yourself in danger. Do you even have a plan? What about backup? If this is a suicide mission, Dak, then count me out."

"Fine! I'll fly the plane myself." Wanting to change the subject, Dak finally asked the question he'd been wondering about all day. "Was Amelia okay?"

Syl stared at him for a minute. "I wondered how long it would be before you asked me about her."

"Just answer the question, Syl."

"Yes, Amelia was okay. It was obvious she hadn't wanted to leave."

Dak drew in a deep breath. "I didn't want to send her away, but I had no choice. It would have been too dangerous for her to stay."

"Did you tell her that?"

"Yes."

"At least you did that much. I can tell she cares for you, Dak, and she's worried. She made me promise to take care of you. Seems to me, the two of you are more worried about each other than you are about yourselves. I wonder why."

Refusing to be baited, Dak stared out the windows in his bedroom—those same windows that had saved his and Amelia's life. Amelia had promised to text him the minute she arrived back in the States. Instead of flying on to Charlottesville right away, she'd decided to remain in New York for a few days to shop and take in a Broadway play.

He glanced back over at Syl. "What about Peggy?"

A frown settled on Syl's face. "What about her?"

When Dak had told him that he would be sending Amelia away, Syl suggested sending Peggy away, too. She would rejoin them in London when it was time to make a stop there on their return trip home...whenever that was.

"Did Peggy get off okay, as well?"

"Yes. And she didn't want to leave either."

Dak waited to see if Syl would say anything about the relationship he'd obviously started with Peggy. When he didn't, Dak decided to leave it alone. If he didn't ask Syl about Peggy, then Syl wouldn't question the way he felt about Amelia.

Hell, he missed her already. He hadn't known how much of an impact she'd had on him until she'd left. Even this house, this entire compound, felt empty with her gone. He was just about to close his luggage when his cell phone rang.

He clicked it on. "Yes?"

"Raven, this is Sparrow."

Dak felt his body tense at the sound of the familiar greeting. He hadn't expected Sparrow to call back so soon. "Yes, Sparrow?"

"It didn't take me long to find out something. Just like I thought, the attack on your compound had nothing to do with Kovalenko. The USN has been keeping its eyes on anyone they thought was connected. They're all dead. However, in their research, they discovered something interesting, and it involves someone who's staying at your compound."

The hairs on the back of Dak's neck stood up. "Who?"

"Amelia Courson."

"Amelia?" Dak asked, shocked.

"Yes. It appears she was the intended target."

"What the hell!" he said, his hand tightening on his cell phone. "Who would want Amelia dead?"

"Unfortunately, it's a case of mistaken identity. A few years ago, Kimberly Watson, an American woman who'd been a sex trafficking victim, managed to escape from a

South American businessman by the name, Sante Al'toria. She became a federal witness and it was her testimony that sealed the deal and put him away. Miss Watson was subsequently placed in the witness protection program, and she's still there."

"And?"

"And according to a CIA informant who has infiltrated a group that is now run by Al'toria's son, Sargrasso, the CIA was tipped off that Sargrasso got a call that Kimberly Watson was spotted at an American airport with a wealthy businessman. Sargrasso had her followed, and he sent his henchmen to Indonesia to dispose of her."

Dak rubbed his hand down his face. "What does any of this have to do with Amelia?"

"It seems Miss Courson shares a striking resemblance to Kimberly Watson. I'm sending you a photo, via text, of the woman, so you can see the resemblance for yourself. Al'toria died in prison and Sargrasso wants revenge for his father's death. Sargrasso has been on the CIA's most wanted list for years, but he's been quiet. For a while, it seemed as if he'd dropped off the face of the earth. None of our agents, including our informant, have ever been able to pinpoint his hiding place. However, to avenge his father's death, Sargrasso intends to come out into the open. Too bad he's targeted the wrong woman."

When Dak's phone pinged, he glanced at the photo, studying it closely. The woman appeared to be a year or two older than Amelia, and he would admit there was some resemblance between the two women. But anyone with a sharp eye for detail could see it was not the same person.

A thought then crossed his mind. "Level with me, Sparrow. Is there a chance that Amelia Courson was 'recognized' because she was with me?"

"Why would you assume that?"

"Well, as much as I'd love to think my past is firmly behind me, I'm sure there are still people who watch my comings and goings. So, if Amelia was seen with me—someone who was involved with the USN—wouldn't it make sense for someone who believes she's Kimberly Watson to think she hooked up with me for protection?"

"I checked out that angle and that's not it. Although there's a possibility you might be on some unsavory person's radar because of your time as an Army Ranger, and all those kick-ass techie contraptions you've created, your involvement with the USN is as airtight as it can get. Those records are not just sealed, they are in a vault somewhere, buried hundreds of feet below the earth. There is no connection between this and the USN, trust me. Like I said, it is merely a case of mistaken identity."

Then Sparrow chuckled. "Shit, even if you *had* been on their radar because of the USN, those bastards would have been smarter to leave Dr. Courson alone. With all those damn techie creations, the last thing anyone wants to do is incur your wrath, Raven."

"Too late now," Dak said.

"And there's something else you should know, Raven. The CIA has wanted Sargrasso for years and now that he's coming out of hiding, they have no qualms about using Ms. Courson as bait."

Sparrow's words sent a chill up Dak's spine. "Like hell!"

"That's what I say. Our saving grace is that Owl's in charge of that particular CIA team, and I've alerted him of your involvement."

"Owl?" Montana Tabaston was another former In-Flight team member. His code name of Owl fitted him perfectly. Owls were known for their paranormal wisdom, regal silence, and fierce intelligence. Tabaston had all three. They often teased and called him 'The Professor' because he was like a damn walking encyclopedia. He could store a whole damn book to memory and could invade a room without the occupants knowing he was there until he was ready to make his presence known. "Last I'd heard, he'd settled comfortably into civilian life."

"Comfortably? Owl doesn't know the meaning of the word. He tried doing the normal-life thing for a few years, but decided he liked the cloak-and-dagger world better. Now he's with the CIA and out there kicking ass, as usual. I told Owl that Ms. Courson is with you, so he knows she's safe."

Sparrow's words hit Dak low in his gut. "Damn. She isn't here with me, Sparrow. I put her on a commercial flight back to the States to keep her safe." *Oh, God...* What if Sargrasso had figured out that she was on the plane and arranged for his men to be waiting for her when she landed in New York? What if...?

"Shit! I'll contact Owl to let him know. Give me her itinerary, Raven."

Dak rattled it off. "I'm going to be there to meet her plane when it lands in New York, Sparrow," he said, rushing across the room to open the drawer to his nightstand. He pulled out his Glock, and then he reached under the bed to pull out a black case that contained his other weapons. He knew Syl was watching him and although he could only hear one side of the conversation, Dak figured Syl was putting two and two together.

"Her plane is at least fourteen hours ahead of you, Raven. There's no way you can get there in time to meet her plane."

"Watch me." He clicked off the phone, and pulled a bag filled with more weapons from beneath his bed.

Glancing over at Syl, he said, "Amelia's in danger. I'll give you the details on our way to the airport."

• • •

"Dammit, Dak, let me at the controls before you kill us both," Syl said, narrowing his gaze at Dak.

"I've got this, Syl. If my piloting is making you nervous, go in the cabin and have a drink."

Dak was aware that he was breaking every aviation rule in the book, but he didn't care. He was going to get to Amelia on time, even if had to fly seven-hundred miles an hour, which was two hundred more than a normal flight. And he was. But he had a lot of hours to make up. And he didn't care that he wasn't following the flight plan Syl had filed for them to take, or that the jet was at an altitude of fifty-five thousand feet instead of the forty-five designated for private planes. So far he hadn't come into contact with any other aircraft and hoped like hell that he didn't. Of course, at that moment, a commercial airplane appeared in their path, and he had to do a sudden climb to avoid hitting it.

"Damn it, Dak. Let me pilot this thing."

He glanced over at Syl, noticing that the color had drained from the man's face. "Leave me alone. Go have that drink, but don't get drunk. You'll need to fly us out of New York."

"I will, if we don't crash first. Of course, if we do manage to get there in one piece, we'll probably be arrested." Cursing under his breath, Syl unsnapped his seatbelt and made his way out of the cockpit.

In a way, Dak was glad he was gone. The last thing he needed was Syl questioning what he was doing. All he could focus on was making up for the hours that Amelia had ahead of them.

"Granger-Aire, 44 Alpha Tango 275, do you read me?"

Dak let out an annoyed sigh, not surprised someone from air-traffic control was contacting him. He'd honestly expected a connection sooner. "This is Granger-Aire, 44 Alpha Tango 275, I read you. Over."

"What are you doing?"

"Flying to New York."

"You're off course and climbing without permission. Do you read me? Over."

"I read you." There was no sense trying to explain that he was racing against time.

"This is a traffic alert. Traffic at 12:00 and 10 miles. Boeing aircraft please report in sight."

He saw the Boeing 747 headed toward him...or they were headed toward each other. "This is Granger-Aire. Boeing in sight." Dak immediately tilted his jet to climb again and could actually hear Syl cursing in the main cabin.

"Return to your correct flight level, Granger-Aire. You're entering congested air space due to severe thunderstorms in the area. Return to your flight level of 450."

Dak didn't intend to argue with them, but nor did he plan to do what they said. They would all have to share this particular airspace. No sooner had that thought crossed his mind, than he saw another Boeing directly in his path. He immediately climbed higher. He had given Granger Aeronautics specifics on what he wanted his jet to be able to do, although he'd never expected to put it to the test like this. But his jet handled the sudden movements like a dream.

He glanced at the controls—he'd already made up six hours. The only thing that mattered right now was getting to Amelia before Sargrasso's men could. He wasn't going to depend on Sparrow, with the USN, or even Owl with the CIA, to protect her. Amelia was his responsibility.

*His.*

The high altitude obviously had him thinking crazy. He'd never claimed any woman as his before. Deciding to check on Syl, he pressed the intercom. "You okay?"

"Hell no. Regardless of what you say, I need to get drunk."

Dak shook his head. "Stay sober, Syl. I'll need you to fly us out of New York. I'll be too busy trying to explain to Amelia what the hell is going on."

"Where are we headed when we leave New York? That is, if they allow us to leave. After this stunt, I can see them putting us in federal prison and throwing away the key."

Dak rolled his eyes. "We're going to my island in the Maldives. So you'd better get some rest."

"I will when you stop flying this plane at seven hundred miles an hour."

Dak ignored Syl and went back to the controls. This wasn't the time to tell his friend that their speed was now at eight hundred.

• • •

"Syl? Where are you? What's going on?" Peggy asked.

Syl tried to keep his voice calm—not an easy feat, at the moment. "It's a long story. Bottom line is that the men who attacked the compound were after Amelia, not Dak."

"Amelia!"

"Yes. It's a case of mistaken identity. These assholes can't tell one woman from another. But now we're on Dak's plane, trying to make up time so we can reach New York before Amelia's plane lands."

"Can you do that? Her plane left hours ago."

"Tell that to Dak, He's determined to get there in time or kill us both trying. The reason I'm calling is because I wanted to warn you to be careful. You were seen with Amelia, so these guys know who you are. Are you still visiting your friends?"

"Yes, but I leave later today. I'd planned to check into a hotel."

"Okay. That's fine. But please don't go out to do any shopping. Stay in your hotel room as much as you can, and if you see anything or anyone suspicious, let the authorities know." The thought of Peggy being in danger was more worrying to Syl than his fear that Dak would crash the plane and kill them both.

"I'll be there as soon as I can."

"You're coming here?"

"Yes. I'm coming for you, Peggy. We'll make a pit-stop in London, once Dak rescues Amelia. Then we're headed for his island in the Maldives. One of Dak's friends from the CIA will send someone to pick you up at the hotel and have you at the airport when we get there."

"Okay. And Syl?"

"Yes?"

"Please be careful. I love you."

A lump formed in Syl's throat. He didn't want her to love him, because he wasn't sure he could love her. Although he now considered her to be his, he couldn't say he loved her. Not now. Maybe not ever. So instead, he said, "I want you to be careful, too, Peggy. I'll see you in a few hours. Goodbye."

# Chapter 22

*"WE HAVE DESCENDED TO ten thousand feet. The captain has turned on the fasten seatbelts sign and we will be landing at JFK Airport in thirty minutes."*

Mellie heard the flight attendant's message and snapped her seatbelt in place, glad the plane was about to land. She had enjoyed Peggy's company as far as London, and had done her best to sleep during most of the flight to New York. But now she was wide awake and missing Dak. She hoped he was okay, and would text him, like she'd promised, after picking up her luggage from baggage claim.

She was looking forward to spending a few days in New York. After the wonderful time she'd spent with Dak, she wasn't ready to return home just yet. She'd even thought about calling Whitney, to see if she was up for some company in California. It had been a long time since they'd spent any girls' time together.

As they had the whole trip, her thoughts drifted back to Dak. She hoped he was okay, and that the authorities found the other men involved in the assault on his property. She wanted to believe Dak was wrong about the attack on his compound, that it had been a botched robbery attempt and had had nothing to do with him personally.

But she knew there was more to it. He'd said something about his enemies. What enemies? He was the only man she knew whose life had been threatened because of a business deal gone bad. But what if there was more to it? Stonewall had told her that Dak ran a legitimate business. But did Stonewall know that for certain?

She forced those thoughts from her mind. Of course, Dak ran a legitimate business. Then how did he end up with enemies? Enemies like the guys who'd shot up his compound? Just what was he involved in? She needed to know, and she intended to find out. Instead of texting him when the plane landed, she would call him. She needed to hear his voice. She had to know he was okay. And more than anything, she needed answers to her questions.

Feeling someone's eyes on her, she turned around. That same man was staring at her again. She remembered him boarding the plane in London. Every so often, she could sense him watching her. But why? She had ignored him, then drifted off to sleep, hoping he would find someone else to make uncomfortable. But now that she was awake, he was staring at her again. It was as if he was intentionally trying to intimidate her, and she didn't have a clue why. But then, maybe she was just imagining things. That night at Dak's compound still had her somewhat rattled.

Mellie closed her eyes when the plane touched down for a landing, trying to calm her nerves. She thought back to Dak's method of making her feel better, when he'd taken her into his lap and kissed her until the jet had landed in

Indonesia. She wished he was with her now. They had made love until just before it was time for her to leave to catch her plane. Then he had walked her to the car, where Peggy and Syl had been waiting. Dak had kissed her goodbye in front of them, and it hadn't been a peck on the cheek. It had been the kind of kiss a couple would share in private. She wasn't sure how long it would have lasted if Syl hadn't interrupted, reminding them that she and Peggy had a plane to catch.

She opened her eyes when the plane came to a complete stop. The man was still watching her. He gave Mellie the creeps, and she decided, since he was seated across the aisle a few rows ahead of her, that she would wait until he got off before she disembarked. Hopefully by the time she left the plane, he would be long gone.

• • •

"Unidentified aircraft, who are you?" an American air-traffic controller asked.

Dak glanced at the time on his controls. He should be arriving ten minutes before Amelia's flight. When he didn't respond quick enough, the controller then said, "The Air Force has been dispatched to intercede."

"Now you've done it," Syl said, sliding in the seat across from Dak. "One of those fighter pilots will probably shoot us down, thinking we're terrorists or something."

Ignoring Syl's comments, Dak responded, "This is Granger-Aire, 44 Alpha Tango 275. Contact the CIA for approval to land without interference."

They were less than thirty miles from JFK. It seemed to take forever before someone finally came back on. "Approval granted. Land on runway 22L. It has been cleared."

"Granger-Aire landing at 22L. Over and out."

"That will put you at Gate B12," Syl said. "Do you know what gate Amelia's plane will arrive at?"

"D41."

"That's a long way. I hope you make it in time."

Dak hoped so, too. "I need you to gas up while I'm gone and be ready to fly out as soon as I get back."

"Fine. I'm making a stop in London to pick up Peggy. I refuse to be on your island alone with you and Amelia. I want to take a woman of my own."

Dak slanted Syl a look. "The last time we talked, Peggy was the last woman you wanted to get tangled up with."

"I can say the same about you and Amelia Courson."

Dak frowned. "Who said I'm tangled up with her?"

Syl laughed. "Any man who risked his own life and mine to fly a plane at breakneck speed, with little sleep and no breaks to rescue a woman, isn't doing it out of the goodness of his heart, Dak. And don't hand me any BS about you doing it because of your friendship with Stonewall. You care for her. Admit it."

Dak wasn't about to admit to anything. "You do know there's a chance Sargrasso's men will know I am taking her to my island. That means there might be trouble."

"Then why are you taking her there?"

"She's safer with me than anywhere else. Unlike at the compound, I'll be ready for them. And knowing Owl, he'll have a trap ready to catch Sargrasso when he surfaces."

"You don't have a problem being used as bait?" Syl asked.

"I welcome the chance to fry those men's asses for even thinking they could harm a hair on Amelia's head. Besides, the island is the best place for a showdown—one I welcome. I refuse to have Amelia looking over her shoulder for the rest of her life. But, knowing what might be going down, you might think twice about bringing Peggy."

"Just like you believe Amelia is safer with you, I think Peggy is safer with me. I figured Sargrasso's thugs know by now that Peggy and Amelia are friends, since they left Indonesia together. That means Peggy might not be safe either. And that's a risk I refuse to take."

"Have you checked on her?" Dak asked, hearing something in his friend's voice that he hadn't heard in a long time...or ever. Fear. And love.

"Yes. I contacted her when we hit ten thousand feet. She hasn't noticed anything unusual so far, and she'll be at the airstrip in London when we get there, ready to fly out. I told her that a friend of yours from the CIA will pick her up and take her to the airport. I need her protected until we get there, so make it happen, Dak."

"Of course." Dak didn't say anything else for a long moment as he concentrated on landing the plane. He could only hope that if he couldn't make it to Gate D41 by the time Amelia got off the plane, Sparrow or Owl's men would.

• • •

An annoyed frown settled on Mellie's face. That irritating man was still sitting in his seat, not moving as others exited the plane behind him. Then again, maybe he wouldn't. There was a chance that New York was just a stop on this flight, and the plane would be headed somewhere else once it left here. That had been the case when they had reached London. She had remained on board while others, including Peggy, had departed.

When it was time for her row to disembark, she got up and started to walk toward the exit. The hairs on the back on her neck stood up when the man quickly scooted behind her. She didn't like him being so close. He was practically breathing on her neck.

As soon as she cleared the plane's door, she increased her pace, refusing to look back. However, she could sense him gaining on her, and before long, he was almost right on her heels, far too close for comfort. She kept walking, increasing her pace. When she reached the terminal, she was tempted to take off at a run, or locate a security person when suddenly, the man reached out and grabbed her arm, then leaned in close and whispered, "If you resist going with me, I will break your arm, then break your neck. I won't hesitate to kill you."

Fear raced up her spine. Who was this guy? Was he allied with the men who'd tried to kill Dak? Had someone seen her leave the compound, and decided to use her as bait to bring Dak out in the open?

As if to prove he meant business, the man tightened his hold on her arm, to the point that she nearly cried out in pain. But that was all it took. Mellie wasn't Granny Kay's granddaughter for nothing. And she refused to be any man's victim.

When Mellie pretended that she was about to trip, he loosened his grip enough for her to twist her body and kick her leg, aiming the toe of her Chucks to his balls. He anticipated her move and grabbed her feet, nearly making her lose balance. That's when she hit him in the face with her carry-on bag as hard as she could, stunning him, and making him loosen his grip on her leg. Then she quickly swung her body around and kicked him hard in the balls with a force that brought him to his knees. He let out a huge howl, and just for good measure, she used that same foot to kick him in the head, knocking him flat on the floor.

"Amelia!"

She turned, convinced she'd heard Dak. But that couldn't be right. She'd left him in Indonesia. People started to crowd around her, and then out of nowhere, another man grabbed at her. She fought him off, then suddenly, Dak appeared, knocking the man out cold and grabbing her arm.

"Come on, let's go!"

*Dak*?

He held tight to her hand as they began racing through the terminal. Security ran right past them, on their way to the area they'd just left. "This way, Dak!" some man called out, holding an elevator for them so they could avoid using the escalator.

"Thanks, Sparrow," Dak said.

Mellie noticed the man didn't get on with them but stayed by the door to make sure no one joined them. When the doors swooshed shut, she fought for breath. She couldn't recall the last time she had run so hard. "Where did you come from, Dak? How did you get here? I left you in Indonesia."

"I'll tell you everything when we get onboard my jet, Amelia."

When the elevator door swung open, Dak tightened his hold on her hand, and they began running again. To others, it probably appeared that they were rushing to catch their plane. That much was true, but Mellie knew they were also running for their lives.

She had a lot of unanswered questions she needed answered, but right now, all she cared about was that Dak was here and for the time being, she was safe, although she had no idea where they were going. Would they return to the compound or was he taking her home to Charlottesville?

She was glad when they finally reached his jet. Syl was standing by the steps, not wearing his usual pristine uniform but instead had on the same jeans and t-shirt he'd worn the last time she'd seen him. He smiled when he saw her. "Welcome aboard, Amelia."

She smiled back. "Thanks, Syl."

"Take off as soon as possible," Dak said, before pulling her up the steps to the jet's door.

Once in the main cabin, he sat and slid her onto his lap, strapping them both in.

"We're safe now, Dak. Can you *please* tell me what is going on?"

Instead of answering her, he captured her mouth. The moment his lips touched hers, she felt her heart do an actual kick in her chest, at the same time heat filled other parts of her. Although their movements were somewhat restricted, she managed to wrap her arms around his neck and cling to him for dear life. She wanted this kiss, she *needed* it. What if those men had kidnapped her...or worse? What if she hadn't taken those self-defense classes? What if Dak hadn't arrived just as the second man had tried to grab her?

At that moment though, an even bigger question came to mind. How had Dak managed to meet her in New York when she had left him in Indonesia? Needing some answers, she broke off the kiss.

"How did you get here from Indonesia so fast?" she asked him.

"I told you my jet was specially designed by Granger Aeronautics, and had more speed than most luxury jets, right?"

Yes, she recalled him saying that. "But how did you find out they were planning to use me as bait?"

"I found out your life was in danger hours after you'd left. However, their intention was not to use you for bait."

She lifted a brow. "Then what did they want with me?"

"They wanted you dead."

She remembered the man's threat to kill her. "But why?"

At that moment Syl's voice came over the intercom letting them know they had reached an altitude of forty-five thousand feet and could move around. Dak unsnapped their seatbelts, and stood with her in his arms, moving toward his bedroom.

After he'd placed her on the bed, she realized that he had not answered her. "Did they want me dead to get back at you, Dak?"

He paused after removing his shirt. "My assumptions were wrong, Amelia. I was never the intended target."

"Then who was?"

Shirtless, he walked over to the bed and sat down beside her. Taking hold of her hand, he said, "You."

Amelia snatched her hand away from him. "Me? That's the craziest thing I've ever heard. I don't have any enemies, Dak."

He stood and pulled his phone out of the back pocket of his jeans. She watched as he flipped through a few screens before handing it to her. She saw an image of a woman. "This woman became a federal witness in a crime that involved sex trafficking. Her testimony was essential in getting a conviction that sent the ringleader to prison. The man died less than a year later, when he was knifed by a fellow inmate. The man's son, a CIA fugitive, wants revenge on the woman who's now in the witness protection program. And he thinks that woman is you."

"What...?"

"Take a good look at that photo, Amelia. The woman resembles you."

His words made her take a second look. And indeed, she and the woman did share a resemblance. The shape of their faces was the same, as were the eyes, and high cheekbones. But the nose and lips, not so much. Moments later, she glanced back at him. "So, for some reason, this CIA fugitive thinks I am her?"

He nodded, solemnly. "Yes. And he wants you dead."

# Chapter 23

DAK WATCHED AS AMELIA eased off the bed to stand in front of the window. The jet was now high above the clouds and the sky was such a beautiful blue, it should have been a perfect day. Unfortunately, that wasn't the case. He didn't have to imagine how she felt, knowing someone wanted her dead. He'd been there before, more than a few times. He'd tried to pretend that he hadn't given a shit. But he knew she did.

Amelia was a healer and hadn't lived the kind of life he had. She didn't have enemies. But now, all because of a case of mistaken identity, she had a deadly one. Now that he'd had some time to think, he understood what had been driving him when he'd left the compound and raced to New York. He cared for her. And he would protect her, even if it meant his life.

Moving across the room, he went to stand behind her. Wrapping his arms around her, he simply held her close. He'd started to miss her the moment she'd left the compound, and had been very tempted to go after her then, but for a totally different reason.

Amelia twisted slightly in his arms, then tilted her head and looked directly into his eyes. He felt a deep thump in his chest, and he suddenly needed to kiss her, carry her over to the bed and make love to her. For hours. But even if he were to do that, the issue with Sargrasso would still be between them. What she needed now, more than his lovemaking, was his assurance that no matter what it took, he would keep her safe.

"Nothing is going to happen to you, Amelia. I give you my word."

She gave him a smile, one that surprised him, considering the situation she was in. "I know you will, Dak. Are we headed back to the compound?"

Her faith and confidence in him turned that thump in his chest into a hard kick. "No, not there."

"Where then? And what's the game plan?"

His sexy doctor was something else. Unable to resist any longer, he leaned down and kissed her, needing her taste and everything else that was Amelia Courson.

She turned fully into his arms and put her arms around his neck. He continued kissing her with a need he felt all the way to the bones. This was the kind of kiss that could make a broken man whole, and a strong man weak. It might even convince a man who'd sworn never to love, to rethink that vow. That thought made something snap inside of him. He ended the kiss and took a step back. He wasn't ready for those kinds of thoughts.

"Let's get out of here and go someplace where I can concentrate on talking to you, without being tempted to pull you into bed with me," he said.

She nodded, then took his hand as they both left the bedroom, and temptation, behind.

• • •

Sitting at the bar in the entertainment room, Mellie glanced around as Dak poured them both a glass of wine. She couldn't help but remember what had happened the last time she'd spent time in here. Dak had pinned her up against the wall and made love to her—hot, erotic, mind-blowing love. It was something she'd never, ever forget.

"Here you are," he said, placing the wine glass in front of her.

She thought it was pretty full. Did he think she'd need it? She still had a lot of unanswered questions. "Thanks," she said, taking a sip. "So, what's the plan? Where are we going?" she asked again.

"Right now, we're headed to London to pick up Peggy. Syl is worried about her and for good reason. Sargrasso's goons have seen you two together, and would likely assume you're friends. They might decide to use her as bait."

Fear clutched Mellie's chest. "Is she safe? Has Syl talked to her?"

"Yes, to both questions. I've contacted a friend of mine in the CIA. He's assured me that the agency will keep an eye on her until she's safely onboard. Then we'll fly to my private island in the Maldives. The plan is to let Sargrasso discover our location, so he'll come after you there. But we'll be ready for him. He's wanted by several international and domestic agencies. They've been waiting for him to come out of hiding for years, and now that he has, they're going to be ready for him. Even now, they're in the process of setting up a trap for him on the island."

"And using me as bait," she said.

"Unfortunately, yes. But it's better than having you continue to look over your shoulder for the rest of your life, Amelia. That's how it would be for you, if Sargrasso isn't captured."

"Why can't someone just tell the creep the truth? That I'm not the woman he's after?"

"He wouldn't believe it. And from what I've read in the bastard's profile, I wouldn't be surprised if he decided to kill any woman who looks the slightest bit like Kimberly Watson, hoping his actions will force her out of the witness protection program. He's made it clear that he intends to avenge his father's death, no matter what."

Mellie didn't say anything for a moment as she took it all in. Then she asked, "What about Syl and Peggy? Will they be safe on your island?"

"I suggested they stay in a hotel at the airport until it's over, but Syl won't hear of it, and he refuses to let me handle this alone, even with the CIA backing me up. He's always been overprotective of me, all because of that promise he made to my father."

"A promise?"

"Yes. I told you that Syl had been a friend of my dad's. But there was more between them. When I was in my early teens, Dad thought it was important for him to be home with me at night, so he traded his job as a beat cop and became an instructor at the police academy. Syl came in as a recruit and Dad took him under his wing. Syl admired Dad—most people did—and they became good friends. Before he died, Dad made Syl promise to look after me, and he's kept that promise ever since."

Mellie couldn't help being glad that Dak had Syl there to look after him, even if he didn't think it necessary. She, too, had asked Syl to watch over him when she'd left Indonesia. "But why is Peggy going? Wouldn't she be safer somewhere else?"

"Syl wants Peggy with him. He believes that no one can protect her better than he can."

She nodded. "Does Peggy know of the danger?"

"Yes, but she still wants to stay here with Syl. Just like at the compound, there are guest cottages on the island. They'll be staying in one. I figure it will take at least a few days for Sargrasso to figure out our location and come after us."

"Won't he suspect a set-up?"

"There is that possibility, so I've put together a plan B, just in case. The security on the island is even more advanced than the system I have set up at the compound. There's no way he'll get off my island alive."

She heard the hard coldness in Dak's voice and saw the grim determination in his eyes. She'd never considered him a violent person. Even when his compound had been under attack, he'd seemed rather calm about it, totally unrattled. But now, she was seeing a different side of him. Gone was the smooth, sophisticated businessman, and in his place, she saw a warrior.

"I hate that all of you might be in danger. I still can't believe this is happening to me," she said, her voice cracking. The reality of the situation was finally starting to sink in.

He reached out and caressed her cheek, and the touch nearly made her melt inside. God, she loved him. "Like I said, Amelia, I will protect you with my life." Then, out of the blue, he chuckled.

"What's so funny?"

"I was so worried about not getting to you in time. But then I saw what you did to that guy. Not only are you a sexy doctor, Amelia Courson. You're an honest-to-God badass. That second guy didn't know how lucky he was that you didn't beat the crap out of him, too."

His words made her smile. "I'm just glad you got there when you did. There might have been others."

"There were. Two more, in fact. Sparrow took care of them."

She remembered the man he referred to as Sparrow getting them on the elevator at the airport. "Is this Sparrow a friend of yours? From your military days?"

He dropped his hand from her face, then turned away and took a sip of his drink. There was something he wasn't telling her. She knew it. But then again, she knew that a lot of people who'd been in the military preferred not to talk about the things they'd done. If that was the case with Dak, she could and would respect that.

He placed his wine glass down. "Your faith and confidence in my ability to keep you safe? Is it because of the things I did in the military as an Army Ranger?"

Mellie nodded. She knew the Rangers were the most elite-fighting force in the army. "Yes. Isn't it?"

"Somewhat. However, what very few people know about me is that after my stint in the army, I was recruited to work for the USN, the United Security Network. Have you ever heard of them?"

She shook her head. "No."

"Most Americans don't even know the USN exists, although it's been around for years. It is a secret agency within the United States' government. Whereas the CIA's job is to collect and distribute foreign policy intelligence and analysis, the USN's role is to take that intelligence and analysis and work behind enemy lines, to eliminate threats, or to protect the United States and their allies from terrorism."

How long were you with them?" she asked.

"Five years. And while I worked for the USN, I developed a number of high-tech security devices for the US government. That's how I met Sparrow, which isn't his real name. It's his code name."

"Do you have a code name, Dak?"

He nodded. "Raven."

She smiled. "Raven. I like it."

He chuckled. "I'm glad. We were members of the In-flight Team, so all of us were named after birds. At some point, you'll meet Owl. He's now a top official in the CIA. Sparrow is the only one of my team members still with the USN, and he's now one of their top officials. So, as you can see, I have two men I trust explicitly—Sparrow and Owl—guarding our backs."

"Thanks for telling me the truth. It helps, believe it or not. Is there anything else I need to know?" Given the way he was absently studying the wine in his glass, she had a feeling there might be.

"Yes. It's about Stonewall."

She lifted a brow. "What about him?"

"I made contact with him before boarding and apprised him of the situation. I also told him I had everything under control."

"He believed you, right?"

"Of course. He knows my history with the Rangers and USN, so he's very aware that I'm more than capable of taking care of you. But he won't tell Granny Kay unless there is a need."

Mellie nodded. "He won't tell her until it's over. She might decide to come save me herself."

Dak chuckled again. "You're probably right." He put down his wine glass. "You must be hungry. I can find something for us to eat."

At that moment, food was the last thing she wanted. But there was something she desperately needed. Her gaze roamed up and down his muscular frame. Like Syl, he was dressed in jeans and a t-shirt, but in her mind, he stood there in all his naked glory.

"Amelia?"

Her gaze traveled from his midsection to his eyes. "Yes?"

"Are you okay?"

She shrugged. "I'm not really sure. But I do know I'll feel much better after you make love to me."

A smile spread across his lips, and it caused a shiver of anticipation to run down her spine. Without saying a word, he walked over and swept her into his arms.

• • •

Sargrasso was livid! "What do you mean the woman isn't dead, Miguel?"

"She had help. That man she was with in Indonesia somehow got to New York ahead of her plane. He managed to take her away before my men could deal with her."

"Where is she now?"

"On his jet. Our informant says they are headed to London, probably to pick up that girlfriend of hers."

"And why hasn't her friend been dealt with yet?"

"Both CIA and British Secret Intelligence have joined forces to protect her. Taking her out now is too risky."

Sargrasso became even more furious. "Make sure your men are punished for their incompetence. The last thing I want is to have them spilling their guts to the authorities. Then I want you to return here." He intended to carry out his own brand of discipline when Miguel returned.

"What do we do now, Sargrasso?"

"As soon as you discover the woman's final destination, let me know. I will handle things myself." Then he angrily clicked off the phone.

# Chapter 24

AFTER STOPPING IN LONDON to pick up Peggy, they had proceeded to fly to the Maldives International Airport. From there, Dak chartered a boat that would take them out to his island. Because of the lateness of the hour, they checked into one of the hotels near the airport, with plans to set sail at high tide in the morning.

Dak had spoken with both Sparrow and Owl when they arrived. He could count on both men to have his back. Once at the hotel, he had checked their room from top to bottom. He and Syl had rooms across the hall from each other, on the first floor. If they needed to make a hasty escape, they wouldn't have to deal with elevators or stairs. Syl's former law enforcement skills had come in handy when he'd rigged a couple of exit doors, just in case they needed to make a quick getaway.

Dak placed his cell phone on the desk in the room, and sat down, thinking about what was to come. According to Owl, it was just a matter of time before Sargrasso discovered their location. After the fiasco at the airport, Owl believed that Sargrasso would no longer count on his men to do his dirty work. He'd come for Amelia himself. After five years of hiding, he'd finally come out in the open. And when he did, they would be ready.

Getting up, Dak walked over to the window and looked out at the waters of the Indian Ocean, thinking about the conversation he'd just had with Sparrow. Every single man they'd arrested at the airport was dead. Someone had gotten to them before they could be taken to the police station for questioning. The coroner had ruled that their deaths had been caused by cyanide, shot from a dart gun. Evidently, Sargrasso had little tolerance for men who failed to get the job done.

"I missed you in the shower, Dak."

He turned and his gaze raked over Amelia, who was wearing one of the hotel's robes. Since she hadn't had time to claim her luggage in New York, she didn't have a stitch of clothing with her, except for what she'd been wearing. It was a good thing she and Peggy were about the same size, and Peggy had offered Amelia some of her things. According to Sparrow, Amelia's luggage should arrive tomorrow.

"Trust me, if I hadn't needed to make a few phone calls, I would have joined you."

"Any new developments?" she asked, crossing the room to stand beside him.

There *were* new developments, but she was better off not knowing most of them. He wouldn't even tell her the fate of the men who'd attacked her at the airport. There was no sense in scaring her any more than she already was. "Nothing you need to be concerned about."

"Okay."

It always amazed him how trusting she was of whatever he told her. Granted, she had an inquisitive side and would certainly ask if it was something she really wanted to know. But so far, when it came to this situation, she seemed to believe that he had everything pretty much under control. And she had, even before she'd known of his experience with the USN. Her faith in him only made him more determined to get Sargrasso out of the picture, so Amelia could have her life back.

"I do have some information about your luggage. It will be delivered to the island sometime tomorrow."

"That's great news. Thanks. Do you always have to travel by boat to get to your island?"

"No. I have a chopper pad, too. Usually, that's my preferred mode of transportation."

"So why aren't we taking the chopper?"

"There's too much fog in this area, and I understand it will last for a couple days. The route the boat will take is a different one—one not affected by the fog, just the tide. I meant to ask you earlier... Are you okay on a boat? You don't get seasick, do you?"

She shrugged. "I don't think so. I've taken a lot of cruises, and they never bothered me," she said, going over to sit down on the sofa in the suite.

"This won't be a cruise ship. And this time of year, the waters in these parts of the Indian Ocean can be rough."

A smile touched her lips. "Thanks for the warning. I'll make sure I don't eat anything before we leave. By the way, I meant to ask you about Chef."

Dak listed a brow. "What about him?"

"Wasn't he supposed to return to Indonesia to fly out with us? He's probably wondering where everyone is."

"I talked to Chef before I left for New York. He's been apprised of the situation, and he's more than happy to spend more time with his family."

"I bet he will enjoy that." Amelia got up, and Dak tried not to notice the quick glimpse he got of her thigh when her robe parted. He had to get a grip. Yes, he wanted her. But then, he'd wanted her the minute she'd walked into the room.

"I guess I'll be going to bed now. It's going to be an early start."

He moved away from the window. "I'll be in to join you soon."

• • •

*The man grabbed Mellie's arm, and she fought back, kicking and screaming. "Let me go!"*

"Amelia, it's okay. I'm right here."

Mellie recognized Dak's voice and stopped struggling. She opened her eyes to total darkness, and when Dak pulled her closer, she clung to him and held tight. "Sorry, I woke you, Dak. I was dreaming about that man in the airport. He had me, and I couldn't get away."

Dak softly stroked her back, and the adrenaline still racing through her system started to ease. "The bastard didn't get you. You're here with me, sweetheart."

They stayed like that for almost half an hour, until Dak's phone rang on the nightstand. He quickly picked it up. The room was pitch-black, but she could make out his features, thanks to the light from his phone. "Okay, we're moving out."

Without saying anything to her, he punched in a number and then said, "Code orange. We're leaving now, Syl."

He clicked off the phone, placed it back on the nightstand, then turned to her. "Amelia, I need you to listen to me very carefully, alright?"

She noticed he was whispering, and she decided to do the same. "Alright. But aren't you going to turn on the light?"

"No. From here on out, the only light we'll have is from our phones. That call was from Sparrow. He's advising us to leave the hotel now."

She nodded. "Will we be going to your island?"

"Yes."

"But I thought we had to wait for the high tide."

"We're going to take our chances."

She nodded again. "Okay."

They both got off the bed and using the light from their phones, they began to get ready to leave the hotel. "Why aren't we turning on the lights?" she couldn't help asking.

He glanced over at her. "Someone is out in the parking lot, watching our room. It's close to three in the morning. If we turn on the lights, whoever it is will figure we've been tipped off and are making our escape. If he doesn't see a light, he'll assume we're still asleep."

"When in essence, we will be escaping," she said.

"Smart woman," he said, cramming stuff into his duffel bag. Since she didn't have much except for the few things she'd borrowed from Peggy, he stuffed them into his bag as well.

"Ready?" he asked her in a low voice.

"Yes."

She watched as Dak scanned the room. Even though he couldn't see much in the darkness, she knew he would make sure they hadn't left anything behind. Once outside their room, they avoided the lit corridor and slipped out through an exit door that led to a courtyard where Syl and Peggy were waiting.

"The boat is already there," Dak said, as the four of them walked toward the pier. Adrenaline was racing through Mellie. What if the person watching their hotel room suspected something, and decided to circle around the building? What if...?

Dak placed his arm around her, and his touch calmed her anxiety. "It will be all over soon," he whispered, brushing a kiss on her cheek.

Mellie cuddled closer to him. Dak had a way of making her feel safe, even when danger was around them. When they reached the boat, a man suddenly appeared out of nowhere. Since Dak didn't go on the defensive, she figured it was someone who'd been expecting them.

"All set?" the man asked.

Dak nodded. "Yes." Then he took her hand and led her onto the boat. When they got to their seats, he dropped his duffel bag on the deck, and put his arm around her shoulders again. "Are you okay?" he asked her, once the boat began moving.

Syl and Peggy were seated on the other side of the boat. Syl had his arm around Peggy, and he was leaning in to whisper something in her ear. Whatever he'd said made Peggy smile. It was strange how differently people reacted to danger.

She looked up at Dak. "I'm okay. What about you?"

"You're here with me and I know you're safe, so I am more than okay."

Mellie cuddled closer to him as the boat moved away from shore. And she'd thought her week with Dak in Bali had been an adventure....

• • •

"I never dreamed your island would be so big, Dak. It's beautiful."

Holding Amelia's hand, they walked toward his estate, rounding a huge row of trees that seemed to reach hundreds of feet toward the sky. "And I've only shown you a fraction of it. But thank you. Of all the places I own, this island is my favorite."

There was no reason to tell her that she was the first woman he'd ever brought here. The island was where he came to relax and unwind whenever he needed time alone. Last year, he had spent an entire month here after he'd clinched a big deal that he'd worked his ass off to win. He had celebrated alone. That was the way he'd wanted it.

Now, the very woman who'd consumed his thoughts for the past two years was here with him, in his private domain. And although he would admit that while on this island, he'd gone to bed many nights thinking about her, he'd never imagined her ever being here with him.

He wrapped his arm around Amelia as they headed back toward his home. Fierce winds were brewing on the ocean—it was a good thing they'd set out that morning when they had. Winds that powerful could have capsized their boat easily. The waters surrounding his island were hundreds of feet deep, and he'd only been here once during a cyclone. This was the time of year for them, and it would be bad if one popped up now. He could only hope backup arrived before the bad guys. But if they didn't, he had an ace up his sleeve. Sparrow had alerted him earlier that Sargrasso was aware of their location, and was planning an attack. Ha! Let the bastard try it. He'd see the surprise Dak had for him, with or without backup.

"Why is this island your favorite?" she asked, bringing him back to the moment.

He gazed at her, thinking how beautiful she looked in khaki shorts and a blue top. Her luggage, which should have been delivered by a chopper by now, hadn't arrived yet. Chances were, with the high winds, it wouldn't. Luckily, Peggy had enough clothes to share.

"This is the last place Dad and I came together. I didn't own the island then, but visiting the Maldives was on his bucket list. We stayed at the same hotel we escaped from last night, and one day, we took a boat out to see some of the islands."

"Was he ill then?"

"Yes, but I hadn't known it. The doctors had given him the news, but he hadn't shared it with me yet. This was one of the islands we came across on that trip. It was deserted at the time and we docked here and walked around. Dad said that of all the islands we'd seen that day, he liked this one best, because of the trees. He'd never seen trees that tall before. Neither had I."

She tilted her head to look up at them. "You're right. They are really tall."

He nodded. “After I lost Dad, I’d heard that some of these private islands had been put up for sale, and I’d hoped this was one of them. When I discovered it was, I took some of the money Dad left me and bought it. It was years later before I was able to build anything on it.”

“I think it’s wonderful how much your father is connected to all that you do, Dak. It says a lot about how much he meant to you. He would have been so proud.”

Dak hoped so. His father had always told him that as long as he used his head, he would be successful. So far, so good.

When they reached the house, he opened the door for her. He hadn’t seen Syl or Peggy since they’d arrived on the island nine hours ago. He figured they had their reasons for staying inside. And since the cottage had been stocked with plenty of food, he wasn’t worried about them.

Hours later, Dak was in the kitchen, whipping up a salad and steaks for dinner when his cell phone rang. He checked the caller ID and saw it was Deijon, the guy who owned the chopper service.

“Yes, Deijon?”

“I’m on my way with the luggage.”

“In these high winds? Are you sure that’s safe? We can get by without it for another day or two.”

“It’s no problem, Mr. Navarro.”

The hairs on the back of Dak’s neck suddenly stood up. “Okay then, I’ll be here.”

As soon as he clicked off the call, Dak placed one to Syl. “Putting plan B into place.”

Then he looked over at Amelia. “I’m taking you underground. Syl will be bringing Peggy there to join you.”

"Why? What's going on, Dak?" she asked, getting up from the table.

"That was Deijon, the chopper pilot for the islands. He called to let me know he's bringing your luggage."

"What's strange about that?"

"He called me Mr. Navarro. Deijon has never called me that in his life. I believe he was warning me that something is going on."

Just before he took Amelia to safety, Dak made another call. "Sparrow. Somehow Sargrasso has slipped through and has taken over the chopper that's headed here with Amelia's luggage. Whatever plan he has concocted, he's going to live to regret it."

# Chapter 25

"MAKE YOURSELF AT HOME, Amelia. Peggy will be here shortly."

Mellie glanced around at the place that resembled a second house beneath the house. This secret area, which was the size of a spacious condo, was located just below Dak's home, accessed through an underground tunnel. A secret door in his master bedroom led to the tunnel through a wide lit corridor. He showed her another door, but told her he was keeping it locked for now. Behind it was a surprise he intended to show her later.

She'd heard about rich men who were into all kinds of state-of-the-art security devices, but Dak was taking it to a whole other level—and he seemed to have an arsenal of it at his disposal. But now she knew why. During their walk around the island, he'd told her more about his time as a Ranger and with the USN, and the talent he'd discovered for creating high-tech military equipment.

"Step over here for a minute, Amelia. I need to show you something very important."

She moved over to where Dak was standing beside a panel box that was built into the wall. It contained several buttons. "What's that?"

He directed her attention to a bright red button that was larger than the others. "This will activate my personal army."

She tilted her head at him. "Your personal army?"

"Yes. My drones."

*Drones*? Now she'd heard of everything. "Are you serious, Dak?"

"Absolutely. If I haven't returned by the time the timer goes off, I need you to push this red button. I have the timer set for an hour, but I should be back long before then."

Mellie drew in a deep breath, not wanting to think what it might mean if he didn't return before the timer went off. "What about your cell phone? Can't you call me if—?"

"No, we're leaving the phones here, where they can't be traced or give away our location—or yours—behind these walls."

She nervously rubbed her hands together. "Are you sure there's nothing I can say to make this Sargrasso guy see reason?"

"The man is crazy and dead-set on revenge. I'll take care of Sargrasso. No one will be able to locate this underground facility, so you and Peggy will be safe here. However, I'm leaving those loaded guns, just in case," he said, indicating the revolvers he'd placed on a table.

She nodded. "When the drones are released, won't they go after you as well?"

"No. My physical ID is stored in their brain cells. Now I need you to press your hand against this screen here, so your ID will be scanned into their brain cell as well. Syl's and Peggy's ID's have already been scanned, so they're safe too."

"What about the guys you were expecting to help you? Sparrow and Owl? What if they arrive? How will the drones know the good guys from the bad?"

"They won't. That's why I told Sparrow to stay back, at least for now." He pulled her into his arms and placed a kiss on her forehead. "Don't look worried, Amelia. I honestly don't think the drones will be necessary. We're only dealing with a few men—three at the max—since they're arriving in a chopper that can only carry four people, including the pilot. Once I know for certain Deijon is safe, I'll deal with the others. I should have no trouble getting back before the timer goes off. But if I'm not, you know what to do."

She really didn't like what he was insinuating. If he didn't make it back, that meant something had gone wrong. He might be hurt somewhere. Or worse...

"I'll be back, Amelia."

She flattened her palms on his chest and frowned up at him. "You don't know that. Not for sure."

Dak smiled. "Trust me. I let you leave an island without me once. I'm not going to do it again."

Then he captured her mouth with his. His kiss was hard, deep and possessive. It was as if he'd known she'd needed it that way, and was using his tongue to communicate to her what he couldn't—or wouldn't say.

She knew things could still go wrong. And she knew Dak was trying to distract her from thinking about the risks he would be taking. And he was almost doing a good job of it. Mellie felt the heat generated from the kiss spread all through her—even went down to her toes. She returned his kiss, needing to believe that he would return to her. She would never forgive herself if the man she loved lost his life protecting her.

He broke off the kiss and released her at the sound of a door opening. Moments later, Peggy and Syl walked in. One glance at Peggy and Mellie knew the other woman was just as scared as she was.

"You know what would be nice, Amelia," Syl said, grinning, trying to lighten the mood.

"What?"

"How about teaching Peggy to play pool while we're gone."

Mellie glanced over at Peggy, nodded and forced a smile. "No problem. But don't blame me if she beats you the next time you play."

Syl just smiled. Dak checked the monitors one more time, then without saying anything else, he and Syl walked out the door...leaving them alone.

• • •

Dak and Syl circled the house, looking for anything that appeared to be out of the ordinary, but didn't see anything. Then they made it to the area where the chopper pad was, changing positions often as they darted between shrubs and trees, just in case they were being watched...or in the target on someone's scope. For all they knew, a sniper could be sitting in a boat off-shore, armed with a rifle that could hit a target miles away.

"And you're certain Sargrasso's in the chopper, Dak?"

He glanced over at Syl. "I'm not certain of anything. But I'm not taking any chances. That bastard has eluded the authorities for five years, which tells me he's cunning, and has resources. I told Amelia what to do if we're not back in an hour."

Syl didn't say anything, but Dak had an idea what he was thinking. Something about this scenario just didn't feel right. "I feel it too, Syl. It's too easy. Sargrasso has to know the CIA and USN is on to him. He's not going to make it this simple for us."

Before Syl could respond, they heard the sound of the chopper and both looked up. "Take cover," Dak said before zigzagging through several trees near the clearing. There was no way he would show himself. If Deijon wasn't alone, then an ambush was planned.

Dak crouched on the ground, positioning himself so he could see everything, while still keeping out of sight. The only person who knew his precise location was Syl. Removing his AR-15 off his shoulder he leveled it, readied, aimed and cocked. The chopper landed and through the whirling blades, he could see Deijon and another man. Just one?

That didn't sit well with Dak and using his audio transmitter and receiver, he said to Syl, "Only one man is with Deijon. I smell a trap." But how?

He glanced around and wondered if more men were coming from another route. Even though the wind had died down, the ocean was still a little too choppy to travel far by boat. But a desperate man would do just about anything. It had been incredibly dangerous to fly in on the chopper, and yet, he'd done it. That told Dak that they were dealing with someone who wasn't playing with a full deck.

When the chopper blades came to a complete stop, the door opened and Deijon and the other man got out. The man was holding a gun to Deijon's head. "I don't know where you are, Mr. Navarro, but I'm sure you're out there…." the man yelled in a heavy South American accent. "Show yourself now or I will blow your pilot's head off."

Dak had no doubt the man would do exactly as he said. He muttered into his phone, "Cover me."

He ignored Syl's cocky response of, "Don't I always?"

Dak eased up with his gun still aimed at the man. "Let him go!" he ordered.

"Not until you turn over the woman."

Like hell, Dak thought, knowing that, at the moment, Syl was moving in on the man from the side, while the guy was focused on Dak. "What do you want with her?" he asked, stalling for time, giving Syl time to get in place.

"That's not your business."

"It is my business if you're asking for the woman who I consider to be mine," Dak responded. It was only then that he realized the words he'd spoken were the truth. Amelia *was* his.

Suddenly, the man swung his gun away from Deijon, and turned it in Dak's direction. But before Dak could fire, the man crumpled to the ground. Syl had taken him down. Dak ran toward Deijon to make sure he was okay.

"It was a set-up," Deijon blurted out. "He isn't the leader. The others have arrived on a private submarine on the other side of the island."

"A submarine? What the hell," Dak exclaimed, just seconds before several shots flew by them, some a little too close for comfort. "Get down!" Dak said and the three of them hit the ground.

"How many?" Dak asked Deijon, handing him the Glock while he readied his rifle. Shots were coming from every direction. He had a sinking feeling they were outnumbered and surrounded.

"Not sure. Maybe ten. Even more than that. They planned to keep us pinned here while the leader and a few of his men raided the house, searching for the woman," Deijon said. "And he has some kind of device that can locate hidden rooms—even those underground."

"Sonofabitch!" both Syl and Dak said at the same time.

• • •

Mellie had been trying to teach Peggy how to play pool, but the woman's heart obviously wasn't in it. Neither was hers. She couldn't help but worry about Dak, and she was sure Peggy was concerned about Syl, too. They both began pacing the room, and Mellie could feel her sense of dread growing stronger with every step she took. But why? Dak could take care of himself.

Still...

Nobody was immune to bullets—even Dak. Out of the corner of her eye, she saw Peggy finally take a seat, and figured she might as well do the same. "You okay?" she asked.

Peggy looked over at her and forced a smile. "As much as I can be, not knowing what's going on outside. I figured they would be back by now."

So had she. She glanced at the clock on the wall. Unless Dak came back soon, she would be pressing the big red button. She could only hope it didn't come to that.

"When did you realize you loved Dak?"

Mellie blinked at Peggy's question. She could easily deny it, but why? Evidently, it was pretty obvious. Well, maybe not to Dak. But definitely to a woman who was feeling the same way about another man.

"I think I fell in love with him the day we met at my brother's wedding, two years ago. But I only just admitted it to myself a few days ago. And you? When did you know you loved Syl?"

A smile touched Peggy's lips. "Like you, I fell for him the day we met. The chemistry between us was powerful, right from the start. Syl sensed it, too, so he avoided me like the plague. His first wife really soured him on marriage. From what I've gathered, he has no intention of ever getting seriously involved with a woman again." She chuckled. "I intend to change that. I'm at the age where I go after what I want."

And if the way she'd seen Syl look at Peggy lately was anything to go by, Mellie figured Peggy had already caught her man.

"I was engaged to be married once. When I was twenty-five," Peggy said. "I left my fiancé standing at the altar."

Mellie's eyes widened. "You did? Why?"

"On my wedding day, I discovered he had been fooling around on me. So, instead of saying, "I do", I slapped him and walked out. I've never regretted it, especially after finding out later that there was more than one woman."

"Wow," Mellie said. "And I thought Ivan was an ass." She was about to tell Peggy about him when Peggy suddenly got to her feet.

"Do you hear something?" Peggy asked.

Mellie stood as well. “No. Maybe the guys are returning.”

“I don’t think so. Listen,” Peggy said. “I hear gunfire.”

“Underground?”

“It’s happening above ground. I can hear it through the P-waves.”

Neither Mellie or Peggy said anything for a long moment and then they both heard it—a continuous barrage of gunfire. Had help arrived, after all? Or were Dak and Syl outnumbered and fighting for their lives? She glanced at the timer and saw she had thirty minutes to go before she was to press the button. But what if Dak needed his personal army now?

“I don’t like the sound of that,” Peggy said. “Syl said he and Dak would have their rifles, but that’s too much gunfire to be just them.”

They both began pacing again. It sounded like World War III above ground. They could also hear a lot of noise right above them. It sounded like doors being opened and then slammed closed.

“What do you think is happening?” Peggy whispered.

“I don’t know,” Mellie whispered back.

Dak had told her that the tunnel couldn’t be found, but what if that wasn’t the case? “Can you shoot?” she asked Peggy.

“I do okay. I grew up on a farm. What about you?”

“I do okay, as well. My grandmother and I used to spend a lot of time at a shooting gallery.” Mellie looked at her watch again. Then she made a decision.

“I’m pressing that button.”

# Chapter 26

DAK GLANCED OVER AT Syl. They had taken cover behind the chopper, but Deijon had taken a hit. He was alive but needed medical help. "Our ammunition is running low and we need to hold them off for another thirty minutes. Now I wish I had set the timer for earlier."

All Dak could think about was that while those damn thugs had them pinned down here, Sargrasso and his men were searching his house for Amelia. What if the man was able to find the underground tunnel with the device Deijon said he had? What if…?

At that moment, a bullet barely missed his head. "Will you keep your damn head down, Dak," Syl snapped, returning fire. "They've got to know they have us cornered. Sooner or later, they'll make a move to take us out."

Dak didn't like that. Nor did he like the fact that Deijon was injured. "Stay with Deijon."

"And just where in the hell do you think you're going?" Syl asked.

"I'm heading to the house." He needed to make sure

Amelia and Peggy were safe. And then he'd release the drones.

"Are you crazy? That's probably what they expect you to do. It's a trap. You won't get ten feet from here before they kill you. Let me go."

Dak swore a blue streak, then said, "No. I'm going. You need to stay. The drones will be released in about thirty minutes regardless. Deijon isn't ID'd. As long as you're with him, he's protected."

"Don't do it, Dak. The women are okay."

"I have to make sure, Syl. And don't pretend you're not as worried as I am."

"If you go, then take all the ammunition."

"And leave you defenseless? Bullshit."

Syl was quiet for a minute, then said, "If you make it and I don't...tell Peggy I love her."

Dak stared at the man who'd been his father's good friend and was now his. They'd been together through thick and thin. And through it all, Syl had always had his back. This time, he'd have Syl's. "I suggest you keep your ass alive and tell her that yourself."

Dak rolled on the ground, dodging bullets, until he was behind a cluster of trees. He was about to make another move when out of nowhere, a man with a gun appeared in front of him. But before he could take aim, the man fell at his feet. He didn't have to look back to know Syl had taken the guy out. He crouched down, and began quickly zigzagging through the trees, dodging bullets, until he was close enough to see the roof of his house.

He saw something else as well. The drones had been released. He threw his head back and laughed, happy as hell. Amelia had pressed the button early! Somehow, she had sensed they were in danger.

He would definitely show her his appreciation later on tonight. But in the meantime, Dak grinned as the drones took Sargrasso's men by surprise. Their weapons were almost useless, given the sheer number of drones, although they managed to shoot one or two out of the sky. But another one would quickly follow, coming out of nowhere, and firing on them. Many of the thugs fled to the beach and jumped into the ocean, thinking themselves safe—much like a person would do when attacked by a swarm of bees. Instead, the drones hovered over the water, waiting for them to surface. The tide turned red.

Dak continued moving as fast as his feet could carry him. A few drones circled around him, almost acting like a shield, as he ran toward the house. Sargrasso's men were still shooting at him but the drones returned fire, and were bringing them down.

When he reached his home, he saw the door had been kicked in. He entered slowly, keeping his eyes peeled. He was seriously regretting his decision about programming the drones to stay outdoors. As he moved slowly, his rifle aimed, two men came out of nowhere and fired on him. He dived to the floor, firing back and taking both down.

He heard voices and when two other men ran out from the back, guns blazing, Dak shot them as well. Then he stealthily moved through the house, wondering where in the hell Sargrasso was.

• • •

"I hear a sound outside that door," Mellie said.

"Hopefully, it's Dak and Syl returning," Peggy added.

Mellie hoped so, too. "But just in case it's not, let's get those guns."

"Okay."

They grabbed the guns off the table and checked them for readiness. She hoped like hell that they wouldn't have to use them, but she had a funny feeling about the noise outside the door. Suddenly the door was smashed in, and a bearded man was standing in front of them.

"I found you!" he said, in a deep foreign accent. He had a gun trained on them. "Drop your guns," he ordered.

She and Peggy didn't move. "Where's Dak?" Mellie asked.

"Dead. He and his men. All dead." She heard Peggy's sharp intake of breath before the man ordered again, "I said drop your guns. Or I will kill you both."

"You're going to kill us anyway," Mellie said, barely getting the words out. If Dak was dead, she had no desire to live.

"That's right. You should never have testified against my father, Miss Watson."

"I'm not Miss Watson. You have me mixed up with someone else."

"You lie!" the man screamed. "I don't give a damn what you call yourself now. One of my father's most trusted men identified you. That's good enough for me. And your lady friend will pay as well. But first, she will watch you die."

Suddenly, a shot rang out. But instead of the bullet hitting Mellie, the bearded man crumpled to the floor. Although blood gushed from his chest, he was able to lift his arm holding the gun. He took aim...and another shot came from somewhere behind him. Sargrasso dropped the gun and took his last breath.

Mellie glanced frantically across the room and saw Dak come into the room. She raced over to him, throwing herself in his arms. Finally, she was safe.

"It's over, sweetheart," he whispered, stroking her back.

She lifted her head and looked up at him. "He said you were dead. He said everybody was dead."

"He lied," Dak said, holding her tight.

"Where's Syl?" Peggy asked in a fearful voice.

"Syl's fine, Peggy. Deijon got hit and Syl needed to stay with him. Deijon isn't ID'd."

Mellie pushed herself out of Dak's arm. "How bad are his injuries?"

"I don't know for sure."

"We have to go get the First-Aid kit I saw in your kitchen cabinet, Dak. Hopefully, he's not hurt too badly."

They raced downstairs and after Dak grabbed the kit, they headed for the door. The moment Mellie opened the door, she was greeted with twenty or more drones hovering just outside, ready to fire. Mellie fought back a scream and fell back against Dak's hard chest. "Dak, call off your army."

"They won't hurt you. You've been ID'd. If you hadn't been, you'd be dead by now."

Wasn't that a comforting thought? "Please, Dak, call them off."

"Not until we reach Syl and Deijon. We'll need the drones to be our escorts, in case some of Sargrasso's men are still around." No sooner had he spoken, than they heard gunfire. "See what I mean."

Now she understood. Still, as they headed toward the chopper pad, she thought how weird this must look. The three of them, running through the forest, with a bunch of drones circling them, shielding them from enemy fire. When Mellie caught sight of the chopper, she increased her pace. Peggy took off running and didn't stop until she reached Syl.

Seeing the coast was clear, Dak looked up at the drones hovering around them. "Retreat."

Mellie watched as the drones regrouped and then headed back toward a structure built into the ground that suddenly opened up, just for them. Wow!

But she didn't have time to stand there in amazement. She had an injured man to take care of.

• • •

"Remind me to never come after your woman, Raven," Sparrow said.

"Same here," Owl chimed in.

Dak didn't say anything as he took a sip of his bourbon and eyed his two friends. At any other time, he would have quickly corrected them, denying that Amelia was his woman. But he'd realized that she was, at least until he safely returned her to Virginia.

After Dak had given the order for the drones to return to their ground-control station, four boatloads of CIA and USN agents had appeared. Better late than never, he guessed.

"And another thing," Sparrow was saying. "How in the hell did you manage to bring weapons like those drones into a country where it's illegal to import weapons, firearms and ammunition?"

Dak glanced over at Owl and could tell from the man's expression that he was wondering the same thing. "When I bought this island, I came to an understanding with the authorities. Although I respected their laws, on my island, I was the law. Besides, I periodically pay enough to the government to give me some slack."

"Hell, the way I see it," Owl said, "they've given you a lot of slack. We were off-shore, watching what was going on. It looked like the battle of the drones. We made sure we stayed far enough back that they wouldn't go after us. But they didn't give Sargrasso's men a chance." He took a sip of his own drink. "At least now we know how Sargrasso evaded capture all these years. The man was living in a damn submarine. One that couldn't be detected by radar."

"That concerns us," Sparrow added, frowning. "Where would he get technology like that?"

Dak shrugged. "That's the nature of the beast. Modern technology is advancing every second. You have to keep up."

"So says the man who was probably born knowing about drones before they were even invented," Owl said grinning. "You and your private army."

"Well, I'm glad you guys arrived when you did, so you could at least collect the bodies and take a couple of prisoners. I would have been tempted to feed them to the sharks," Dak said, glancing at his watch.

Amelia was probably in bed by now. It had been one hell of a day. After she'd seen to Deijon's injuries, patching him up as much as she could, Syl had flown the man to the nearest hospital. Peggy, who refused to let Syl out of her sight, had gone with him.

A government cleanup crew had arrived shortly afterwards, and Amelia had walked around the island with Dak as he surveyed the damage. Luckily, there hadn't been much after the bodies were removed.

And Dak had introduced her to Sparrow and Owl. He could tell his friends had been impressed with Amelia, and not only for her beauty. Her obvious intelligence, professionalism and the calm way she handled situations under pressure had won her their admiration. After all, most women would have succumbed to panic attacks after going through what she had.

He stood. "The two of you are welcome to stay the night, if you'd like," he said.

"Thanks, but we're leaving at high tide. Chances are we won't be here for breakfast," Sparrow said, grinning. "Give Amelia our regards."

"I'll do that," he said, hugging his two friends. "And thanks for everything."

"Hell, we didn't get a chance to do anything," Owl said, laughing. "As usual, you found a way to kick ass without us, using your techie toys. All we ever get to do is clean up the bodies. That's the way it was that time in South America, when you single-handedly took on Kovalenko's men. I'd thought, now that you're a respected businessman, that you'd have cleaned up your act."

Dak chuckled as he drained the last of his bourbon. "Good-night guys."

Leaving his friends, Dak walked into his bedroom that had now been returned to a semblance of normalcy. Syl had texted that he and Peggy would check into a hotel, and would remain on the main island for the night.

When he got into the bedroom, he found Amelia stretched out on top of the bed, asleep, wearing a cute pair of shorty PJs. The midriff top was showing a portion of her bare stomach and he felt his body harden, just looking at her.

Easing out of his jeans, briefs and shirt, he moved over to the bed, thinking about the way she'd tirelessly worked on Deijon to keep the bleeding under control. And after she'd finished with Deijon, she had walked around checking on Sargrasso's men. Most were dead, but she'd come across two, who were barely conscious, and she'd worked on them until the medic boat had arrived.

What a woman his Amelia was. Those men had been sent to kill her, but it hadn't mattered to her. She was a doctor and they were injured. She was in her element—providing medical care and saving lives. It had been simply amazing to watch her—and a total turn-on.

The more he watched her, something more, something other than lust, had taken hold of him. But he was fighting it—he had to. As much as he'd loved his father, Dak would not follow in his footsteps in one major way—he'd never love someone so much that if he lost that person, he'd lose everything. Michael Navarro's last words still rang in Dak's ears. He'd said that dying didn't bother him, because he and his wife would be back together again.

Dak couldn't help comparing Michael to Larry Smalls, who bashed women and relationships all the time, once again. They were two different men. One had loved a woman so deeply, he couldn't manage without her, and the other could only tolerate them in his bed.

Dak had learned one thing from both examples—a man was stronger without a permanent woman in his life.

Dak couldn't help thinking about the way he'd reacted when Deijon had told him that Sargrasso had entered his home, looking for Amelia. He'd been terrified, in a way he'd never been before. And in a way he never wanted to be again.

He believed his father had had a good life after losing Tabitha. Michael had told him that all the time...and he'd said it was because of Dak. But Dak had known there were moments when his father had missed his wife desperately, and had probably wished she was there with him. With them. Dak couldn't imagine how it would feel if Amelia was taken from him, the way Tabitha had been taken from Michael. But that could have happened today. And then where would he be?

Dak was about to get into bed and pull Amelia into his arms when she began thrashing around, obviously in the throes of another bad dream. He quickly went to her, scooped her into his arms and cooed, "Shh, baby. It's okay. It's over, Amelia. I've got you."

Amelia stopped fighting and slowly calmed down, slumping against him. When she opened her eyes to meet his gaze, she whispered, "Don't ever let me go."

He swallowed. "I won't."

"Promise?"

"I promise."

Then she buried her face in his neck and drifted back off to sleep.

Dak continued to sit there, holding her. Dak was a man of his word, and never made a promise he couldn't keep... until now.

• • •

Holding Peggy's hand, Syl entered the hotel room, tossed the passkey on the table, then pulled her into his arms and kissed her with everything he was feeling at that moment. This had been one hell of a day and for a while, he'd been afraid he'd never have the chance to do this— hold her and kiss her—again. But she *was* here, with him, and he couldn't get enough of her.

Needing to show her how much she meant to him, he swept her into his arms and headed straight for the bedroom. He placed her on the bed, then joined her. But he wasn't ready to start undressing. There were a few things he needed to say first.

Gathering her up into his arms, he said, "I told you about my first marriage, how disastrous it was, right? And that I'd promised myself I wouldn't ever go through that again."

Peggy nodded. "Yes, you told me. And do you remember me telling you about what happened on my wedding day?"

Syl laughed. "I remember saying how you smacked the guy, right in front of the minister."

"It took me nearly ten years to get over it, Syl. So I understand what you're saying. I didn't want to love again, either. But..."

"But what?"

"But I met you. And even when you acted like you didn't want to have anything to do with me, I knew better."

He tilted his head. "And how did you know?"

"I just did. I could tell you wanted me, and I believed that one day that desire would turn into something more."

He didn't say anything for a minute, because she was right. It had. "I was so worried I wouldn't ever see you again. I even gave Dak a message to give you. I told him that, if I didn't make it, that he was to tell you that I loved you."

He saw tears welling up in her eyes. "But you did make it."

Syl smiled. "Yes, I did. And now I want to say those words to you myself. I love you, Peggy. I don't know what I'd ever do without you."

With tears in her eyes, she reached up and cupped his cheek. "And I love you, Sylvester Wright. No matter what pain we've endured, we *will* make it. Because we're stronger together." She let out a little laugh. "After the past few days, I think we'll be able to handle anything life throws at us. Don't you?"

Leaning toward her, he answered her question with a kiss.

# Chapter 27

MELLIE WOKE UP TO find a hard naked body spooning her. Dak was so close, she could feel the heat of his even breathing on her neck, and his strong muscled thigh was thrown over hers. She closed her eyes and relived yesterday's terrifying events—she and Peggy waiting underground, hoping they'd be safe; Sargrasso and his men invading the island; Dak and Syl risking their lives to protect her and Peggy....

*Then there were the drones.*

Dak's private army. If she was the creative type, she could write an action-packed thriller about the real Dakota Navarro, the warrior—and it would be better than any movie Hollywood put out.

She still couldn't wrap her mind around the fact that it had all been due to a case of mistaken identity. And revenge.

Sargrasso had died, believing she was to blame for his father's death. She had to wonder, why didn't he put any blame on his father? Did Sargrasso not care about the sex trafficking that had landed his father behind bars in the first place? Did he not care that Kimberly Watson was in the witness protection program because she had been his father's victim? And that by testifying, she'd made sure it couldn't happen to others?

Obviously not. He'd likely been even more evil than his father. Had the older man been equally unbalanced? She shuddered. Now that was a scary thought. Although it was horrible to say, she was glad both men were dead.

"You're awake?"

Mellie opened her eyes to the sound of the masculine voice. She rolled over on her back to stare into his handsome face. He was the man who'd risked everything—his home, his friends...his life—to keep her alive. "I'm awake."

"Good."

And then he leaned in and kissed her. And if she'd had any lingering doubt about whether or not she loved him, that kiss took care of it. No man kissed like Dak, and just his touch sent her libido into overdrive. His tongue mated with hers, as if they'd been doing this all their lives. When she felt his hand slowly caress her thigh, she realized something—she still had her pajamas on. That meant...

She pulled away. "We didn't make love last night."

"What makes you think that?"

"I still have clothes on." Whenever she and Dak slept together, they were always skin-to-skin.

"By the time I wrapped things up with Sparrow and Owl, you were asleep and I didn't have the heart to wake you."

"I wouldn't have minded."

"I would have. After yesterday, you deserved to rest." He reached out and brushed a strand of hair back from her face. “You were incredible yesterday, Amelia. I never knew I was sleeping with such a sexy badass. And I’m so glad you released the drones when you did.”

“I wasn’t sure what to do. But when Peggy and I heard noises, I knew you needed me to do something. So I took a chance.”

She paused, remembering the way Sargrasso had aimed his gun at them, intending to kill them both. Only Dak had ended up killing him first. “Thank you for saving my life, Dak.”

“Thank you for saving mine, Amelia. Sargrasso brought more men with him than I’d imagined. Who would have guessed they’d arrive by submarine? But our ammunition was getting low and we were outnumbered. If you had waited until when I told you to release the drones, there’s a good chance some of us would not have survived.”

He leaned down and kissed her again, licking the tears she hadn’t realized she’d shed. She didn’t want to think about what could have happened. It was just too terrifying.

Right now, she was just glad to be alive and with him. “Make love to me, Dak.”

She had never asked a man to make love to her, but she needed Dak inside of her now, to make her forget the events of yesterday...and to celebrate the fact that they were both alive. He seemed to understand, and didn’t waste any time removing her clothes, then sheathing himself in a condom. Returning back to the bed, he eased down beside her. Then, holding her gaze for a breathless moment, he leaned in and recaptured her mouth as he slid his naked body over hers.

He entered her in one smooth thrust and the moment he did so, it felt like everything was right with the world.

Pleasure consumed her, overtaking her senses, and she was helpless to do anything but writhe beneath him. When it came to lovemaking, Dak was the best she'd ever had. He was so giving, so passionate, so...virile. He was never in any rush, and seemed to delight in taking his time, while making sure she was enjoying everything he had to offer. Everything he was intent on sharing.

He broke off the kiss and looked down at their bodies as they moved together in sync. His strokes had started out long and deep, but now they were longer and deeper. "There is nothing like the feeling of being inside of you, Amelia. You take my breath away, baby," he said, increasing his strokes.

Her body matched his rhythm, almost of its own volition. She couldn't have slowed down if she'd wanted to. The sensation of having him so deep inside of her was making her blood rush through her veins, and sending electric waves to every part of her, especially where they were connected. There were times when the magnitude of her desire for him stunned her, and she'd hoped that, maybe he loved her, at least a little. But then, her common sense would kick in and she'd talk herself down. She had to accept that Dak was all man. Everything he did, he made sure he did well—including making love. And he was a true master, making her feel as if she was the only woman in the world for him. But she knew that wasn't true.

And then it happened—a climax of epic proportions. She felt her body explode in mindless ecstasy, and he followed right after her.

This moment belonged to the two of them, and it would have to be enough for her. In a few days, maybe even tomorrow, they would be leaving the island, and she didn't want to think about what might be next for them. It could very well be nothing. When he returned her to Charlottesville, there was a good chance he would simply walk away, their time together just another one to add to his list. At that moment, she tried to convince herself that it didn't matter. She would always have this.

When the spasms of their bodies finally subsided, he reached out and cupped her chin in his hand, then looked deep into her eyes. It was as if he had something on his mind, as if he wanted to say something. Only he didn't. Instead, he just lowered his head and took her mouth in another deep, drugging kiss.

• • •

Five days later, they were back at Dak's home in Vermont. He hadn't been ready to take Amelia straight home to Charlottesville, although he knew he'd have to, eventually. And he knew that unlike other weeks—and other women—the memories of their time together would linger in his mind for a long time.

The morning after Sargrasso's invasion, he had awakened her again to make love. Then he had shown her the areas in the underground part of the house that he hadn't revealed earlier. The surprise he'd told her about were bedrooms, ones that extended past the shoreline and were underwater. They had spent the rest of their days there. At first, she was nervous about spending the nights in a room made of glass, sixteen feet below sea level, but he'd convinced her.

After that first night, she became more comfortable with the sea world watching them make love. And afterwards, they would just lay there and watch as the sea creatures swam by.

As Dak stood at his window, wondering how he was going to walk away from her, Amelia came into view. Knowing this was their last day on the island, she'd decided to get up early and walk around the estate, taking in all it had to offer. He had intended to go with her but he'd received an important business call, and she'd said she would be fine by herself.

Watching her, he couldn't dismiss the feeling of how right she looked on his property. She had paused to stand beside one of his waterfalls. He wondered what she was thinking. Their time together had been filled with danger, but she'd told him she'd enjoyed it.

He had, as well. And he'd miss her.

Dak knew that and accepted it. But in time, he would move on and eventually forget her. It would probably take a while, but eventually, the memories of what they'd shared would fade.

As if Amelia felt his gaze on her, she turned and saw him at the window. She smiled, then waved and blew him a kiss. Instinctively, he blew one back to her.

Moving away from the window, he headed for the door, deciding to spend every moment of his time with Amelia. And then maybe tomorrow, he'd be able to say goodbye.

• • •

Mellie had felt Dak's penetrating stare, which had prompted her to turn around and see him standing at his bedroom window. As usual, the emotions she felt whenever he looked at her with those mesmerizing dark eyes descended upon her, making her dread tomorrow when they would part ways.

She had already spoken with Granny Kay, Stonewall and Joy, assuring them she was okay and telling them all about what had happened. She knew Stonewall had already heard the details from Dak, but figured he'd wanted to hear her version of the story. Everyone was glad the CIA had stepped in and had assured her there was no longer a threat to her life.

The full details of what had happened on Dak's island hadn't made the news, just the watered-down version the CIA had let out. Basically, that Sargrasso was dead, as were most of his men. There was no mention of her, Dak, Syl or Peggy. Only two of Sargrasso's men had survived. They'd been taken into custody, and once there, they'd sung like canaries. In the submarine the CIA had confiscated, they'd discovered a journal in which Sargrasso had listed a number of other hits he'd planned to make—including the judge who'd sentenced his father to prison.

Mellie turned back to look at the waterfall, basking in the rays of the warm summer's sun. She could understand the reasons Dak's father had loved them so much. The sound of the water made everything seem so peaceful. She'd be quite content to sit by this spot for the rest of the day. Unfortunately, she needed to start packing. Dak would be flying her home first thing in the morning.

"You've never looked more beautiful than you do now, Amelia, with the sun behind you. You take my breath away."

She turned and smiled as Dak walked toward her.

"Thank you." Mellie almost told him how much she loved it here but decided against it. The last thing she wanted was for him to think she was sending hints that she didn't want to leave. Especially when she knew she had to leave.

"Have you heard from Syl and Peggy?" she asked.

Dak nodded. "I talked to Syl earlier. Peggy is staying at his place in town. For a man who did everything he could to avoid her for the past year, he's very possessive. He won't let her out of his sight. It's a good thing they both work for me or I might have a problem."

"I'm glad," Mellie said. She had spoken to Peggy, as well. She sounded happy and Mellie was happy for her.

"You didn't walk far," Dak said, glancing around.

No, she hadn't. "I was taking in the beauty of your property. It's vast."

"Why didn't you take the golf cart?"

"I just felt like walking." No need to tell him that in addition to her heart staying behind, her footprint would as well.

He nodded and then took her hand. "I'm glad you didn't venture too far. Now I can walk with you."

They had satisfied their physical hunger that morning, but the moment their hands touched, she grew hungry all over again. She glanced over at him. Would she ever get enough of him? Probably not. She'd just have to find a way to live with it.

"What are your plans when you return home?" he asked.

"I'm going to spend a few days at home, checking my mail and looking after a few things. Then I'm going to visit my best friend Whitney in LA for a few days. When I get home from California, I want to paint both of my bathrooms. That should keep me busy." She glanced over at him. "What about you?"

"I return to work on Monday. There are a number of items that need my immediate attention."

She nodded. "I'm sure there are a lot more security devices to create."

"Always," he said, smiling.

And there was no doubt in Mellie's mind that he would be making them. He'd probably be so busy, he wouldn't have time to think of their time together, or to remember their nights spent behind those ricochet windows, or under the sea. Those memories she intended to hold close to her heart would eventually become nothing more than a blur to him.

They continued walking in silence, as if they were both deep in thoughts. Maybe that was a good thing. The last thing Mellie wanted to do was to give away her feelings for him. That wasn't part of their deal. When they made love for the last time tonight, she would try to tell him with her body what she refused to say in words—that when she left the island tomorrow, a piece of her heart would stay behind—with him.

• • •

"You don't have to see me home, Dak," Amelia said as they waited for Syl to bring her luggage off the jet.

Dak shoved his hands in his pockets. "I want to." He couldn't help but remember the way she'd shown up unexpectedly at his house weeks ago. His life hadn't been the same since.

She gave Syl and Peggy big hugs and when Chef appeared, she gave him a hug, too. Then she made them promise to take good care of Dak. She turned around when the car arrived on the tarmac, but he'd seen the tears in her eyes and knew she felt sad at leaving her friends behind.

The chauffeur opened the door, and when she slid in the backseat, Dak joined her. He knew he should probably leave her alone, but for some reason, he couldn't do that.

When he heard her sniffing, he handed her his handkerchief. "You okay?" he asked.

She nodded. "I'm just going to miss everyone."

"And I'm sure they'll miss you." Then deciding to be honest with her, he said, "I will miss you, Amelia."

She looked over at him and he saw more tears gather in her eyes. "I'll miss you, too, Dak."

He broke eye contact and looked straight ahead. No matter how much he might miss her, he wouldn't be seeing her for a while. It would be an intentional move on his part. He had to put some distance between them, for his own sanity.

Looking anywhere but at the woman sitting beside him as they drove through the streets of Charlottesville, Virginia, Dak noticed how bright the sun was shining through the trees they passed. It was a beautiful day. Then why did he feel so blue.

"I'm also going to miss your jet, Dak."

At her words, he looked over at her and smiled. He didn't have to wonder why. "We did have some good times on it, didn't we?"

"We definitely did."

And he knew he would remember every single thing they'd done, each time he stepped on the plane. Hell, he might as well name it after her. Damn! Now he was thinking crazy.

Far too soon, the car pulled up in front of her house. The driver brought the car to a stop, then came around and opened the door for him. He slid out, then offered Amelia his hand.

He felt the sizzle that raced up his spine the moment their hands touched. They had practically made love all night and several times that morning before finally getting dressed and leaving for the airport.

"I'm home," she said, looking at her house.

"You are, indeed." Still holding her hand, he walked her to the door.

"You don't have to escort me inside, Dak."

Oh, but he did. Dak had thought that the kiss they'd shared before landing would have been enough—enough for him to finally let her go. But he'd been wrong.

When she opened the door, he followed her inside, then closed the door behind them. Then he pulled her into his arms and kissed her one last time.

He needed to make a clean break.

Taking a step back, he whispered, "Take care of yourself, Amelia."

"You do the same, Dak. Thanks for everything."

He nodded and while he still could, he turned, opened the door and walked out.

# Chapter 28

"OKAY, GIRLFRIEND, WHEN ARE you going to shut down the pity party?"

Mellie glanced over at Whitney. The two had spent the day shopping in LA, then had gone out to dinner. Now they were back at Whitney's condo, sharing a glass of wine. "What do you mean? I've been nothing but fun."

Whitney rolled her eyes. "You've *tried* to be fun, but I know you, Amelia Ursula Courson. You've only been pretending. And really, I'm not surprised after all you've been through. I can understand some hero-worship on your part for Dakota Navarro."

Mellie took a sip of her wine. "It's more than that, Whit. I love him."

Whitney chuckled. "Don't you think I know that as well? I remember you being smitten at your brother's wedding. All you talked about for weeks was Dak. Even when you stopped talking, I knew you weren't over him. Like I said, I know you."

Mellie shrugged. "Dak is wonderful. And he saved my life. I wouldn't be here if it wasn't for him."

Her brother had admitted that the only reason he hadn't immediately caught a flight to the Maldives was because he'd been to the island with Dak before. And he knew all about Dak's private army. Stonewall figured she was in good hands.

"I'm sure you told Dak how grateful you were to him for saving your life, but did you also tell him how you felt about him, Mel? That you loved him?"

"Of course not! That wasn't part of the deal. And it wouldn't change anything, anyway. It's not Dak's fault that I fell in love with him."

"But what if he fell in love with you, too?"

"He didn't. Men like Dak don't fall in love. They enjoy women, but they don't get serious about them. I knew that and fell for him anyway. It's all my own doing. And I don't regret anything I shared with him."

"So, what do you plan to do now?"

"Not much. I'm going to enjoy my week here with you and then return home, paint my and Granny Kay's bathrooms and then get ready to return to work. And I'll have a new niece or nephew to play with sometime early in the new year. Being an auntie will definitely keep me busy."

"So, you're going to give up on love, Mellie?"

Mellie shrugged. "Some things just aren't meant to be. I never thought I could change Dak. I just wanted to enjoy my time with him. And even with all the danger, I did enjoy my time with him, Whit."

She finished off her wine. "I thought I loved Ivan, but I was wrong. What I feel for Dak is so much more than anything I've ever felt before." She then took a deep breath. "Enough about me. What about you? When are you going to tell me who pushed your buttons at Stonewall's wedding? Was it Locke, Shogun or Macayle? I've told you all about my love life. It's time you did the same. So talk."

• • •

"It's been almost a week, Dak. When are you going to end this self-torture?"

Dak refused to stop playing pool and glanced up. He'd known the minute Syl had come down the stairs, but he wasn't ready to hear any advice. "Don't you have something else to do?"

"Nope."

"Then go spend time with Peggy, like you've been doing for the past couple of weeks or so," Dak suggested.

"She left this morning to visit her parents. I miss her already."

"So now you've come to pester me?"

"No, I thought I'd come talk some sense into you."

Dak cursed when he missed his shot. When he straightened, he glanced over at Syl and found the man smiling. "What the hell is so funny?"

"You. You need Amelia in your life, the same way I need Peggy."

Dak rolled his eyes. "Speak for yourself."

"I'm speaking for both of us. I finally saw the light and now I want you to see it as well."

"That won't be happening," he said, hanging up his pool cue. "You know why. Remember my history with Larry Small and the woman who birthed me?"

"Yes, I know your poor excuses for parents, both of them. But then Michael came into your life."

Yes, he had, Dak thought. "But you also know how hard it was on Dad to lose his wife."

"I also know how much joy he felt when he found you, Dak."

Yes, Michael would tell him that all the time. But still... Going over to the bar, he poured two glasses of bourbon. He handed one to Syl, then he took a sip of his own. "But he still grieved for her. For years he was unhappy, Syl. You know that as much as I do."

Memories flashed through his mind of walking in on his father as he stared at Tabitha's picture, or going on camping trips with his dad, and Michael would say how much he wished she'd been there with them. "That's why Dad couldn't love again, Syl. Ms. Janice never had a chance against Tabitha Navarro's ghost."

"And it seems like that same ghost is haunting you."

He stared at Syl. "What the hell do you mean?"

"Just what I said. Mike loved Tabitha, we both know that. She was his wife, so losing her devastated him. He missed her...but he did manage to get on with his life. He was happy more days than he was sad. And he had you. So no, he didn't remarry. But it wasn't because he didn't want to."

Dak frowned. "What are you saying?"

"He wanted to marry Janice. He even proposed, engagement ring and all. He wanted to make a life for you, him and her. A family."

Dak swallowed the lump in his throat. "And?"

"And she turned him down, Dak. She said that she was afraid to commit to anyone. She'd never been able to get over how badly her first husband had treated her. Michael hung in with her for as long as he could, but your dad was smart enough to know when to cut his losses and move on when her thoughts about marriage didn't change. She was satisfied for the two of them to date exclusively for years, but Michael wanted marriage."

"I didn't know that."

"And Michael didn't ever intend for you to find out. He knew how much you liked Janice."

Syl was right. He had liked her. She had come to his dad's funeral and cried all through it. At the time, he'd thought all those tears had been for a man who hadn't been able to return her love. Now he knew the truth.

"Even if Michael hadn't decided to fall in love again, that doesn't have any impact on the way you live your life," Syl said. "Look at you? You're grieving for Amelia and she's not even dead. But you're willing to walk away from the best thing to ever happen to you, out of fear that you'll lose her. Take a look, Dak. You've already lost her."

Dak stared hard at Syl. "Are you finished?"

"Nope. But I'm sure you don't want to hear anything else. Just take it from a man who knows. There's a life worth living if you're willing to take a chance. Hell, if I can do it, anyone can." Then Syl turned and stalked up the stairs.

Three days later, Dak was again in his entertainment room. Only he wasn't playing pool. Instead, he was sitting in his wingback chair, staring up at the ceiling and replaying Syl's words over and over in his mind.

That night, he hadn't wanted to hear a thing the man had said...but that hadn't stopped him from listening. And what he'd grasped from Syl's sermon was that life was meant to be lived.

That made him think about just how close he'd come to losing Amelia. What if he hadn't made it to the airport in New York in time? What if he hadn't managed to get back to his home on the island in time to stop Sargrasso from killing her? He knew the answer to both questions.

He would be doing the same thing his father had done, spending the rest of his life mourning the woman he'd loved. Syl was right. He was already grieving over losing her, and she was alive.

He lowered his gaze and stared at the floor as he accepted the truth—he had fallen in love with Amelia. Not in Indonesia or the Maldives. Not even on the flight back to the States. He'd loved her from the moment Stonewall had first introduced them. And possibly even before that, when he had walked into that wedding rehearsal and had first seen her. What other reason could he have had for going two years without female companionship? He hadn't wanted anyone else.

He stood up and began pacing. Hell, he hadn't saved her life just to treat her like she was dead. What Syl said made sense. Why let a difficult past overshadow a new beginning? He knew, just as certain as he was that there was a moon in the sky tonight, that Amelia was the best thing to ever happen to him.

*And he'd told her goodbye and walked away.*

He stopped pacing, then tilted his head back and looked up at the ceiling again. What had he done? God, he'd messed this up. He wasn't even sure what he wanted out of life anymore. There was only one thing he knew for certain—he needed Amelia to be a part of his future. He knew it, and suddenly realized, he'd always known it. He just hadn't been willing to accept it. Until now.

Then another thought crossed his mind. Just because he could now admit that he had feelings for her, that didn't mean she felt anything for him. She'd never said anything, but then she probably wouldn't have. He'd made his position clear, right from the start.

But just because she hadn't told him how she felt, that didn't mean she didn't love him, too. And if she didn't love him yet, he'd do whatever he could to convince her.

The one thing he knew how to do better than anything was how to seduce a woman. But Amelia deserved better than that. He would pursue her properly—ask her out on dates, fly her to exotic places, and make sure she got to know the real Dakota Navarro. Although he had shared more about himself with her than any other woman, there was still more. And he wanted her to know everything about him. He wanted her to be part of his life. A permanent part.

Picking up the phone, he called Syl. "Get the plane ready. We're flying out in the morning."

"For Charlottesville?"

Dak heard the excitement in Syl's voice. "No. I have a matter to take care of in St. Louis first. That might take all day. Then we'll fly to Charlottesville."

"Now you're talking."

"And...thanks, Syl. I needed to hear everything you said that night."

"I know you did. You've been focused on business long enough. It's time for you to accept there is more to life than making deals and growing your wealth. I'll see you in the morning."

• • •

The door opened and a man wearing a white coat walked into the office where Dak waited. "Sorry to keep you waiting. I was dealing with a medical emergency. My secretary said you had an important matter to discuss with me, Mr. Navarro."

Dak got up and faced Dr. Ivan McIntosh, offering the man his hand. "That's right. I figured you would be rather busy. That's why I decided to wait until the end of the day."

"Thanks for that," Dr. McIntosh said, moving around to sit behind his desk. "So, what do we need to discuss?"

"It's about this building. I recently purchased it."

Surprise showed on the doctor's face. "There was no need for you to make a trip here just to let me know where I need to send future mortgage payments."

"For me, it was," Dak said, sitting back down in his chair. "I bought this entire strip mall for my fiancée. She's also a doctor and it's going to be my wedding gift to her." Okay, so Amelia wasn't his fiancée yet, but she would be one day soon. He'd make sure of it.

"That's quite a gift. She must be some woman."

"She is. I think a lot of her, and I make it my business to look out for her best interests."

"Then you did good by purchasing the entire mall. You might even want to consider finding other tenants in the medical field. A huge medical complex was just built a block away, and the referrals I get from them are fantastic."

"My future wife will be pleased to hear that."

Dr. McIntosh nodded. "Where will her office be located?"

"In this building."

The man's brow lifted questioningly, as he sat up straight in his chair. "This building?"

"Yes."

"You're mistaken. This is my building."

"Not anymore."

A deep frown settled on Dr. McIntosh's face. "You might have purchased the entire strip mall, but I have a separate contract with the owner about this building, and it's ironclad."

"I suggest you reread your contract. It states if your mortgage is bought, the buyer has an option to renegotiate the terms."

"Yes, but I was assured something like that wouldn't happen."

"Sorry to disappoint you. Maybe this is the time when I should mention my fiancée's name. You might remember her. Dr. Amelia Courson."

He saw surprise flare in the man's eyes. "Amelia?"

"Yes. I understand you used some of her money as a down payment and you never paid her back," Dak said.

"It was a gift, not a loan."

"Go tell that lie to someone else, Dr. McIntosh. We both know it's not true. Amelia trusted you to do the right thing and you turned out to be an asshole. You have thirty days to pay back the amount you owe, plus the interest that's indicated on this invoice," Dak said, tossing the document on the doctor's desk. "If her loan is repaid in the stated time, I will allow you to remain here as long as your mortgage payments are on time. Otherwise, I'll expect you to pack your little black bag and vacate the building. And don't even think about contacting Amelia about it. It's a surprise gift and if you ruin her surprise, Doc, I will ruin you."

Then Dak stood and walked out the doctor's office.

# Chapter 29

DAK PARKED HIS CAR in front of a white frame house and immediately saw Granny Kay sitting in the swing on the porch. The older woman smiled when he walked up the steps. "Hello, Granny Kay."

"Dak. You're back."

"Yes, I'm back."

The older woman nodded. "Mellie's not expecting you, you know."

"I know." He then told the older woman something that made her smile.

"Good luck. I'll leave the two of you alone." Granny Kay opened the door and invited him in. "She's down the hall in the bathroom on the left, painting."

Just as he moved in that direction, she reached out and stopped him. "Thanks for taking care of her, Dak. She told me what all you did, and I appreciate it."

"I would do anything for her, Granny Kay."

The older woman stared at him for a minute, then nodded. "I need to get to my own house and start dinner,"

Granny Kay said. Then she got her purse off the table and left.

Dak strolled down the hall, following the scent of paint, and stopped when he came to the bathroom. Amelia was standing in the middle of the room dressed in a pair of skimpy shorts and a t-shirt that bared her midriff. Her hair was pulled back in a ponytail. Her back was to him as she leaned against a ladder and surveyed the room that she'd just finished painting. More than anything, he wanted to pull her into his arms and tell her how much he'd missed her, wanted her and needed her. How much he loved her.

Evidently sensing someone behind her, she said, "So what you do you think, Granny Kay? Am I good or what?"

"You are very good, my sexy doctor."

Amelia jerked around, nearly knocking over a can of paint. "Dak? What are you doing here?"

He didn't quite know where to begin. He certainly couldn't tell her about his visit to her ex-boyfriend. Not yet. He would save that for later.

"I came to see you."

"You said goodbye weeks ago. Why are you here now?"

That was a good question, one he hoped he could explain. "Can we go sit in your living room and talk?"

She tilted her head, concerned. "Is the smell of the paint getting to you?"

He fought back a smile. She was forever a doctor. If only she knew that *she* was what was getting to him. Today, she looked sexier than ever. "No. Please, we need to talk."

He suddenly saw fear in her eyes. "Is it about Sargrasso? Did the CIA discover something else? Are they—?"

"No, Amelia. You're still safe. My visit has nothing to do with that."

She released a deep breath. "I was about to make lunch. You want to join me?" she asked, walking out of the bathroom.

"I'd love to."

When they reached the living room, she glanced around. "Where's Granny Kay? Did she leave?"

"Yes. She said she needed to start dinner," he said, following her into the kitchen.

"Oh. You can sit at the table. Chicken salad and iced tea are on the menu today."

"Sounds great," he said, pulling out a chair to sit down. He glanced around. She had a nice place. This was the first time he'd seen this much of her home. He'd never made it past the foyer a few weeks ago, when he'd kissed her goodbye.

He watched her move around the kitchen, hoping she hadn't planned on going out wearing shorts that short. They were even more revealing than Daisy Dukes', but he had to admit that they looked good on her. But the way she looked was not the main thing on his mind right now. Telling her how he felt about her, was.

She placed a glass of iced tea in front of him. "I know you prefer your tea unsweetened."

"Thanks, Amelia. Do you need help with anything?"

"No, I've got this, Dak." She placed a plate with a sandwich in front of him, and then joined him at the table with her own lunch.

"Did you visit your friend in California?" he asked after they'd said grace.

She nodded. "I was at Whitney's place for a week. She was able to take some time off, and we had a lot of fun." She glanced over at him. "Did you go back to work last week?"

"No."

"Oh."

He knew why she was surprised. He'd been surprised too. And he had intended to jump right back into his normal life. Only his mind hadn't been on work. It had been on her. "What did you do in LA?" he asked.

"Shopping, dinner, you know. We spent one day in Beverly Hills. And I saw the Hollywood sign for the one-hundredth time. Then there was more shopping. We even went to a party given by one of Whitney's clients. She's an entertainment attorney."

"Sounds like you enjoyed yourself."

"I did."

Dak nodded. "It was good seeing Granny Kay again."

"I'm sure she was glad to see you, too."

He decided to hold off until after lunch before he broached his reasons for coming by. He wanted to make sure she heard and understood everything he said.

They made more small talk during the meal and when they'd finished, she discarded their trash and put the plates and glasses in the dishwasher.

"Thanks for lunch, Amelia."

"You're welcome. Now we can talk in the living room. I hate discussing things on an empty stomach. If you want to go on in the living room, I'll be there in a minute."

He stood. "I'll be waiting for you."

• • •

*"I'll be waiting for you..."*

Dak's words were still ringing in Amelia's ears when she joined him in the living room a few minutes later. He stood there, facing the door to the kitchen. Her gaze raked across his dark slacks and those broad shoulders that filled out his light blue dress shirt.

He couldn't seem to take his eyes off of her, either. In fact, his intense perusal was making her a little nervous, and she began gnawing on her lower lip. She wondered what had brought him back here, but figured she would find out, soon enough.

When she sat down on the sofa, he took the wingback chair across from her. If she didn't know better, she would think Dak was nervous. But that couldn't be right. He had nothing to be nervous about. If this wasn't anything about Sargrasso, then what? There was only one way to find out.

"So, what brings you here, Dak?"

"You."

Lifting a questioning brow, she said, "Me?"

"Yes. I miss you."

She tried to make sense of what he was saying. When she finally figured it out, a sad smile touched her lips. "You miss sleeping with me."

He tilted his head and looked at her with those penetrating dark eyes. Whether he knew it or not, he'd just broken her heart, now that she knew the only thing that had brought him here was sex.

"My visit has nothing to do with that."

Now she was confused. "Then maybe you need to explain your purpose in coming then."

He didn't say anything at first and then he reached out his hand to her. "Come here, please."

Amelia knew he wanted to kiss her. Didn't he know by now that their kisses always led to the bedroom? But still, she needed a kiss from him as badly as he apparently needed one from her. She would call herself all kinds of fool later for being so weak where he was concerned.

Standing, she crossed the floor to him, and took his hand. He drew her close, then tugged her down into his lap. The moment he had her cradled in his arms, she couldn't help but think of all the other times she'd been this way, with her head resting on his heart.

She looked up at him and he dipped his head and captured her lips, tasting her slowly, and then with a hunger she felt all the way to her toes. What was he trying to do? Remind her just how well he knew her body? That he was capable of making her scream, especially if he touched her back. By the time he released her mouth, she was panting hard, trying to bring herself under control.

"Like I said, Amelia," he whispered close to her ear. "I missed you. It took me a little more than a week to realize the reason I missed you so much was that I'd fallen in love with you."

His words surprised her so much, she tried to scramble away from him, needing some distance, and almost fell out of his lap. He tightened his hold on her, stopping that from happening. "What's wrong?" he asked.

*What's wrong*? Dak had the nerve to ask her that? "Why would you say something like that?"

He lifted an arrogant brow. "Why not? It's the truth."

"No, it isn't. You're incapable of loving anyone. You told me that yourself."

"I was wrong, Amelia. Let me explain."

"Please do." This was so unlike Dak. Why was he suddenly saying things like this? He'd told her that he only wanted her for a week. And she'd agreed to that. So why was he messing with her now?

He didn't say anything for a minute and then in a low, husky voice, he said, "I told you all about my dad and how he grieved for his wife until the day he died."

She nodded.

"What I didn't tell you was how knowing what he was going through, affected me. Although Dad smiled a lot, I would often see sadness in his eyes, and sometimes I'd walk in on him when he was staring at his wife's picture. The pain of loving someone that deeply—and then losing them—was something I never wanted to experience. And so, I decided to erect a wall between me and any woman who got too close. Losing Dad was hard enough on me. I couldn't imagine facing anything worse than that."

He paused a moment. "My biological parents were really messed up. Larry drilled it into my head that women were good for fun, and nothing else. And when I met my mother, I understood why he thought that. She hadn't wanted either of us." He let out a long breath. "All of that stayed with me. I thought I had pretty much had my heart protected until that day I met you. Even before Stonewall introduced us, I'd caught a glimpse of you at the rehearsal... and knew you were a threat."

She frowned. "A threat?"

"Oh, definitely. A threat to my peace of mind and my way of life. If you recall, I left the wedding reception early. After dancing with you, holding you in my arms, I had to get away from you and the emotions you could stir inside of me. I figured that once I was alone again, I could pull myself together. I didn't see you and I didn't ask Stonewall about you. I thought that if I kept you out of sight, you'd be out of mind. But it didn't work. I dreamed about you, all the time. Thoughts of you made it hard for me to concentrate at work." He paused for a moment.

"I couldn't wait to see you again at Drew and Toni's wedding. I hadn't been with a woman since I met you. I just didn't have the desire to be with anyone else."

He shook his head. "I thought by spending time with you at the wedding, then dancing at the nightclub, I might see that you were nothing special, just another woman. Then you invited me to your room, and I knew I needed more than a night with you, Amelia. I wanted a week," he said.

"Just like all those other women?"

"That's what I'd thought. A week with you should have been more than enough to get you out of my system. But in the end, it wasn't. And even when I brought you home, I knew I was in trouble."

"You were?"

"Definitely." He held her gaze. "The cycle started up again. I went to bed thinking about you, I dreamed about you, and I couldn't concentrate on work. I've been in a foul mood ever since I brought you home and Syl finally called me out on it. He made me realize what I was going through...and why."

She swallowed a lump in her throat, and asked, "And what exactly were you going through?"

Dak adjusted her position in his lap, making sure he had her total attention. "I had fallen in love with you, Amelia. But I was trying to deny it. Finally, I couldn't take it anymore. So here I am, begging you to come back to me."

Mellie blinked back tears. "Are you sure?"

"I'm positive. I almost lost you once, but I didn't. And I'm so grateful for that. And the more I think about it, I believe Dad would have wanted me to experience the kind of love he shared with Tabitha, instead of hiding myself away."

More tears welled in her eyes, and she didn't know what to say."

"I refuse to lose you again, Amelia. Last month, I invited you to share my world. Now I'm asking you to share my life. I know I have to win your love first. But I have a plan, and I intend to follow through on it. After all, desperate times call for desperate measures. I will do everything in my power to convince you that I am worthy of your love. My mission in life is to prove that I can't live without you, and that you love me, too."

Mellie swiped at her tears. "Oh, Dak, you can consider that mission accomplished. I do love you. I have since the moment I first met you."

When he saw the truth in her eyes, he held her tight against his chest and kissed her again.

"I need to ask you something important, Amelia."

"What?"

"Will you marry me? Wear my ring, take my name, have my children. Travel to exotic places with me on my jet? And before you answer, I just want to let you know, I called Stonewall to let him know what I was planning. I told Granny Kay as well. They were both happy about it."

"And I'm happy, too. Yes, Dak, I will marry you."

A huge smile appeared on his face, and he leaned in and kissed her again. In his heart, he knew that this was a love that would last. He'd make sure it did. He had found his partner, his love, his destiny. And she would be by his side for the rest of their lives.

# *Epilogue*

*Ten months later*

DAK WAS USED TO seeing Amelia cry at weddings, so he wasn't surprised to see tears fill her eyes at their own. But instead of handing her his handkerchief, he used it to wipe away her tears himself. It was hard to believe ten months had passed since their Bali adventure. Neither of them had wanted to wait a whole year for a June wedding—waiting for today to finally get here had been hard enough—so here they were, on a beautiful day in April, standing before the minister as they pledged to give their lives to each other.

His bride-to-be looked breathtaking. The moment she had entered the church on Stonewall's arm, he had choked up, amazed that such a wonderful human being loved him as much as he loved her.

"I now pronounce you husband and wife. Dakota, you may kiss your bride."

The minister's words reclaimed his attention. This was the part Dak had been waiting for. When he drew Amelia into his arms, he would be doing more than simply sealing their vows—he'd be sealing their love and lives from this day forward. His sexy doctor was now his sexy wife.

He released her mouth and when she smiled, flashing those beautiful dimples, he felt the urge to steal her away and get her behind closed doors. Leaning in, she whispered, "I love you, my husband."

"And I love you, my wife." He was about to kiss her again when Syl, his best man, whispered a reminder that he and Amelia needed to turn and face the audience.

When they did, the smiling minister said, "I present Dakota and Amelia Navarro."

While the entire church clapped and cheered, Dak decided now was just as good a time as any to pull his wife into his arms for another kiss.

• • •

Hours later at the reception, Stonewall was telling his friends how wonderful it felt to be a father. Four-month-old Garrett Sheppard Courson had been born on Christmas Day and was named after the three men Stonewall admired the most—his grandfather and father, who shared the name Garrett, and the other man who'd had such a huge impact on Stonewall's life, Sheppard Granger.

Stonewall's friends, Striker Jennings, Quasar Patterson and the Granger brothers – Jace, Caden and Dalton - were offering tips on ways to persuade Garrett to sleep through the night. Although Stonewall was listening, his attention was divided between his friends advice and the seventh man standing with them—his boss and good friend, Roland Summers.

It was understandable that Roland wouldn't have anything to contribute to the conversation. He was a widower and hadn't been lucky enough to have children. However, Stonewall couldn't help noticing how Lennox Roswell, a beautiful woman standing across the room at the buffet table, seemed to be holding Roland's attention. Lennox was a medical examiner with the police department and was a friend of Mellie and Joy's.

Their obvious attraction shouldn't have seemed odd. After all, Roland was a man in his prime, and Lennox was definitely a looker. It was just that no one in their inner circle of friends had ever known Roland to show any interest in a woman before. In fact, it was pretty much a foregone conclusion that although Roland dated on occasion, it was to merely satisfy his physical needs. He'd told them that his deceased wife Becca would always have his heart, and that he had no interest in remarrying. Stonewall couldn't help wondering if that mindset was about to change.

When Striker, Quasar and the Grangers decided to go find their wives, Stonewall turned to Roland. "You're still thinking about selling your house, Roland?"

Roland had shocked them all when he'd mentioned last month that he had decided to sell his home. Although he hadn't lived in it for years—Roland had been renting it out while living in an apartment—the decision had to have been a hard one to make, since the house was the one that Roland and Becca had once shared together.

"Yes. In fact, it sold last week after being on the market less than a month. I'm also moving out of my apartment and into a condo. I signed a lease on it the other day," Roland said.

He was about to ask Roland where his new condo was located when there was a tumult of clapping and cheering. The newlyweds were leaving for their honeymoon, and everyone was giving them a joyous send off.

• • •

Mellie's head jerked up. "What did you do?"

Dak simply smiled at her. She was sitting in his lap, all strapped in, as the jet took off. Their destination was Argentina for four weeks, and then Dubai for two.

He had just handed her an envelope that contained a check for forty-two thousand dollars. Her eyes widened when she saw the signature on the check—Dr. Ivan McIntosh.

"What makes you think I did anything?" he said.

She tilted her head and gazed at her husband. "How did you get my money back from Ivan? And it's more than what I loaned him."

"I paid the good doctor a visit and told him he owed you the amount of the loan, plus interest."

"And he agreed to pay it? Just like that?" she asked.

"Not exactly."

She fought back a smile. "Then I will ask you again, Dak Navarro. What did you do?"

He shrugged muscular shoulders and said, "I simply gave him a choice."

Mellie's eyes widened. "You threatened a doctor?"

"No, I threatened an asshole. But it really wasn't a threat. I made him see it was really in his best interest to pay back the loan with interest, since you now owned the building and could ask him to vacate anytime you wanted."

Her brows bunched. "I own the building?"

"Actually, including his building, you own the entire complex. It's my wedding gift to you."

Mellie opened her mouth, then closed it, shocked at what he'd said. Finally, she cleared her throat and said, "Let me get this straight. As a wedding present, you bought me the strip mall in St. Louis where Ivan's practice is located?"

"Yes, and I told him as long as he paid you what he owed you, I wouldn't kick him out of the building...yet."

Mellie fought back a smile and shook her head. Dak had already given her a number of wedding gifts, including her own little island in the Caribbean and a cute little sports car. "I wished I could have been a fly on the wall during that meeting."

"I'm glad you weren't. Now enough about him. Let's talk about us. Are you happy?"

She reached out and wrapped her arms around his neck. "Extremely. And I'm happy for Peggy and Syl, too."

Their two friends, who were accompanying them to Argentina as pilot and flight hostess, would be getting married as soon as they got there. Roles would be reversed, and Dak would be Syl's best man while Mellie would be one of Peggy's bridesmaids. As a wedding gift, Dak had insisted on flying Peggy's family to Argentina for the wedding, as well as picking up the tab for their hotel. And he would be paying for the couple's honeymoon stay at an exclusive resort there, while Mellie and Dak would be staying at his home in Buenos Aires. She couldn't wait to see it.

"I love you, Dr. Amelia Navarro."

"And I love you, Mr. Dakota Michael Navarro."

He lowered his head for a kiss that seemed to never end, until Syl came on the intercom to let them know they could move around the cabin. Dak unbuckled their seatbelts, and then with her still in his arms, he headed for the bedroom.

Their honeymoon was about to begin. And it was only fitting that their first night as husband and wife would begin among the stars.

COMING IN 2022!

BOOK 3 IN THE “MEN OF ACTION” SERIES,

*Infinite Possibilities*

ROLAND SUMMERS’ STORY

# About the Author

**Brenda Jackson**, *New York Times* and *USA Today* Brenda Jackson, New York Times and USA Today Bestselling author of over 140 books and novellas, and 15 million books in print, earned a Bachelor of Science degree in Business Administration from Jacksonville University. She worked in management for State Farm Insurance where she retired after thirty-seven years. Forty-nine years ago, she married her high school sweetheart, Gerald and they have two sons, Gerald Jr. and Brandon, ages forty-three and forty-one, respectively. She is a member of Delta Sigma Theta Sorority, Inc.

Her professional writing career began in 1995 with the release of her first book, Tonight and Forever. Since then, she has received numerous national and literary awards and has made many trail-blazing accomplishments, which includes being the first African American author to make the New York Times Bestseller's List and the USA Today's Bestseller's List in the romance genre, and the Nora Roberts Lifetime Achievement Award and the Vivian Stephens Lifetime Achievement Award.

With the belief that if you aren't invited to the table, then you create your own table, Brenda Jackson has partnered with Hollywood's film writer Bobby Smith Jr. (Jason's Lyric fame) to launch a film and television company to develop and produce titles from Jackson's collection of over 140 romance novels. The pair are excited to bring love stories by Brenda, as well as by other romance authors, to life on the screen.

Visit here for a printable list of all Brenda's books -
https://www.brendajackson.net/books/printable-book-list/
Visit here for information on Brenda Jackson Movies –
https://www.brendajackson.net/movies/
Visit here for Brenda Jackson monthly newsletter -
https://www.brendajackson.net/media/newsletters/
Visit here to visit Brenda Jackson's website –
www.brendajackson.net